D1393265

Phil Hogan was born in 1955 in West Yorkshire. He writes a weekly column for the *Observer* and lives in Hertfordshire with his wife and four children. *Hitting the Groove* is his first novel.

hitting the groove

PHIL HOGAN

An *Abacus* Book

First published in Great Britain in 2001 by Abacus

All characters in this publication are fictitious and any resemblance to real persons, living or dead, is purely coincidental.

A CIP catalogue record for this book is available from the British Library.

ISBN: 0 349 11453 6

Typeset in Erhardt by M Rules
Printed and bound in Great Britain
by Clays Ltd, St Ives plc

Abacus
A Division of
Little, Brown & Company (UK)
Brettenham House
Lancaster Place
London WC2E 7EN

For Mum and Dad

hitting the groove

flying

I've always loved heights. I don't mean I have a head for heights though; I don't mean you'd catch me putting my name down for charity parachute jumps, or checking out the thermals over the Eiger, or being cranked slowly towards the top curve of one of those white-knuckle rides with no turning back and only the sickening rush of gravity to look forward to. But give me a solid viewing platform at the top of the Eiffel Tower or Canary Wharf or, now, just *this* – this polycarbonate glass pod rising above the Thames, rising steadily, undramatically, by degrees, as the big wheel turns, lifting us high into the starry above – and I'm in a heaven of sorts. The London Eye, they call it, all-seeing. Climbing slowly. Undramatic, steady. Just like me. But up here you can take the world in at a glance, its bewildering range of possibilities reduced to grids and patterns. Its chaos ordered. When we talk about putting things in perspective, this is what we mean. This world as a monument to architects and engineers. A glimpse of things as they really are for those of us who fear the unknown. Those of us who in the normal run of things are happy to be spectators.

So what makes a spectator suddenly leap from the parapet? I'm speaking metaphorically of course. This is not a tale of action-packed adventure or extraordinary deeds. In fact, you might say it could have happened to anyone. I mean, given the right class of trauma. A new job? That was me. Moving house? Yup. Death of a loved one? Check. Divorce proceedings? You'd have to ask Cathy about that one.

Even up here, now, I can't quite put my finger on it. Maybe it was my way of handling the excitement. Because, in case I forget, it *was* one of the most exciting times of my life. I don't know. I'm not a psychiatrist. But let's take it one trauma at a time. Let's start with my best friend Dean, without whom none of this would have been possible. Or, rather, necessary.

It didn't happen often, but I remember once catching myself talking to him as if he was in the same room. 'Wake up, Dean,' I was saying. 'Wake up and tell me what you're thinking.' Because everyone had said their piece – Cathy's mum, my folks, everyone at the Lion, my sister, the postman, Sadie, Sadie's classmates, Sadie's boyfriend, Sadie's dog. It's funny how people kept telling me how we'd miss the old place, as if they were giving us some fantastic, insightful piece of advice. Really? Blimey, I hadn't thought of that. Maybe we won't go after all. Did they think I didn't know we'd miss it? Did they think I didn't know what a massive change it would be? The point is, I'd already missed too much for any more to matter. Dean had seen to that one well enough.

I'd been busy answering chirpy e-mails promising to keep in touch with people I knew I'd never clap eyes on again. It made me stop for a minute. It made me think about the days when the two of us used to while away the odd lunchtime exchanging e-mails – the days when e-mails were a novelty worth whiling away a lunchtime with – me at my desk at the *Echo*, him at Drive My Car (prop. D. Scholes, est. 1989). I used to imagine him sitting there prodding at the keyboard in his red Lotus overalls eating a bacon sandwich with his thumbprinted Beatles book open in his lap, trying to catch me out with European tour trivia from the Epstein years. From that to this seemed like a charmed lifetime ago.

The last time I drove by, the business was for sale and boarded up. I stopped the Renault in the street and ran to look. I could still see Tony's perennially unwashed Leeds mug on the workbench through the gaps in the chipboard panels on the window and Dean's grimy office at the back, with his computer and his 1985 Pirelli calendar and the French *Hard Day's Night* poster in its frame above his desk that I used to wish was mine. I knew it would break his mum's heart to let it all go, but what could she do?

I realised that talking to Dean in his absence was probably not that healthy. I realised it was probably a subsection of denial. And it wasn't even as if what he thought mattered any more. I'd already said my goodbyes to him. But there was just something else before I left the scene for good.

I was thinking about the Ringo story, the 'Hey Jude' story with the four of them in the studio getting ready for a take when Ringo nipped off for a pee just before McCartney started to count everybody in, and nobody knew he was missing until he came rushing back, falling over himself to get into the drum booth just in time to snatch up his sticks and stop it all happening without him. Adding up the journey time, zip-operation, high-level flush, it must have taken him about forty seconds. Was it a leisurely pee or a hurried one? We both loved that story. How Ringo came in right on cue, sixteenth bar, just ahead of the first bridge.

A comic moment in pop.

But here was the tragedy. The tragedy of what that song reminded me of now when I heard it. It reminded me of swaying out of the toilets at a Christmas party at the Bricklayers in Headingley in my first year at college. It reminded me of seeing Dean and Cathy leaning against the wall, chatting. It was a long time ago but I could still see the way he offered his bottle of Newcastle Brown to her and the way she took a swig without wiping the top first. The two of them had been dancing and her cheeks were pink and she was sweaty, with her lovely long hair (as it was then) all over the place and they both looked at me at the same time, still both grinning the same grin that was left hanging over from whatever rubbish they'd been saying to each other over the noise of the place. And I remember gazing down amid that drunken clamour and seeing the little coloured flecks on my shoes where I'd thrown up and feeling vaguely that something wasn't quite going to plan.

I'm not saying it mattered. She wasn't my personal property or anything. I probably hadn't even mentioned her to Dean. I'd met her on the coach from Leeds to Oxford, her going to proper university, me to the poly. I'd bumped into her a couple of times that first term, and then seen her again on the bus home. I was two years older than Cathy, and impressed her by the way I had fucked up my A-levels twice before scraping into college. I'd asked her along to the party with as much undergraduate come-as-you-are swagger as I could muster without collapsing with nerves. So, in fact, it didn't matter. I could have written it – her – off. I remember when I walked in with her, Dean made one of those thumbs-up signs with his eyebrows that meant, Blimey, old Matt's with a girl who isn't his sister, so he has to have his tongue in her ear at least, right? But I shook my head and frowned coolly, as if he were still some *Homo erectus* while I'd moved up into the kind of circles where a young man and woman in the full bloom of higher education could easily turn up at a party as platonic friends, possibly with a common interest in Brechtian dramaturgy or Renaissance cathedrals. It never occurred to me that she might fancy him, even though he'd had more fully penetrative sexual encounters by then than I'd had unwholesome fantasies about all three Charlie's Angels, and just possibly had something going for him that my smattering of fresher's culture couldn't compete with. What was I thinking? That students didn't sleep with garage mechanics? Did I think a foundation course in medieval studies could withstand the forces of animal magnetism?

'This is Cathy,' I'd said. 'Friend from Oxford,' I added.

'Hi,' Cathy said.

He smiled. He always had very good teeth. 'Any friend of Matt's,' he said, bowing slightly and shaking her hand in a mocking, formal way. 'You both OK for a drink?' he asked. 'I know how hard-up you penniless students are. Or at least that's always Matt's story . . .'

Off he went grinning, shouldering a way through the crowd. The bar was heaving, but Dean was one of those people who always got served at heaving bars. Not by frantically waving a crumpled fiver (that would have been me) or by shouting above the racket, but just by standing there knowing he'd be served. You either have that or you don't. Dean was good at all the kind of stuff that people value you for socially when you're young and growing up – ordering drinks, being untacklable at football, getting girls to sleep with him, knowing how engines worked. I was his anomaly. I was an odd person for him to mix with, and if we hadn't lived on the same street and got hooked on box guitars and mouth organs and kazoos and the Beatles when we did, we would never have been having this conversation years later. I wouldn't be introducing him to Cathy. And even more years later I wouldn't be talking to him when he wasn't in the room.

So the Cathy moment shouldn't have mattered, except. Except that . . . well, Dean and I had always been John and

Paul, right? And now here I was, suddenly relegated to Ringo, a novelty act with a large nose and sloppy grin, a left-hander sitting at a right-hand kit, playing everything backwards. (No offence to Ringo, obviously.) I never asked Cathy about it until it was way too late, though I did make her count up all the other men she'd slept with before me (five), in return for all the other girls I'd slept with before her (zero) during a heated dispute on our honeymoon in a two-crown guest house in Stratford. In the end we managed to wake Sadie, who had been snoozing nicely in her carrycot on one of those slatted bench things where your suitcase is supposed to go, and I ended up spending an hour not officially consummating our new legal status, but wearing the carpet out between the wall mirror and the trouser press with a baby perforating my eardrum and thinking FIVE! FIVE! FIVE! And not five-all, or five-four, but five-nil. I mean, *fuck*, she was only nineteen by the time I eventually made some progress with her by going to a silent comedy starring Jacques Tati, who was supposed to be the French Charlie Chaplin, which meant I had to go to all the trouble of laughing like a drain and slapping my thigh along with the rest of the audience because that's what sophistication used to be when you were a student confronted by something European. But it did work. I did get the girl.

Talking to a dead person isn't against the law, though I admit that, to those uninitiated in the ways of bereavement, it might seem a bit demented. But you don't just file people away. Especially someone like Dean, a person who (in a strictly wholesome, non-homosexual, big brotherly kind of way) was an important part of my life. And now, to complicate things, there was this Cathy moment that shouldn't have mattered suddenly, for some reason, mattering. I remember sitting in my study, switching off my Mac, switching off the Anglepoise lamp and sitting for a moment in the dark, just listening.

Cathy snoring lightly in the next room, still beautiful to me, still a mystery in enough small ways for me to get things wrong sometimes, to misread her moods and expectations, to be surprised at my own clueless fumblings in the dark. The thing was, I realised, you made a fierce intimacy in the heat of love and marriage but you couldn't live inside each other's heads. I was listening to her now . . . What did she dream about? Because there were always secrets. There had to be. Not necessarily bad ones. Little fears maybe, unspoken wants, irrational regrets, moments of shame born in the swell of youth, only to surface, rippling, years later, in the rapid eye movement of sleep. Secrets not really worth telling, but secrets nevertheless untold. Secrets that stopped two people becoming one. I loved her when she snored. That was one of my secrets.

It was during those last few days that Tony dropped by, standing there on the doorstep grinning. I assumed he'd come to say goodbye, so I asked him in and gave him a cup of tea. It was odd seeing him sitting there in his baggy overalls without Dean in *his* baggy overalls, but we chatted for a while about how the England cricket team were doing (I'd no idea) and what was going to happen to Dean's garage (ditto). He told me he was working at the Ford dealership on the ring road earning better money than Dean had paid him, so we had a laugh about that until we stopped. And still he was hanging around, not mentioning our move south, even though I gave him one or two cues in case he hadn't noticed all the packing cases. And then . . .

'Sold the Alfa by the way,' he suddenly said.

'Sorry?'

'You know – the white Spyder. Just sold it this morning. This QPR supporter came all the way down from London for it.'

'Up, surely . . .' I said, trying to stop myself saying it but too late, because now I had entered into a conversational compact with Tony, who for some reason had begun to see me as someone who knew which side of a car the petrol cap was on.

'Take a gander at these,' he said, bringing a Kodak wallet of photographs out and spreading them over the coffee table – thirty-six colour snaps of the car he'd just *sold*, for goodness sake, taken from various angles, none of which made the car seem any more interesting to a casual observer who might just have been thinking of maybe spending the afternoon preparing in some small way for an adventure that would affect the rest of his life. Specifically, packing up my CDs.

'I found an old film hidden under the dash and had it developed,' he said. 'This is the man who had it before me,' he went on, pointing at some grinning bloke with a moustache and his hand on the bonnet. 'And this must be his girlfriend, I suppose . . .'

'Why didn't you give these to the new owner?' I said, thinking this might be an uncontroversial question, but Tony looked baffled. Then it suddenly struck me that the only reason he was showing these pictures to me was because he couldn't show them to Dean, and I suddenly felt really sorry for him. That was why he was here on a Saturday. He was lost. In fact I felt so sorry for him that I found myself asking what motor he was driving now, if he'd just sold the Alfa. I mean I actually said 'motor'. I actually went *outside* with him and let him show me how the hydraulic suspension worked on a 1965 Citroën something or other. And in the pouring rain.

Cathy gave me earache afterwards because I'd let Tony sit in the blue chair in his oily filth from the Ford garage on the ring road. Funny, but until Tony turned up, I'd never really thought about it before, though I should have – this idea that Dean had a whole other parallel world that was nothing to do with me. I mean, I'd got a job, but it wasn't something I'd want to enthuse about with my own parallel version of Tony.

I'd only had Dean. There was no default position as far as intimates were concerned. He was it.

Dean, meanwhile, had history wherever you looked. Cathy did finally tell me she'd slept with Dean but only because I did finally ask her. She shrugged and said she'd always assumed I already knew and what did it matter anyway? She assumed Dean would have told me. After all, he was supposed to be my best mate. But he had never mentioned it. And neither had I. It was nothing to get hung about, as he used to say. Except he didn't say it that time, and by the time it *was* something to get hung about it was too late to say it. I brought the subject up about three weeks after the funeral. I don't even know why I asked her. It would have been better not to. But she sighed and told me she'd only seen him two or three times during those Christmas hols. 'Do you really expect me to remember this?' she said. But I would have remembered if it had been me. I would have remembered them all.

The day I heard about the accident – not straight away, but later, in the evening, after I'd got back from Dean's mum's – I was sitting with my guitar in the dark with just the light from the computer, and Cathy came in and caught me singing 'A Day in the Life'. The bit about the man killed in the crash not having noticed that the lights had changed.

'Matt, I really don't think you should play that song,' she said in her soft, concerned voice. I didn't say anything and she went off, shutting the door quietly, thinking she was being sensitive by not starting an argument, like you do with sick or old people. She probably thought I was being maudlin rather than provocative, but I knew Dean wouldn't begrudge me a moment of reflection, or whatever it was. Self-pity, I suppose. Or rather pity for both of us. And, of course, that song would have plopped to the surface of his mind too if it had been the other way round, even though, strictly speaking, there had been no lights to change, just a rise in the road, a bend, a tractor, a dry-stone wall and a sign that said 'Caution, slow vehicles turning', which in the usual run of things means quite the opposite.

You can never believe it when somebody close dies suddenly. But what I found hardest to believe was that Dean was capable of doing something so stupid when he'd spent his whole life effortlessly doing everything right. He might have looked like the drifting type – casual, unhurried – but everything he had done had been a positive choice, even down to dropping out of sixth form to mend cars. He was one of those people who could absorb something new or see to the heart of a problem just by standing next to it. I'd be fiddling around for days trying to work out something difficult on the piano and he'd just come along and do it by ear. 'Wait a sec, listen,' he'd say, reaching across to plink the keyboard. 'I think that ought to be . . .'

And he'd look at me with that triumphant grin.

He even once saved me from a fight I got caught up in after school. It was nothing major. Three boys from our year – the usual line-up of one tough guy and two ugly eggers-on – pushing me around at the bus stop over something I was supposed to have done or not done when I should have. I'd managed to get a split lip. But Dean didn't save me by wading in and throwing punches. He just grabbed me by the lapel and dragged me away, like an older person would. 'Come here, you fucking idiot,' were his exact words. But he only muttered them. He wasn't shouting the odds. He hardly even acknowledged the others, except to let them see how inconvenienced he was by the whole thing. Naturally, they stood their ground with standard-issue sneers on their faces but none of them said a word. He had this quiet assurance that no one had ever challenged, and of course by then it had crystallised into a reputation. What Dean had managed to grasp by then was what all grown-ups knew – that bullies were cowards rather than psychopaths, and that what they really needed was someone to come along after a decent interval and allow them to retreat without loss of dignity in front of their stupid mates. We went back to his house so I could clean up. He was in the little dining room tinkering with an old 1940s stand-up valve radio that he was turning into an amp.

'You've got to make it look as if they've won,' he said. 'That's the trick.'

With him it was instinct. He saw the systems behind things. He understood herd mentality. He saw beauty in engines. And of course he loved great songs. A song was something you could take apart and put together again. A great song was like a performance motor, he said.

I envied him his certainty. You had to envy a guy like that. Someone who knew how everything worked.

You have to be dead to have these things said about you, and Dean for one would have been surprised to hear me say them. But he would have done the same for me, at a push. He would have told you what he envied about me. My hearth and home? My devoted wife? My uncertain command of musical theory? It goes without saying.

I'd stopped talking about Dean with Cathy by now, mainly because I got the feeling she thought it was time to move on. Of course she'd noted more than once that I hardly picked up my guitar any more, even though up until then it had been part of her job spec to tell me to put the bloody thing down for God's sake and repaint the lawn or change the bulb in the hall with the light fitting that wouldn't unscrew. Plus there was a new baby to think about. And Sadie, growing up fast, thinking she was old enough to have her own steady boyfriend with acne.

The big news was, though, that we *were* moving on; though not in a way Cathy could ever have predicted a couple of years before, when I'd been content enough to build up my pension at the *Echo*, run through some tricky harmonies with Dean every other Wednesday and have sex with her once a fortnight – or, since Ellie was born, once every old re-run of *NYPD Blue* starring the original short ginger-haired one. And, actually, I suppose I *was* quite happy to carry on doing that. Undramatic, steady, solid, remember? Until Dean made his one false move I was perfectly fine. Dean in a yellow Ferrari. OK, so it belonged to one of his clients who didn't know what growing up was, but Dean still couldn't resist driving it, cruising Leeds city centre after work, attracting admiring glances from secretaries at bus stops. If it hadn't been for him, the absence of him – him not now turning up unannounced in our kitchen to eat our biscuits and strum my guitar and irritate Cathy while she chopped carrots – I don't think I would have been seized with that sudden, restless enthusiasm to uproot everyone and everything, regardless of the opportunity that had come my way like a sign from a benevolent god. Apart from anything else, Cathy had a pathological dislike of London, possibly because it was full of women from her college who were now barristers or derivatives dealers or forensic scientists – women who decided not to get themselves pregnant in their final year but do well in their exams instead.

Sadie gave me hell on an hourly basis too, about moving – GCSEs next season and all that – and I'd sometimes come down quietly in the middle of the night, sit and let my senses just go, surrender to the deep tick of the hall clock. The truth was, it almost didn't matter, at this stage, whether it was actually the right thing to do. I could already see myself up there now, hair blasted back in the wind, smiling, eyes trained on the uplit pink horizon, astonished that I was off the ground and moving with such force. The way it had happened was like a gift. It meant I wasn't running away from anything, but drawn to something fantastically compelling. On the other hand, it wouldn't be human not to have some misgivings. It wouldn't be human not to wake up in the small hours and sit in the light of an open fridge drinking milk and eating your teenage daughter's Terry's Chocolate Orange. As someone once said, flying might be a miracle, but landing was all about technique. So I ate the Chocolate Orange and drank the milk. It didn't do to think in metaphors. It didn't do to put spanners in the works at this stage.

At the office things were steaming ahead. It was Wednesday afternoon and I was supposed to be clearing out my desk but I couldn't be fagged, and I'd got as far as going to the canteen for a large espresso and a Snickers bar. I tried to make a joke about reincarnation to the girl behind the counter (about Snickers being Marathons in a previous life) but she wasn't old enough to understand it and neither was anyone else in the queue, which was slightly depressing. I'd just got back from a kind of farewell lunch. The editor had stood up and toasted me and said I could come back any time I wanted – which with all due modesty didn't strike me as surprising since I practically wrote the entire features section for next to nothing, well at least the worthless, shallow showbiz features and TV stuff. Still, it was nice of him to say it. I remember thinking it was lucky I'd stopped noticing girls, because there was this one girl – or woman, as I had learnt to call them by then – who was snogging my leg with hers the whole time after her fourteenth glass of carbonated mouthwash. Ruth something she said her name was. I was telling her I'd be forty in October. I was telling this Ruth something that in all likelihood, I would come to the end of my life never having owned a brand-new pair of football boots. Two second-hand pairs saw me through school, and I'd always worn trainers for the odd kickabout in the park. She was pretty fascinated. Nice too. Not that I would ever. Not with anyone else.

Even so – even though I never had, and never would with anyone else – I could have told Dean a thing or two he didn't know about women. Long-term things he couldn't know about. OK, Yoko eventually broke the Beatles up by eating

George's chocolate biscuits without asking him. But it was bound to happen. You couldn't blame Lennon. It was just like Mowgli going off with the girl from the man village in *The Jungle Book*. We fall in love. We want to shag women we love the whole time, and devote our lives to them and admire their fantastic uncontrollable hair and bury our noses between their breasts for ever. Sometimes we haven't got time to be in the most successful pop group the universe has ever known as well. Even me and Dean. Even we had to take an extended musical break when I was at college being in bed with Cathy twenty-four hours a day except during lectures. (Why did Dean never meet the right girl? All those Julies and Mandys and Zoës. And a trick, optional question that didn't matter anyway: who decided it was a two-night stand – was it Dean who didn't ring Cathy, or her who didn't ring him all those years ago? Who gave who up, after only two (or three) shags? I mean, which would be worse – him dumping the person I love, or him still fancying her? A girl giving Dean the elbow for the first time in his life, thus making him mad for her, or Cathy secretly wishing it was Dean that got her pregnant and wishing it was his face she saw when she looked in Sadie's pram fifteen years ago? Or neither? This was how much it didn't matter.)

As I said, things were moving on. By now Cathy had dismantled the entire house. I'd no idea where we were all going to sleep for the next three days.

Love and marriage. What I couldn't quite bring myself to admit, even to myself, was how it all ends when you're not looking, even when you're still theoretically happy. How women give us up when they have babies. I mean they let us have sex, and let us have a hobby, and let us watch *Match of the Day*, and let us change the bulb in the hall, and let us bring money into the house, and let us pretend to be over the moon when they buy us an unfortunate checked shirt for our birthday. But that other stuff – the *real* stuff – has ended. Because whatever great sex might still happen in bed occasionally, they're saving their cooing and stroking and tenderest thoughts for their beautiful children. I could never imagine my mum and dad holding hands in the street or kissing at the bus stop. When does that stop? It goes on for ages and ages, and then one day you realise you're not doing it any more. That's what I missed. That's what I could have told Dean.

Three days to go . . .

I vaguely remember that night standing there in my socks, rocking slightly, blithely aware that standing there in your socks and rocking slightly was the kind of thing you did when you were drunk and your wife was elsewhere in the house, ostentatiously turning off lights, unplugging the TV, locking the front door, checking the baby, tucking the dog in, bringing you the pint of water you could only ever be arsed to get for yourself when you were too sober to need one. I maybe closed one eye and looked at myself sideways in the long bedroom mirror, which had been unscrewed in preparation for the move and propped against the wall, the screws in a small polythene bag stuck with masking tape across one corner of the frame by someone (Cathy) organised enough not only to think in advance but to think in advance in detail. I turned this way and then that. The glare from the unshaded ceiling bulb cast everything in ugly, black relief, in particular my goosebumped flesh in the cold, adding extra tramlines to my frown, an extra portion of fries under the droop of each buttock. How did things get this bad? How did you fill an absence like Dean's? How did you fix an unfixable hole? I pulled in my stomach and clenched those buttocks and narrowed those eyes. Drink famously altered your perceptions. It was not inconceivable that I would look younger, fitter, more crucial to events in the morning. Anything could happen. I heard Cathy padding upstairs and got into bed quickly, socks on, teeth unbrushed, prayers unsaid.

Two days . . .

The Lewis household was in a state of no small disarray as I tapped out a short, humorous, final valedictory speech on the laptop I bought myself as a reward for winning last year's Critic of the Year, regional section (northern, evening, open to males, medium height), which – I suppose I should mention – was how all this started. Naturally there were a small number of envious persons at the office who were unkind enough to suggest that the field had been a bit thin that year, but they had to eat their own spineless tongues when I landed my fantastic high(ish)ly paid job on the *Sunday Post* in London which I was hugely looking forward to/secretly frightened to death of starting the following Tuesday.

The fantastic thing was, I was only supposed to be going for a free lunch, and to take a look at how a big national paper was run, and even then it was only because one of the judges had been the deputy editor, Jeremy McVie, who I'd been chatting to after the awards, who had said he liked my work, who had invited me down to have a look around. Obviously, I did think there might be a bit of freelance in it for me and it was brilliant to have those kind of contacts. But then, right there in the restaurant the next day, he offered me the job. Right there over the pudding and custard. TV Editor. T-V. ED-IT-OR. Editor (TV!). 'Obviously, I'll have to think about it,' I said, though in my mind I had already spat on my palm, kissed him on the lips and walked on my hands all the way back to King's Cross. I couldn't wait to get back up to Leeds to tell Cathy. She was excited too, to start with – possibly because I was jumping up and down so much and she hadn't seen me do that in a while – and then she remembered Sadie's education, our substantial three-storey Victorian house and garden, the amateur dramatics thing she'd just started again, our good friends Laura and

Mike and Sally and Ray (who were actually her good friends and her good friends' husbands – though I might occasionally bump into Mike, who used to go to Dean's garage with his red Lotus Turbo Attention-Seeker), all her National Childbirth Trust cronies, and the fact that she was thinking of going back to work part-time. But look at it this way (as I explained for hours and hours until she finally surrendered with a selfless whimper of congratulation): when Chris Tarrant asks if you want to take the £1,000 or answer another four infant-school questions and turn it into sixteen grand, what do you say? You say the right thing. You open champagne.

Anyway I was using my laptop because my Mac was in a crate somewhere. Cathy's ex-pupils had been turning up like little groupies to pay their last respects ever since they heard we were heading south, even though she hadn't taught a class since starting maternity leave when Ellie was on the way, which must have been getting on for fifteen months before that. Cathy still hadn't quite got over the way I got her pregnant again at thirty-five years of age (and just when they'd decided to make her Head of English), but of course she was crazy about Ellie, except in the middle of the night, which is when I was supposed to be crazy about her.

One . . .

Cathy's mother came round trying to make things more difficult by helping, the three of them wrapping glasses in newspaper while I fed the baby, Sadie's face as long as a bargepole, if you could see it for those curtains of hair. Anyway, this was the scene:

Cathy's mother (leaning over, conspiratorial): 'Don't worry, darling, you'll see Alan again – you know you can come and stay with me whenever you like. I've got lots of room . . .'

Sadie: 'It's Adam, Gran . . .'

Cathy's mother (pained smile): 'You know, Catherine, I do hope you're not making a mistake. I hear they have terrible drugs problems in some of those schools. And the crime – did I tell you, when Mrs Elliot went to the flower show last year . . .'

Cathy (laughing lightly): 'For goodness sake, Mum, we're not moving to . . . [searches 1980s memory-bank for address from hell] . . . Broadwater *Farm*. Crouch End is a nice area.' (Looks at me, half-pleadingly for support, half-glaringly because it's all my fault and her mother is probably right.)

Me: 'Actually Bob Dylan was looking for a house in Crouch End at one time. It's quite a cool place. Sadie will like it. There's a park and tennis courts, and . . . oh, I don't know – a hairdresser's. Cathy will be able to go to the theatre in the West End. Just think – Tom Stoppard, Ben Elton, that other bloke who wrote *Educating Rita*. Musicals, operas. It'll be fantastic. It'll be fine.'

Cathy's mother (turning to Cathy, ignoring me): 'But you won't know anyone, dear . . . At least here you have lots of friends – and some family. [Smiles pointedly.] And what a shame to leave your lovely big house and have to move to . . . well, I imagine something rather smaller, am I right?' (Cocks head to one side. This was her last chance to move into our granny flat, which didn't actually exist and never would now, I fervently hoped.) 'I suppose your father is encouraging you in all this. Just to upset me, of course.' (Sniffs.)

Sadie gets up abruptly and leaves the room sighing. Doors bang offstage. Cathy carries on wrapping egg-cups, sighing. Her mother lights her eighteenth cigarette in the past half-hour even though we'd asked her not to smoke while the baby's still between courses. *But I have so few pleasures left, dear*. That's a lie. What about pulling wings off sparrows? Apparently she's not getting any younger, which is a relief. I wouldn't say my mother-in-law was fat but . . . (Actually she's bone-thin.)

My big anxiety? That Cathy was turning into her mother. It was just in the odd expression, the way she laughed too long at something she would never find funny in the old days, the way she piled food up on her fork instead of using all her cutlery as a spoon, like I did. I was worried. Obviously I still loved her. But . . .

Well, Dean again. Sadie was still a toddler and we were still in our little terrace off Kirkstall Road. I'd been doing the all-day shoplifting shift at the magistrates' court, and I was knackered. When I got home, it was just getting dark and there were no lights on downstairs, so I thought Cathy wasn't in. And then there was a crackle on the baby monitor and I heard someone laughing. Just laughing. And then they both came down the stairs. Cathy was carrying Sadie. Obviously it wasn't anything, but it just took me by surprise. And then, before I had a chance to speak . . . I looked at him for a second and didn't realise what it was. And then I noticed. He'd shaved off his moustache. His Lennon moustache. I couldn't believe it. The trouble was, at that time, punks had been and gone and New Romantics were poncing around on *Top of the Pops*. No one had a moustache any more and certainly we had been under pressure for ages to get rid of them by everyone we respected in the Lion, and had resisted. But then Dean obviously just went and did it. We hadn't even discussed it. I didn't know what to say. I felt like an idiot standing there with mine still drooping over my top lip, and of course it had to go soon afterwards (the same night). I know it didn't matter. I just felt let down. As anyone would.

Zero . . .

So this was it. Sitting on the sofa with my hangover. Tea chests. The smell of swept dust and disinfectant. The neighbours had been round to kiss us all. Cathy and Sadie had gone off in the Punto (KEEP YOUR DISTANCE – BABY ON BOARD!) to pick up her mother, who was insisting on coming down to London to help us move in. I'd walked round the empty rooms singing 'She's Leaving Home' to hear the echo.

My work chums presented me with a framed cartoon of myself, drawn by Terry the house cartoonist, and a brand-new pair of football boots. Brilliant. I told my new friend Ruth she could come down and visit any time she wanted. Any time, I said, in that way you do when you invite complete strangers from Tasmania who you meet on the shores of Lake Titicaca to look you up if they ever find themselves in your neck of north-west Leeds. Maybe I could introduce her to a few people, I said. The editor made another speech. I made mine. Everybody laughed at my self-effacing jokes and/or slurred delivery.

I'd been to see Mum and Dad the evening before that. Mum said she thought I was doing the right thing and that I'd been stuck in one job for too long for a man with my abilities. It was never too late, she said. I could get knocked over by a tram (a what?) tomorrow and that would be that, she said. Nobody ever gets asked twice, she said. I needed to push myself, she said. (I loved her for this because I think that, actually, she would have been perfectly happy to have me live conveniently just up the road for the rest of my life.) My Dad just sat around coughing. I gave him a hug, which was a first for both of us. He'd given up the fags, but what was really killing him, I think, was having to give up the brass band. Here was a music teacher who taught classical French horn for forty years and then played in a colliery band. Maybe he would rather have been a miner, then he'd have an excuse for the brass band *and* the cough. He kept his horn behind the door but he couldn't inflate it any more. Mum was still under the impression that he'd get better.

I didn't stay for dinner because Vicky and her interesting husband Richard were up from St Albans. 'You'll be able to come and see us more often,' Vicky said, because she knew how much I loved to talk about the pharmaceuticals industry with Richard while she and Cathy discussed the new Jane Austen adaptation on BBC1. Richard knew practically nothing about the Beatles, which was astonishing for someone of his vintage. What was he up to in 1963? Probably listening to Acker Bilk or Cleo Lane or something. Vicky was fantastic, of course. You couldn't imagine a better older sister. How many older sisters would let you and your best mate sit in her bedroom with her and listen to records? How many would cut your hair into junior Merseybeat mops when everybody else at school had to have a Tony Curtis or a flat-top? Not many. I couldn't believe it when she was doing her A-levels and she suddenly went off the rails and started listening to Cream and Led Zeppelin and Traffic. She'd started going out with some guy – Brian? Barry? – who said he was a student but turned out to be twenty-five and working in the indoor market. Selling pies. Not that she cared. That was Vicky, then.

And even when she was out with him, there we were, Dean and me, raking through her stuff. If you could have seen us there, in her room, like proper brothers, reading her mags, trying to work out how to play 'Eight Days a Week' with only four chords between us. Dean was always round our house (which I suppose was why he found it so easy to carry on even after I'd got married). And then she gave me all her Beatles stuff, bless her – the posters, the albums, the singles, the Yellow Submarine alarm clock. This is a girl who actually went to see the Beatles play live at the Gaumont in Bradford in 1964. I'd still never even seen *one* of them live. (Dean and I did consider queuing for tickets to see Wings – just to see McCartney in the flesh – but the occasion came and went.) There was a defining moment, I remember, when Cathy and I went to Vicky's house and noticed a Dire Straits CD on the stereo. I hoped it was Richard's, but I don't think it was. It was probably what she would call moving on. I know what Dean would have called it.

Anyway, this was it. The end of an era. I was taking all the important things myself in the back of the Renault, because something was bound to get broken or warped or squashed or bent at the corner of the sleeve. I wondered, for the last time, whether I was mad to be moving on. To be worrying about what happened all those years ago. To be talking to a dead person. But I wasn't mad. Just sitting on a sofa, waiting for the van to come.

friends

Just look at me. I was like a born-again junior reporter. I counted those first days and reached twenty-nine. I woke every morning to plant reassuring kisses on Cathy and Sadie, whose understandable frowns I ignored as I crunched through breakfast with my irritating enthusiasm and sprang blithely from the domestic threshold into the swirl of my new metropolitan life like a week-old puppy into the path of oncoming traffic. The sun warmed me. The air was bracing. The rain filled me with vigour. I could find my way to the office without thinking about it. I knew not to talk to strangers at bus stops. I was on 'Morning, Dorothy!' terms with the black woman who whipped up the cappuccino in the staff cafeteria. I bought but didn't read the *Big Issue*. I walked faster. I'd been out with my new colleagues to spend too much money on lunch in an Italian restaurant, even though it wasn't anyone's birthday. I had been careful not to moan about the beer being crap, or to wonder aloud why so many people wore sunglasses on top of their heads in public places whatever the weather. I remembered to stand on the right on escalators, and to get pissed off at anyone who didn't. I was not a sightseer. I was not passing through. I flourished my three-zone travelcard like the badge of a citizen. I knew to gaze blinkered and world-weary at my reflection in the darkened window of the Tube as it thundered towards King's Cross even though the words 'Ich bin ein Londoner' still sang gaily within me to the rhythm of my giddy heart. My name was Matthew Anthony Lewis and I had arrived unexpectedly at the age of almost forty at the brink of some unspecified adventure. I actually smiled to myself in the street, falling short only of swinging my briefcase arm as I walked. *That's* how bad it was.

On the other hand . . . Well, at the office there was me and Alex and Milo, and sometimes Jane, when she wasn't working from home. We sat in a cluster of desks off the main drag of the office, nearer to sport than to features and hidden out of sight in the corner between the fashion editor's frock-room and the double doors leading to the lifts. Don't ask me why I'd been lumped in with Alex, Milo and Jane, since they were all feature writers and I . . . Well, TV, I suppose, was closer in spirit to features than news, obviously, but I was a bit disappointed not to have my own mini-empire. If I'd been TV Editor of the *Echo*, I'd be writing up all the press releases, doing the acerbic weekend column with my engaging picture above it with my eyebrow in the air, checking the finished pages, slipping over to Liverpool or Manchester to interview the latest lesbian teen pregnancy love-triangle interest on *Brookie* or *Corrie*, smuggling in the odd thinkpiece about the enduring strengths of American comedy and still have a shilling left to ring Cathy on the way home to explain why I'd have to go to the pub first. I'd be doing it all except subbing, design and actually shoving the damn thing through people's letterboxes. They'd be *my* pages. But here, I was . . . what?

Jeremy McVie, Deputy Editor, the man who had lunched, hired and sent me a letter of congratulations – and therefore who ought to know about everything pertaining thereof – had run me through absolutely everything on the first day in the five-minute gap he could spare between vaguely remembering who I was and vanishing off to a meeting, never to darken my desk again, or so it seemed. Anyway, it was pretty straightforward, Jeremy had said, hurriedly enumerating the ins and outs of my important duties on the fingers of one hand: any TV celebrity interviews tended to be done by the regular arts writers, so I wouldn't have to worry about those; the main TV column came under arts too, so I wouldn't have to worry about that either; and the seven 'Watch It' previews were all written by the paper's star columnist James Thomas, who also did the 'Weekender' column for the magazine so I wouldn't have to . . .

'So, um, what *do* I have to worry about?' I'd said, half grinning and half not grinning, struggling to find an expression consistent with worrying that I might not have enough to worry about while not wishing to give the impression that I was the sort of person who worried about things on a habitual, obsessive basis.

'Oh – you know,' Jeremy sniffed, looking over my shoulder at something more pressing on the horizon. 'Just the usual – arrange for tapes to be sent out to James, co-ordinate things, rewrite the listings, keep up with whatever the PRs are throwing your way, keep an eye on production and . . .'

I'd found myself nodding forcefully in agreement, but wondering how Jeremy had managed to forget how much he'd admired my award-winning articles and our exciting lunch together at which the words 'Television Editor' had hovered like annunciating angels over the Blackberry Tart With Crème Anglaise. *Hello, it's me*, I felt like saying. True, the contract of employment that had arrived to mixed notices in the Lewis household was a bit short on detail, but it had never occurred to me for one moment that that was because there was no detail to be long on.

'Sounds pretty great,' I'd said, unable to stop myself moistening my top lip with my tongue, a habit that Cathy now read to mean the opposite of whatever I had just told her. 'And will I be doing much in the way of . . . writing?'

'Ah, right . . . Well, I wouldn't rule it out, but I imagine you'll have your hands pretty full.' Jeremy had grinned, clapped me on the shoulder, winked and then strolled off. Afterwards I wondered whether perhaps Jeremy might simply want to see me use my initiative, which, if I ever got through reading the piles of page-proofs that kept turning up on my desk, shouldn't be entirely beyond the bounds of a chap's ambition.

However, at this particular moment, twenty-nine days in, I suppose I was satisfied to be contemplating my first payslip rather than reading the proofs on my desk. Not just the bit at the end that said how much had gone into our new bank account (NatWest, Crouch End, London N8), but the bigger bit at the top where if I multiplied it by twelve I could find out how much more I was worth than I was a month ago before tax, even though I wasn't quite sure yet how I was meant to be earning it.

'How goes it, Mattie?' Alex prodded me between the shoulderblades as he passed, drumming his fingers along the filing cabinet before collapsing into the seat opposite. He pointed. 'You still reading that payslip, mate? I hope they're not giving you too much.'

I smiled, folded my payslip in half and put it in my pocket. I had begun to realise that when Alex called me 'Mattie' or 'Matto' or 'Matts' or even 'Matso' I was being reminded who was the much-admired veteran controlling the midfield and who had just come up from the reserves. Not because footballers had this weird thing where grown men got stuck with these boy-names like Kenny and Teddy and Robbie and Nicky or truncated into playground tags like Becks and Giggsy. No, in fact it would be exactly the same if Alex decided to give me the full Matthew treatment. The point was, if you were the new boy who didn't know where the toilets were or hadn't been given any proper work to do, the Alexes of this world could call you whatever they wanted and there was no point getting offended and chippy about it.

'Anything good on TV tonight?' yawned Alex. Alex yawned as only a midfield veteran could.

I consulted my listings like a good boy. '*Randall and Hopkirk* – Sixties original series?'

Alex shook his head, chuckling and starting to leaf through a magazine. 'Just pulling your leg,' he said, grinning knowingly, and knowingly looking sideways at Milo. But Milo, who had apparently built himself a solid reputation for being the opposite of a technical genius, was too busy following the procedure of switching on his permanently jinxed computer to focus on anything that demanded the amount of nuance that being knowing required.

Jane, trawling through the tabloids slewed across her desk just behind Milo, looked up. 'Take no notice of him, Matt,' she droned, using the same, now familiar, tone she had used on the day I started, when she and Alex had introduced themselves at the coffee machine and Alex had unexpectedly enquired where I had bought my splendid pointed-toed, black Merseybeat boots. Instinct warned me not to tell Alex I'd got them mail order from a Beatles fan quarterly. 'New York,' I'd said. (New York? Where did *that* come from?)

'New York!' said Alex, nodding and whistling appreciatively, looking at my boots again from this side and that, leaving me wondering whether Alex was a bit dim, whether he knew a pathetic lie when he heard one, or whether he was taking the piss because only someone with coal and whippets in their ears would think that jetting off to New York and buying shoes when they got there was the acme of sophisticated living.

I was starting to develop a kind of fascinated dread of Alex, who never seemed to tire of talking about clothes, and was always coming back after lunch slung with expensive-looking carrier bags from Covent Garden and Islington to attract ironic whistles from the sports desk, whose cheerful denizens erred sartorially on the side of wrinkled shirts and not shaving. Today Alex was wearing some Japanese designer jacket that was almost exactly like the ones the Beatles wore for the NME awards in 1965, except without the epaulettes. I felt it was too early in our relationship to mention it, and probably always would be.

But, deep-down, it wasn't Alex's games that bothered me that morning as I sat there reading proofs. It was the fact that I *was* sitting there reading proofs. I didn't mind *checking* proofs, which was just a question of ensuring that, say, the caption under the photograph of Clint Eastwood, starring in *Thunderbolt and Lightfoot* at 12.30 on Channel Four, actually said 'Clint Eastwood' and not, for example, 'Meryl Streep', who happened to be starring in *Sophie's Choice* on Bravo the same evening (and whose picture, given this not entirely hypothetical scenario, I had found on the opposite page yesterday with Clint Eastwood's name underneath). This was someone else's job. Human error? Well, yes, but you weren't talking about genetic manipulation here. You were talking about having two eyes in your head. And I was reading proofs because the two subs who allegedly worked for me three days a week and were supposed to do this stuff – one called Isabel and one called Isobel – not only shared the same name, but were, I had decided, cut from the same plank of wood. Of course, I wouldn't want to be too ungenerous. Isobel, it had to be said, brought an encyclopaedic knowledge of Broadway musicals to the party and Isabel was a vintage comics buff with a heavy bag of pop trivia (1963–83) on her shoulders. And for all I knew, they could both be grandmasters at backgammon. So they weren't bad at everything – just the things they got paid £150 a shift to be good at: spelling, syntax, a facility with words, having a brain that could hum more than one tune . . . The point was, by the time it came to salvaging a little sense from their execrable doings, the pair of them had gone off to the *Radio Times* or *Time Out* to earn another £150, and I wouldn't see them again till next Monday, by which time I couldn't really be bothered to have thc argument, especially since they always turned up bright and cheery with paper bags full of little jammy cakes from the patisserie outside the Tube. And let's face it, you'd employ someone to do that. Alex, on the other hand, you'd employ to keep your world turning happily like you'd employ a donkey to play the piano. 'Don't take this badly, Mattie,' he was saying, 'but what exactly made you think I might want to watch *Randall and Hopkirk* – rather than, say, something from this century?'

I ignored him.

'This is the one where the guy's partner dies but comes back in a white suit and follows him around being irritating, right?'

'Something of a classic, as I remember,' I murmured.

'OK. But, be honest, do you really think Sixties comedy is still actually funny? I mean people go on about Tony Hancock and Morecambe and Wise, but you have to admit it's all a bit post-powdered eggs and ration books.'

'Well, some of it is, but—'

'I mean, I can't believe they still show those old sketches with André Previn and . . . what's her name, for God's sake, the newsreader. Do you remember how shocked we were all supposed to be to discover that women newsreaders had legs?'

'Well yeah, but if you look at *Rising Damp* and *Porridge* and *The Good Life* – they're still pretty watchable.'

'That was the Seventies, mate . . .' Alex leaned back in his chair and folded his arms.

'Please don't get into this,' droned Jane.

I returned to my proofs, while someone came down from IT, picked up Milo's keyboard, pushed the plug in properly and walked off again without a word. The guys in sport applauded.

'Ah, thanks, Jeff,' Milo called after him. Jeff, or someone like Jeff, visited Milo every day.

I watched him log on, only to sit with a blank screen in front of him and leaf through a battered copy of *Social Trends* from the Stats Office. I didn't know what Milo was up to exactly but I'd give him twenty seconds to tell me. I'd got to eleven when Milo gave a snort. 'Ha! Listen to this. Women aged sixteen to seventy-four are more likely than men to think that a suntan is important,' he said. He swivelled round. 'What do you think, Jane?'

'About what, Milo?' The phone rang and she quickly answered it.

I leaned across the desk. '*Sergeant Bilko*.'

Alex looked at me and shook his head as if I were a complete oaf. 'That was the Fifties.'

'Oh I see. So the Fifties and Seventies can be funny but not the Sixties.'

He laughed out loud. 'You're losing it, Mattie . . .'

'I'm not fucking losing it, *Ally* . . .'

'Alex, Matt . . .' Jane had her hand over the receiver. 'Shut up?'

'OK,' I said, after a moment, sticking my thumb in the air ready to count. '*Bewitched*, *Mister Ed*, *Gilligan's Island*, *Hogan's Heroes* . . .'

Alex frowned and smoothed his sideburns, which tapered to the point of ostentation. 'Americans are different,' he said.

'Fine,' I said.

'An uncle of mine used to collect Hancock's radio shows on tape,' Milo said. Alex and I looked at him, but he'd got his head in *Social Trends*. He turned the page slowly, and ran his finger down the contents. 'Men drink twice as much as women. Hmm. Not in my experience . . .'

I picked up my blue pen and scored through a misspelling of 'minuscule'. I didn't look up again. At 1.30 Caroline, who edited the paper's 'Manners' supplement arrived and threw a preview video wrapped in a press release on my desk, saying she thought it might make a piece. I looked at it. I looked at her. 'Oh. Thanks,' I said, my heart suddenly leaping out of bed at the prospect of something that might make a piece. I didn't want her to think I was desperate, so I faked a yawn of the kind used by Alex, apologised with a smile for yawning, and said 'thanks' again, as if actually I was pretty tired of commissioning editors suddenly noticing that I existed and dropping press releases on my desk that might make a piece that might just possibly carry my byline into a national paper before my sixtieth birthday. Of course by now I was gagging to write something. Cathy had actually caught me staring in the bathroom mirror and mouthing the words 'Interview by MATTHEW LEWIS', which in our house came under career masturbation and was therefore banned.

'*Matt?*' she'd said.

'Facial exercises,' I'd said, distorting my right cheek in her direction.

I missed seeing my name in print, except, of course, on the envelopes that kept flopping on to our doormat bearing demands for payment to do with the new mortgage, some unforeseen unsolicited service carried out by our solicitor, and other bills from people I had never heard of but who seemed to want money for the simple job of providing water, gas and electricity.

'See what you think,' Caroline said, and went off. She had glossy hair and make-up and wore the kind of red jacket that women in the 1980s wore to make everyone on the train think they were the boss of something. All the same, I had to love her for this. The tape and the press release sat on the corner of my desk, but the last thing I could do was look at it right now because Alex hadn't spoken for two hours and was due to say something unhumorous at my expense.

'Hey Matt,' Alex said after five minutes. 'Fancy a beer?'

'Love one.'

Laahv, I said in the southern way. Not luv. What on earth was happening to me?

Those first weeks it was obvious that Jane was a surrogate parent to Alex and Milo, who I was grudgingly getting used to. Alex kept making me spend money that my NatWest card didn't have, particularly one lunchtime when I came back with a seventy quid (*hello?*) white shirt. How was anyone supposed to be able to tell I didn't just buy it at M&S, apart from the extra long cuffs for scooping up gravy? I asked. 'Come on – look at the cut,' said Alex, who obviously fancied himself as Rex Harrison to my whatsername Doolittle. But he could be entertaining. And there were worse things in life than hanging out at Eamonn's (one of those themed spit and shamrock bars with pig's knuckle and cabbage on the menu) watching Milo rocking his chair back and forth, rolling a cigarette, untouched Veggie of the Day in front of him, telling us about going on tour with the Stones in the '80s and going out clubbing with Keith Richards, who he seemed to model himself on, especially the teeth.

Milo used to be a music journo, though exactly what he did now was a mystery to me. Nothing ever appeared with his byline. Jane said he wrote the showbiz diary, which didn't strike me as a full-time job. He wouldn't have lasted five minutes at the *Echo*.

But the *Echo* seemed a million years away now. I wondered what they were all doing. And I'd think about Dean, singing to himself, his head in a car engine, or round at ours sitting on the kitchen table twanging the guitar and getting in Cathy's way while I was on my way back from the magistrates' court or a council meeting. I wondered what he would make of white shirts costing seventy quid.

On the domestic front, we had some way to go. I had my first row with Sadie, about her room. Too small, she said.

'Sadie, it's bigger than your old one. Believe me.'

'It's all the wrong *shape*,' she said, throwing an indeterminate item of clothing against the wall to indicate wrongness of shape. 'Look at the ceiling!' she cried. In the end she managed to crack the window with one of her almost completely metal shoes, which I said she'd have to pay for. 'How can I?' she said. 'I don't have a job any more – *remember*?' Of course I remember. By 'job' she meant her paper round, which she had given up about a year before in favour of asking me for money. Sadie was like an unexploded bomb. Except, obviously, she kept going off. And then the following afternoon Cathy rang the office when I was at lunch and left a message on my machine. Kite had run off somewhere in the park and she couldn't find her anywhere and now she'd had to come back to the house to feed Ellie, and it was past three and Sadie would go up the wall when she got home from school, and where the hell was I at three in the afternoon? (Teachers, of course, think lunch is something you do at twelve o'clock on Noddy-size tables and chairs and it has to last twenty minutes and costs £1.75 and involves telling people to keep their elbows off the table.) Eventually she went off to call the police or the RSPCA, cursing the stupid hound and cursing me because apparently I promised to get a new doggy ID thing for round her neck with the address on, so the whole thing turned out to be my fault after all, for a change. And then by the time I called the house *our* machine was on now, so all I got was Cathy's sunny voice, which was the one she saved for public announcements. So after the bleep I told her in a calm, sober and reassuring manner that, yes, of course I'd be home as fast as my legs would carry me, and not to worry, Kite would probably turn up any minute now wagging her tail with a dead squirrel clamped between her slavering jaws. I told her everything she wanted to hear because that's what perfect husbands are for.

The trouble was that, while as a perfect husband I was happy to do whatever I reasonably could to stop Cathy having a mental breakdown over everything (we had just recently moved house, after all), I was also trying to keep one eye out for old Jeremy, who had amazingly broken his silence, or at least his secretary had left a Post-it on my screen saying he wanted a quick word. Excitement! My guess was that he'd remembered who I was at last and wanted to send me to Hollywood to interview Uma Thurman in the bath. I all but sprinted to his office, but of course he was in a meeting.

By this time, though, I had also read the press release that Caroline with the red jacket had given me and skim-watched the video, which turned out to be a trailer for a breathless investigative docusoap called *Cheating Hearts* (ho hum), which, according to the guff, was a thrillingly controversial four-parter charting the decline of romantic loyalty as a moral anchor in post-industrial Britain, whatever that was. Caroline had helpfully put her big pink highlighter against programme three, which was called 'Something for the Weekend' – an exposé that promised to 'lift the lid on the anonymous extramarital exploits of three married men'. OK, not obviously thrilling but it was a start, right? I rang the press office who said they'd bike number three over pronto.

Alex had of course tried to grill me about whatever it was over lunch at Eamonn's, but I told him it was a bit hush-hush, which got him so peeved that he was obliged to disclose that Caroline in the red jacket liked it up the rear, which even if true struck me as a bit ungallant, but remember I was still pretty new and didn't realise you couldn't talk about sexism in smart London without everyone groaning and rolling their eyes. Even Jane couldn't be bothered to disapprove. Plus Alex was assuming in his patronising, twattish way that anal sex was a complete mystery to northerners, which admittedly it was in our household, but then any kind of sex was a mystery at that precise moment, unless the dog was getting some. Anyway Alex reckoned that Jeremy had been 'giving her one' (Caroline, not the dog), a rumour started by one of the Iso/abels, who it seems surprised them with their tongues down each other's throats one evening in the archive room, though how this adds up to anal sex I don't know, but my sausage and mash arrived at this point so to be honest I didn't really feel like reviving the subject.

Until Cathy rang, it had been pretty quiet, mainly because Alex had fifteen hundred words to file and had been banging away like a man with his Katharine Hamnett trousers on fire. Milo, who was a puzzle in anybody's book of nonsense rhyme, rushed off to see a chap about something probably unconnected with whatever he gets paid for, but not before telling us about the top one hundred most intelligent dogs that he found on the Internet, via his new multifunction mobile that kept going off at lunch but which he didn't have a clue how to operate. It turned out that border collies are the brightest dogs and Afghans are the dimmest (maybe they just don't hear too well with all that hair). I suppose Kite's nearest relatives were whippets, which were medium thickos, coming in at number fifty-six and no doubt fully capable of not finding their way home, unless it transpired that she'd legged it back to Yorkshire of course.

Cathy rang again and left another message the *second* I had to go off for a leak. Where on earth *was* I, she wanted to know, but then after one of her dramatic pauses she 'surprised' me by saying she'd got Kite back and everything was fine. She'd explain later. She'd dropped her belligerent carping tone now and had put on this gooey half-forgiving, half-apologetic voice, as if she couldn't quite decide whether not being able to find the dog because of my neglecting to buy a new ID tag was more of a castration offence after all than her losing the idle mutt in the first place. Oh, by the way, she wondered, had I managed to get across town to Hamley's at lunchtime for Ellie's birthday present? Had I? Well of course I hadn't, I'd been too busy having lunch.

Alex, never one to absent himself too long from my personal affairs, thought it was very funny. 'What are you going to tell her?' he said. 'The truth, of course,' I said, which of course was a lie.

'Did you know that three-quarters of divorces are granted to wives for unreasonable behaviour?' he said.

'Christ, don't you start,' I said.

Just after five Jeremy's secretary called me into his office. He waved me into the seat. I could tell straight away that Uma was off the agenda because he wasn't holding first-class airline tickets but a copy of that week's TV supplement with a thick, angry black circle scrawled around something that I couldn't quite make out but I guessed was bad. 'Ah, Matt . . .' He frowned and passed the supplement across the desk like a wad of used toilet paper. 'I gather we managed to run last Saturday's BBC2 listings instead of this week's,' he said, which had the instant effect of dispelling an image that was just floating into my mind of Caroline bending over the photocopier with him standing behind with his suit trousers around his ankles. He didn't go mad but he did have the slightly discommoded air of someone whose favourite son has just achieved the impossible and flunked GCSE art (which, as it happened, I did). Of course he was never likely to give me a major earache over this, because not only a) he was the one who appointed me and didn't want to look like a jerk, so maybe he'd wait until I'd fucked up a few more times before he fired me and impoverished my family, but mainly b) he was in a panic because there had been a train crash in Somerset and people kept coming into his office with pictures and death-counts and layouts for him to see, so obviously he'd got better things to do than think about what was on TV, or rather what wasn't on TV, that Saturday. I muttered something about it being the subs' fault and he looked relieved that I wasn't the kind of idiot who would just roll over and take the blame, and said something about keeping a closer eye on them. His secretary buried her nose in her work as I came out, so no doubt my cock-up had already been around the office twice, carefully missing my desk.

I walked back through the newsroom amid the flurry of activity that you always get with a running story. Eleven people dead and rising. The mystery now was the proximate cause. Signals? Driver error? Bolt of lightning? Cow on the line? I know it's not very newspapermanly of me but I could never see the point of finding out. I mean, whatever it was wouldn't stop the next terrible thing happening. Disasters are like viruses, always mutating, always looking for interesting new ways to wipe us out. They're too clever for us. We fill our public buildings full of sprinkler systems but then someone drops a fag-end at a football match and burns down the fucking stand. You can't legislate for it. And you can't bring dead people back, which is all we really want. I was at the *Echo* when I heard about Dean's crash, sitting at my desk playing Minesweeper. They hadn't identified the body yet. They had a picture of the wreck, but because it was only some twerp driving a yellow Ferrari (so obviously no great loss, you couldn't help thinking) it just seemed like a reasonable-looking evening splash for the front page. Oh Dean, I'm sorry, but the news was not remarkable. Nothing special. I mean, nothing that having eleven passengers in the back wouldn't have made more special. Likewise, I supposed, if this train driver (thirty-five, unmarried) had copped it alone, the news hacks here wouldn't be rushing around trying to give the impression that journalism was a branch of the emergency services. Everyone would be saying how lucky it was that only one person was dead. Except the one person's mum, and the one person's best mate, who was probably expecting to see him as usual, sometime after nine, walking into the Ticketpunchers Arms for a game of pool.

One man's tragedy was another person's good fortune. Of course no compassionate journalist would actually wish for a rail crash to come along and sweep the issue of his dodgy TV listings off the front page of his editor's mind, but since when did you ever get to choose your own gift horse?

I just about got away with it at home too. Well, eventually. I mean once we'd got past the obligatory cooling-off ritual performed in our bijou kitchen, the two of us crouching down, me trying to touch shoulders with her, me pretending to help tickle Kite's ribs while the silly mutt was rolling about on her back panting with excitement and jerking her head this way and that, me pretending everything was fine, which you have to do before it actually is fine. But then Cathy stood up abruptly, as if she hadn't quite decided whether I was fully out of the doghouse, or whether she cared very much for the smell of designer lager on my breath (even though I'd been madly sucking Clorets all the way home on the Tube), which obliged me to follow her into the living room, leaving Kite yelping for more and obviously wondering why we suddenly cared more about ourselves than about her.

So I tried again. We hadn't actually had the chance yet to discuss the Kite fiasco at this point because of the Ellie birthday present rumpus, which was more or less ironed out once I convinced her that it had slipped my mind for reasons of temporary insanity and not because my family meant so little to me now that I'd got this incredibly important new job. She had her arms folded high across her chest and her hair tied back with a rubber band, which were both established signs of hostility in body language with particular reference to sexual unavailability. All the same, something told me she was only going through the motions of being pissed off, and that deep inside she was defrosting, which was why I was still happy to pursue her round the house cooing in her ear about Kite and not stomping up to my little den at the top of the house. 'So let me guess,' I said. 'This woman who found Kite – she rang the old Leeds number that she found on the collar and they gave her our new address, right?'

'Wrong,' Cathy says. 'This *woman* lives six doors away from us. She spotted Kite wandering up and down the high street sniffing at lampposts and brought her back.'

The dog was rolling over again, bleating. Cathy went to sit on our little Habitat two-seater, so I sat beside her. She was just staring ahead, so I knew she was about to say something thoughtful. 'She's nice,' she said, meaning this woman, not the dog. 'Separated, no kids. Nice old black labrador called Malone. She's taking me along to her reading group.' Cathy sipped her coffee. 'Her name's Bev.'

And, this is soppy I know, but she suddenly gave a little smile, as if she'd been holding it back, so now it was a relief, and her eyebrows went up over her coffee cup, and I realised that her eyebrows were going up for me too and I felt a bit choked, God knows why. Well, OK, I did know why. It was because she'd been gritting her teeth for a month, standing by me when Sadie had been a pain, and stopping herself saying that she should have listened to her mother when Ellie's buggy disappeared overnight from the front garden after I couldn't be fagged to bring it in, and only occasionally ringing me at work to complain that BT still hadn't sent the Yellow Pages so how on earth were we supposed to get a fucking *plumber* . . . But now, with this Bev moment, there was just an inkling that she might at last be ready to lay down her hat and ask the neighbours over for a cup of sugar. I knew it was going to be hard for her, of course, but I suppose I didn't want to hear about it. I didn't want to be responsible if it all went wrong. It had been a long time since she'd had to meet new people. You might meet new people at work maybe. Or friends of friends. But not completely new people. Not straight off the street for God's sake. And now she'd done just that. Moving on wasn't just about moving house. It was about having a new map in your head showing where all the different neighbourhoods of your life were. And I immediately realised that for Cathy (because this is how well I know her) knowing the name of this Bev's dog was the first sign of that. So we had a tender moment when I put my arm round her and gave her a kiss, which I'd been wanting to do for weeks but didn't dare because I was too shit-scared of what she might suddenly need to say – like 'take me home' or 'it's not working' or 'I'm not happy'. Now I'd be able to just ask if everything was OK, knowing that, more or less, it would be, and she squeezed my hand as if it was, and we both went quiet, like you do after your first kiss or your first time in bed together or anything else that you can't go back on. I was as happy that night as I'd ever been.

But then there were other times in those first weeks, when the small things came to rattle me in the night, and I'd go sit upstairs in my new den, prodding at my little Wurlitzer electric piano with the headphones on. Sometimes it was the job, sometimes Dean, sometimes Cathy and me. I'd hear the baby wake up and a creak of floorboard as Cathy went to fetch her, which meant Ellie would be in our bed when I went down, which was a drag of Shakespearean dimensions. And then Cathy was pressing me about Sadie, who wanted to go up to her gran's again for the second time in the five minutes we'd been here, which resulted in one of those whispered barking conversations (because Sadie was sulking in the kitchen) about how Sadie couldn't just keep running back to Leeds and how we'd all got to look forward, and how it would cost us a fortune at this rate, and hadn't she got any friends at school for God's sake and how I had been talking to Jonathan next door who was amazed (not to say a bit put out) that we managed to get Sadie into Muswell Hill, because they tried to get whatever their daughter was called in there but couldn't. Obviously this was my side of the argument. Cathy didn't really have one. She just wanted me to give in.

'She just needs a bit of time,' Cathy said, but I knew it had to be about this boyfriend of Sadie's, who I wouldn't mind about if we'd ever actually met him. 'Well, I said she'd have to ask you,' Cathy said. 'And you *have* met him. Adam his name is.'

So perfect. I got to be the bad guy, which soured things a bit after our recent warm feelings. But then later, when we were watching TV, I caught her looking at me in a funny way, which was generally a sign that she was about to say something amusing that would make things OK between us. Of course what amuses one person might leave another person slightly annoyed and it's not as if I couldn't take a joke but . . .

'Matt.' She pointed at my face. 'Tell me that's *not* a goatee beard you're growing there.'

I mean it's not as if we'd ever drawn up a prenuptial agreement about permissible facial adornment. It's not as if I'd ever asked her if she was growing armpit hair. Anyway, she put her hand up to touch it and I pulled away slightly. I wished I hadn't because it was a lost opportunity, and I ended up sitting there with my cheeks going red in the middle of *Newsnight* like a teenager who's been caught by his mum with a copy of *Big Ones*, and I made some joke about there being nothing wrong with taking a healthy interest in your own appearance. And she was smiling, not at the joke, but as if she'd got some secret little thought about it, which annoyed me even more, I don't know why. It was like when the news comes on just before the highlights of a midweek match and they tell you to look away now if you don't want to know the score and I always used to make Cathy look away too. Not because I thought she might give the result away but because I didn't like the idea of her knowing something that I didn't that was more important to me than it was to her. It was all about power, probably, I guessed – or insecurity.

Cathy's mother had stayed a week before we managed to pack her back off to Leeds, hugging Cathy and Sadie and Ellie at King's Cross station as though they were prisoners on death row, and reserving a cold smile for me and a parting lament on the size of the gardens in London. Of course it was a smaller house, but how much space did we need? There were only four of us. And it was big enough by London standards. If anything, the house in Leeds was too big, surely.

I pulled a record from the shelf and blew imaginary removal men's dust from the sleeve. 'All My Loving' – 1964. It was one of Vicky's EPs. I wondered why she'd bought it – she must already have had all the tracks on LPs by then. Maybe it had been a birthday present. Maybe she was like me and had to have everything. I played both sides through, standing at the square window that didn't open, two floors up, and staring at the tangle of garden below. I'd brought all my non-CD stuff up to my new little loft hideaway, and arranged it by size – not, as Cathy might joke, alphabetically or chronologically or by preference or sleeve colour or smell. ('So Matt owns twenty-five different cover versions of 'Yesterday' – that doesn't make him obsessive,' Cathy used to delight in telling people whenever the opportunity arose at a party or a pub, or anywhere else a Beatles song might suddenly charge the air and invite a joke at my expense. She used to turn to me quickly and make sure I was laughing too, make sure I hadn't taken offence, as if it were some weakness or illness – haemorrhoids or jock-itch or something – that she suddenly felt ashamed of exposing.)

Left to right: reel-to-reels, then albums, EPs, singles, cassettes along one shelf, with my old Technics midi-system, Vicky's even older Pye mono player, boxes of sheet music, knick-knacks, Pignose amp, Teac deck and, on the floor beneath, the big headphones I bought twenty-five years ago. Pre-digital tech. My Yamaha acoustic, Wurlitzer and Dean's Rickenbacker were in their cases against the wall, my red trimphone and Apple Mac were plugged in, my favourite Soviet Union *Help!* poster was on the wall with the signed John Lennon tea-towel from 1966 that had been Dean's too. So I was at home, even if the rest of the house looked as though all the furniture that really lived there had gone on holiday and theirs had come to house-sit and didn't know where anything was.

Sadie came up to the loft. She bumped her finger along the tops of the albums, and lifted the lid of the Pye and fiddled with the chrome lever that made the records drop. 'Is this about Alan?' I said, pulling her hand gently out of the record player and lowering the lid.

She looked sullen and sat on the one chair and started pressing the keys on the computer keyboard. 'Dad, he's called Adam. And no, I just want to see my friends, that's all.'

'Look, I'm not sure it's a good idea. Why don't you invite some friends from school round here?'

'Mum thinks it's a good idea.'

'Did she say that?'

'No, but . . .'

'But?'

She stood on her toes to look out of the window. 'I don't want new friends, Dad, I want my old ones.'

'It's hard for everyone, Sade—'

She whirled on me, her eyebrows knitted together in exaggerated fury. 'It's not hard for you. You didn't have to leave anyone behind. You didn't have any friends.' She made a play of storming out but there was no door to slam, and she couldn't clomp down the stairs because they were too steep and she was wearing her breeze blocks. Eventually I heard the door of her own room bang.

I sat for a while. The house was quiet. I could hear Cathy way down in the kitchen drinking coffee and mooning over paint charts with her new friend Bev. Every now and then the sound of a teaspoon or laughter floated up through the house. In a minute Bev would leave, and Cathy would suddenly wonder why I hadn't made a start on clearing the garden. The grass was a foot high where it wasn't completely bald and there were clumps of straggly, dried-up shrubs all over the place. There was a rusting washing machine in the shed.

At the old house, all I had to do was mow the lawn three or four times a year. It was a big lawn but it ended at the apple trees and the little plot where Cathy grew her organic vegetables. We had a swing for Sadie, a place to put deckchairs in the summer, a patio with terracotta pots and a metal table and chairs for having a beer in the evenings, and a wispy creeper that flowered in the summer. When you'd been somewhere ten years, you didn't have to do that much to keep it exactly the same. It was terrible when we'd first moved in. I mean it looked fine to me, and it was OK really, but Cathy said we had to make it ours. She said that was the point. Even if she'd loved the decor, we would have had to change it. But after a while, I started to dread weekends. I found myself just wanting to hang out, or take little Sadie to a pub with a garden, but Cathy would want me to start stripping a floor or put shelves up, even though we both knew I didn't have a clue, and the mere thought of holding the Bosch electric drill she had forced me to buy made me go hot and cold with fear. It was irrational and stupid but it was real at the same time.

Of course, I managed to get a handle on the basics in the end. I had dispelled the lethargy which during the early years used to hit me like a sickness, leaving me inert and quiet, putting a cold distance between me and Cathy for days on end. Of all the moral failings it was possible to be accused of, being useless with a screwdriver or a spanner seemed the weirdest. How did it ever get on the list? When I was about fourteen,

Mr Fletcher, our woodwork teacher, would make a point of gathering everyone round my bench every Wednesday morning for a tutorial in how to make a sow's ear from a nice bit of pine. One week, I'd been working on a box – just a little box to keep my plectrums in – and old Fletcher had come up and started knocking it to pieces with his mallet in front of everyone. He didn't have to knock it very hard. Just a few soft taps with his mallet. He was making a point about slack dovetails, but he seemed to take pleasure in it too ('Just look at this'). You didn't do that to a fourteen-year-old. I hated the idea of Cathy coming along with a mallet and doing the same thing.

Sometimes she'd let me take Sadie off to the park while she got on with the wallpapering. But at other times, I'd sit in our two-seater Habitat armchair getting more and more depressed because I knew we were going to have a row and Cathy would say I was a lazy bastard and unsupportive. Lazy? Hardly. By this time Dean and I had learnt all the words and chords and harmonies for all the Beatles songs by heart. In fact we'd started working out each other's harmonies and inventing harmonies for songs that didn't even have harmonies, him Lennon, me McCartney, sitting with cups of tea in the front room.

I didn't know what it was, but it wasn't laziness. It was more like paralysis, and the longer it went on the harder it was to imagine being able to move. I'd also felt guilty because Cathy's dad had given us £10,000 towards that house, which seemed an awful lot back then – though the truth was that Cathy's father, who had taught at the university, broke up with Cathy's mother and ran off to America with his research assistant when Cathy was about seventeen, so it didn't take a genius to work out what the ten grand was about. Even so, all I could feel was the burden of opportunity that was having to do a ton of work to restore that fantastic big house.

I didn't know Cathy's dad too well, but I couldn't bring myself to blame him for getting out, though I knew Cathy did, even though she must have realised that it was twenty years with her mother that had driven him into the arms of a younger woman. But what else could you do – you've put all that life into a marriage you don't believe in any more, and all you can see ahead is more of the same. Do you just surrender to everyone else's happiness or do you move on? Fleeing to America and being called 'professor' and shagging his research assistant was moving on for Cathy's dad.

Ages ago, there had been someone Cathy and I both knew slightly from the Lion who had split up with his wife. It sounded pathetic but this man's wife had been asking him to put a new fence up for ages – maybe a year – and he had just kept putting it off. He was training to be a solicitor with a firm in Wakefield and being quite brainy got into the habit of doing crosswords on the train. Then at the weekend he'd get busy on one of those hard crosswords without black squares in one of the Sunday magazines. It was like the Rolls-Royce of crosswords. It was one of those crosswords that take even crossword geniuses half the week to finish. So he used to sit around doing just that while the fence fell down around his marriage. The fence was just the breaking point. His wife would have to bully him into doing everything, but the fence never got done. In the end she left him and she divorced him. He didn't try to stop her. Maybe he had expected something different.

Cathy understood completely. She had said it was not about fences at all but about love and support. I remember the two of us standing in our matching blue dungarees in the front room scraping wallpaper together, with Cathy getting madder and madder, and me more and more bewildered. I wondered why this bloke couldn't just have got someone in to fix the bloody fence.

'Don't you see,' Cathy said, 'if you don't love someone enough to work to make a home together, you might as well split up. This is a bit like you, and your bloody—'

'But I do love you – I'm always telling you.'

'I know, but it's not enough to tell someone you love them – it's too easy. You can tell someone you love them and then go off and play guitars with your mate for ever. That's what you do when you're a teenager. When you're a grown-up you have to do things you don't want to do. You have to scrape the wall. Working at a marriage isn't bringing flowers home – it's scraping walls together. And sometimes it's scraping walls on your own.'

'I am scraping the wall.'

'Yes, you are now. But it's just as easy to imagine you doing the crossword.'

'I can't do crosswords.'

So I looked out of the little window that didn't open over the garden. It was a mess. I remembered mowing my first patch of lawn in our first little redbrick terrace off Kirkstall Road. I remembered wondering, as I went backwards and forwards digging up lumps of turf with next-door's Crimean War-issue manual Qualcast what the point was of cutting something down just to watch it come up again. It was like an illness that you had to keep at bay. Marriage was exactly the same. It was a metaphor, wasn't it? If you stopped cutting your grass the marriage got sick and died. They called it unreasonable behaviour but when you thought about it that was the kind of thing it boiled down to. And yet I did love Cathy, as madly as ever. Would she have divorced me over a fence?

Dean had never lived with a woman. I mean, he'd hardly even worked with one, except Judy or Julie or June who did his accounts twice a week. I know he'd been out with a lot of women, and taken them back to his yuppie apartment on the river with its communal gardens and pool in the basement that he paid for but never bothered to use. I was always amazed that he went for a place like that. Walkways and little shrubs and French cafés. He hated all that stuff. What he liked was a bacon sandwich with brown sauce, wolfed down at 10.30 in front of his computer while we exchanged e-snippets about McCartney's taste for jelly beans or his bizarre decision to live with Jane Asher and her parents. Anyway, women were impressed by yuppie apartments, he said. But he never gave me the impression of wanting to step beyond what impressed the women he saw. He never took them home to meet his mum, or even me and Cathy. He was never tempted to move in with one or let one move in with him. What did he talk about? Or did he let the revolving mattress do all his talking? *Next!*

I, of course, immediately moved in with the first one who came along, or rather she moved in with me. I never said anything to Dean, for obvious reasons, but by then I was completely mad for Cathy. I felt lucky that she wanted me, not only because I was at the poly and all her friends were at the proper Oxford, or because she could have had me instead of Dean at that Christmas party ages ago in the Bricklayers, but because I spent so long with her *not* wanting me. I mean, not wanting me in particular. It was because I absolutely ached for her (sorry, but Mills & Boon has it exactly right there) and pursued her under the false pretences of something more casual, and then one day it worked. I knew she kind of liked me, but because I'd always had this sexual jinx following me around, it seemed so impossible. I mean I'd *never* done it, though Christ knows I'd been in all the right places with all the right girls – behind the garages, down the rec near the swings, in the back room when Mum was out having to watch Dad's school orchestra. But for one reason or another I hardly ever got into the opposition's half, let alone the eighteen-yard box. I remember having a fight with Dean over a girl when we were about sixteen. In the snow. It was more of a scuffle really, and the funny thing was he never actually knew what it was about. I could tell his pride was hurt – not because I'd got the better of him (I hadn't in any real sense) but because he'd always been able to head conflict off at the pass and this one somehow got past him. It was one of those things that never came up again. And now it was one of the things that I couldn't do anything about.

I should just say that the thing about Cathy, in the end, was that there was none of that preliminary stuff. One minute we were friends who happened to both come from Leeds and travel on the same bus and go to the arty cinema sometimes to watch Jacques Cousteau or whatever he was called, then suddenly we were having our first fully comprehensive sexual encounter back at my flat-share off Banbury Road. And when I say our first fully comprehensive sexual encounter, I mean, of course, *my* first fully comprehensive sexual encounter. I was twenty-one. So yes, of *course* I wanted to live with her for the rest of my life.

I used to have this unconscious habit at work. I suppose I still do. I close my eyes and inhale women as they pass the back of my chair. Men don't smell at all, but women leave their scent behind as they waft past. It's not perfume, or at least not perfume on its own, just a mingling of their daytime smells. When you live with someone, you get to know all their smells. You want to be intimate. You want them to wear your shirt or your jumper and leave their smell on that. Of course Dean was more experienced. I mean he had quantity and variety, but he had no depth in that way. I never said this to him – I suppose because I didn't want to seem gratuitously indelicate *vis à vis* Cathy – but if you've never brushed your teeth in the same room as a woman busying herself on the toilet, you've never really been in love. I agree it's not love as it appears on TV. I mean you couldn't sell it as an idea. It's not a motivating factor. And yet when you really love someone, that's just the kind of unsavoury thing you eventually get to do. It's like, to start with, you want to rip all the barriers down between you as separate people. You want to be honest with each other. Trust each other. The first time you do it, you're showing someone how close you want to be. So for me, it was part of love. It was holy matrimony.

Then I found myself wondering whether it wasn't also the beginnings of contempt. I mean, if that's what familiarity breeds. Maybe it's not good to know someone too well. You often hear about women talking about their husband's feet or farting in bed. But what do they expect? As a man, you hide yourself and then you give yourself. That's what they ask for. We want it too. We expect it. The Victorians never saw their wives naked. They had their own bedrooms. It sounds terrible, but just think about fourteen years into a marriage like that – when you've never really 'known' your wife in that sense. You've never seen her on the commode. The funny thing is, it's almost enviable. I mean, if you only want what you can't have, and you never get it, then you'll want it for ever, right?

And I'd think about Dean. Buddy. Blood-brother. Kindred keeper of the Fabs flame. John to my Paul. Bright, white-suited Hopkirk to my wizened, bad-complexioned Randall. These were the kind of things I couldn't say. I don't mean that any of it was so unbearable, just that it was the kind of thing you might not want your best friend to know.

And then there was Sadie, walking around wearing one of those tops that would show her pierced navel if I'd let her have one for her last birthday. I'm not a pervert or anything but sometimes I'd look at her and suddenly imagine her having anal sex with Alan or Adam or someone else with eyebrows that met in the middle, and I'd just have to look away. Sexy Sadie. I sometimes wished I'd never suggested that. Cathy had wanted to call her Maisie after her favourite long-winded Henry James story. I don't think Sadie would have thanked her for that somehow. The amazing thing was, Cathy had reached the ripe old age of thirty-seven without even knowing there was a song with that name. Unless Gilbert and Sullivan had covered it. In fact the only time she really took any interest in the Beatles was when I told her they'd almost played at her college, but that they'd had to cancel because it clashed with the band's holidays. (Paul, George and Ringo went to Tenerife, John went to Spain with Brian Epstein.) Odd that. I can't believe he was a secret tortured homosexual or anything. Just looking for a father figure. He was wrong about one thing. Love wasn't all you needed. You needed everyone to be happy too. Which was turning out to be much more tricky.

The four of us were sitting outside the fashion editor's office eating sushi from Pret a Manger and idly watching part three of *Cheating Hearts*. Every now and then I made a note in the pad beside me. And every now and then Alex laughed out loud and smacked the desktop with delight. Jane was undisguised disdain personified. 'For God's sake, Alex, you're sadder than they are.'

'Maybe, but I'm not married. I can sleep with as many women as I want.'

'Ha! You wish. Anyway you *were* married. It amounts to the same thing.'

Alex was even more delighted. 'What? How do you make that out?'

Jane answered with a contemptuous silence. Milo was flicking through *Empire* magazine, looking up from beneath his lank, black crow's-feather fringe and murmuring in vague agreement or vague disagreement when any of the others made a comment. The film wasn't a strikingly original kind of confessional documentary – three case studies spliced together, most of it beamed in from a sofa or a kitchen table, with some sauced-up exterior shots with a hand-held camera and set against a dozy country-and-western soundtrack intended to point up the sentiments on display and show that the makers had a sense of humour. It was one of those set-ups where you didn't hear the questions put by the researcher, just the answers. I'd already sat through the film once and put a begging call through to the producer to arrange my own interview with 'Lawrence', one of the men featured in the programme. Lawrence was the interesting one.

'Just listen to this prat,' Jane was saying.

Despite the teasing reference in the press release about the whole thing being 'anonymous', two of the three philanderers were completely open about it, sitting as reasonable as pie in their front rooms with their sad, understanding wives explaining how sex with other women kept their marriages fresh. The wives looked on uncomplainingly as their husbands talked, putting on a show of intimacy for the camera but betraying touches of discomfort with the occasional facial twitch and eyes that offered flashes of doubt that could be read by anyone except their stupid men, who wittered on about having a modern relationship that kept everyone happy, who spoke without shame or irony about the differing fundamental needs of the sexes. (Neither wife went in for affairs but that was because they didn't need it, the husbands both said, looking intently as their wives replied to this point, holding their hands to help them through it, as if these understanding women might use the opportunity to confess dark thoughts or deeds and launch unexpected revenge attacks to make cuckolds of their husbands on air.) Both men were smug, overtanned, cropped-headed gym-attenders and could have been the same person, except that Paul ran his own haulage company in Nottingham and hardly saw his wife anyway, and Doug was a Norfolk computer consultant, who seemed to think that his job was 'obviously glamorous', and 'obviously had its fair share of temptations'. 'I don't ask him for details and he doesn't tell me,' sniffed Doug's wife, as if this was an agreement 'obviously' hammered out in heaven, rather than all she had left to boast about.

'Can you believe these women?' Alex was saying.

'The *women*?' shrieked Jane. She shook her head.

We watched Amy the fashion assistant tottering by on clunky heels struggling with an enormous bundle of designer-wear in plastic wrappings and trying to unlock the frock cupboard. She had a short fleecy top on, and her backbone stood out as she leaned over. 'Here, let me,' Alex said, leaping up, exaggeratedly gallant.

'Wait, though,' Milo said, 'they're just trying to keep the marriage together. Makes sense. I mean, take *American Beauty* . . .'

'But why on earth should they?'

Milo shrugged. 'I read something recently about Britain having the second-highest divorce rate in Europe.'

'So what? That doesn't mean—'

'Who's got the highest?' asked Alex, coming back, ostentatiously winking at Amy across the office for our benefit.

'Um. I don't know, I think it only mentioned Britain.'

'Hang on, this is the one,' I said. 'This is Lawrence.'

The programme-makers had Lawrence seated in a darkened room answering his case through the voice of an actor. Intercut with this were scenes where the camera followed Lawrence's legs – or perhaps the actor's legs – into the West End: a couple of bars first, both done out in the same flat polished surfaces with waiters flitting around in white aprons (identified by Milo as Brazza's and Tupelo), and then later a smart club, with the actor's voiceover cutting through the music (the Move, the Hollies, the Isleys) and giving an unemotional account (unless emotion had been flattened in the translation) of nocturnal ramblings that led – on an ideal night, Lawrence's actor pointed out – to a discreet, expensive one-bedroom hideaway in the Barbican with a spicy blonde in tow, preferably full of champagne.

'I think you can be a better husband and father by not completely giving yourself up to one single emotional focus. I don't want to lose the passions that make me an individual,' he was saying. 'I'm not comparing it to a hobby exactly, but . . .

well, going out to find sex isn't a sign of dissatisfaction. It just gives me a kind of *extra* satisfaction - the kind that someone else might get from water-skiing or rock-climbing or playing golf.' Lawrence had an adoring wife and two children who loved him and who had been required to appreciate that the price of a big house and holidays and mountain bikes meant the odd weekend away on business or fishing trips with friends.

'Do you fish?' asked the interviewer, missing the point.

'Are you kidding?' laughed the actor.

Milo's phone rang and he rushed over to answer it. He spoke softly for a couple of minutes before pulling his greasy-looking brown suede jacket on and sloping off, giving a short wave as he left.

I was trying to imagine Lawrence at home leafing through a paper, or taking the kids swimming while his wife cooked dinner, or having to go out to find a lost dog in the park, but I couldn't. 'The thing is,' I'd said when I rang Tanya, the producer, 'it might look a bit flat if I just preview your programme. But if I get my own slant on things, I can expand it into a bigger piece – and obviously you'd get better exposure.'

She hadn't been enthusiastic, but I told her the publicity people had been very keen, though in fact they'd had no opinion about it, mainly because I hadn't thought to mention it when I'd spoken to them.

'I think there's maybe a slight weakness in your programme, in that – well, you can't really tell what kind of person Lawrence is. You know *what* he says, but you only have the actor's word for how he says it. How much can the viewer enter into that? Whereas a literal description of how someone speaks or acts is much richer in these circumstances, don't you think? People trust what they read . . .' I waited for her to laugh but she didn't. 'I think a written piece will bring out a bit more depth and tee up the readers nicely for the TV version – it'll flesh him out a bit. What do you think?'

'OK, I'll try,' she said eventually. 'But he won't agree to it. Not in a million years.'

But he had. With the accepted provisos about anonymity and anything else that might give him away, this so-called Lawrence had agreed. Why? Presumably for the same reason that he wanted to appear on TV. Whatever that was. But what kind of a rat cheated on his wife in such a systematic way, and then wanted to tell the world about it anyway? Was it egotism? Or euphoria? Maybe it was just good old therapy. And maybe it was because he had already said yes to Tanya that he now said yes to me so easily. Confession was a bit like adultery itself. Once you'd done it with one person, you might as well be anyone's.

Dean was always saying how nicc and peaceful the old house was in Leeds. Which always struck me as odd. It could hardly be more peaceful than his own house, which had no one in it moaning about homework (Sadie) or barking at the phone (Kite) or clattering about in the kitchen (Cathy). 'No, no,' he'd say. 'You know. Domestic bliss.' Lying back in the chair with a beer after lunch on Sunday, watching the box with one cye open, one foot on our coffee table wagging slowly from sidc to side. I don't know if hc was taking the piss in a lazy appreciative way. It wasn't as if he'd ever wanted anything I had.

Thinking about this, I was finding it harder and harder to think about Dean in any specific way. Outside the set pieces of life – a memorable trip somewhere, a wedding, a crucial gig – it was impossible to divide up our history into anything more detailed than typical moments where the same things were said and done – our house, his mother's kitchen, the Bricklayers. To remember him properly, it seemed I had to remember what really counted.

By contrast, the scenes at this time from Crouch End still

had a fresh separateness about them. Nothing competed for space. It was like a new photo album with only three pictures in it. Everything counted. Everything was still present tense.

Such as . . .

Mum on the phone. 'Hello, Mum . . .'

Dad coughing in the background while she asks me about Cathy and the job and London and Sadie. 'Fine,' I say three times, with a provisional 'Well . . .' for Sadie. But because she's already spoken to Cathy and asked her exactly the same questions, I'm happy to let her soothing narrative wash over me as she dredges up the usual popular wisdoms on settling into a new place, teenage moods, cultural differences, house maintenance and the homing instincts of dogs, though obviously if Kite had had any homing instincts she'd have been a hundred miles up the M1. Dean's mum has phoned her to say the garage has been sold, which brings a lump to my throat. She says there's some Beatles stuff Dean's mum wants me to have. Dad isn't in great health, but the weather's been very fair, they've had chops for tea, Leeds won 4–3 at Coventry. We can't really tell each other anything we don't already know. I don't know why, but I find this strangely comforting.

And . . .

Her: 'What is your problem, Matt?'

Me: 'I don't know. Nothing. I'm just tired.'

Her: 'Well be tired away from me. I can't stand it. Go away.'

Me: 'All I'm saying is, when you put the Hoover back, why can't you hook the pipe back over the . . . the hook? That's what it's there for. Otherwise it sprawls all over the place and you can't get anything else out of the cupboard. It's not difficult . . .'

Her: 'All right, I've heard you. But why is everything such

a problem? And anyway you hardly touch the Hoover, so what would you know about how difficult anything is?'

Me: 'Oh, come on, please don't start on that . . .'

Her: 'I didn't start anything, you did when you started complaining about my shoes and the fridge.'

Me: 'Well what do you expect? I—'

Her: 'Drop it now, Matt, I've really had enough.'

Me: 'Why do always do that? You—'

Her: 'Drop it. Just *drop* it!'

Me: 'OK, OK . . .'

(Ellie starts crying. Cathy scoops her up wearily, exaggeratedly, out of the high chair, and starts to rock her as if I'm the one who's upset her. The dog yelps once and circuits the kitchen sniffing the floor. Sadie slouches in and starts to make a banana sandwich.)

Sadie (looking at me accusingly): 'What is it with you two?'

Me (jocular): 'Don't worry, it's healthy for parents to argue.'

Cathy sighs and takes Ellie into the small dining room.

And again . . .

I'm setting the alarm. Cathy turns to me and says she understands I'm under pressure from my new job, that maybe I should to get out more, start finding new friends. She doesn't mention Dean. I put my arm around her and say maybe I should take up golf or rock-climbing. Her hair's in my face and slightly obstructing my breathing but I know that if I move it, the moment will be gone and she'll turn over and go to sleep.

And me? My mind was on the blink. Dean's mum sent me the *Hard Day's Night* poster from his office drawer (yes!), plus a couple of Beatles monthlies I'd already got, the Overlanders' 'Michelle' single, a nice 1963 handbill from the Slough Adelphi with Roy Orbison. Oh, and an unfathomable orchestral score of 'For No One'. Where did *that* come from? Then I was just about to throw the parcel away when I found a set of old photographs we'd had done for him – ancient pictures of me, Dean, Cathy and Sadie when she was about two on a trip to Liverpool. There was one of Dean holding Sadie outside where the old Cavern used to be. Cathy was bored stiff. We'd run out of money (Dean had insisted we spend our last collective fiver on sticks of Beatles rock for everybody) and my dad had to pick us all up from Leeds station and we had to listen to his tapes all the way back to Headingley.

Dean wouldn't remember how Dad always used to go wild about Dennis Brain, though I would be surprised if I'd never mentioned it. Dennis Brain was the best classical French horn player in the world. He was the John Lennon of classical French horn. It wasn't until about six months after the funeral that I was reading the McCartney biog and found out that Dennis Brain had actually been booked to play on a Beatles session when they were recording *Revolver*. The track was – guess what – 'For No One'. And guess what again – the poor man was killed in a car crash before he could do it. I couldn't think of anything more tragic. He could have been right up there in history along with the man who played the high-pitched trumpet on 'Penny Lane'. What a waste. I'd told Cathy but she wasn't really too astonished.

That was why I'd been playing *Revolver* a lot, but on this particular day, the day the package arrived from Leeds, it was that Harrison song 'I Want to Tell You' (same album, two tracks further down) that was ringing in my head, in particular the line about feeling hung up and not knowing why. I decided then and there that it was a song about finding a picture of your wife that you've never seen before, taken with your best friend's camera (one of those long, letterbox-shaped panoramic jobs), but under your own apple tree, near your wife's vegetable garden, presumably by your best friend. Your wife is massively pregnant with her second child and wearing a big jumper to keep out the cold. Her hair is blowing all over the place. She's not smiling. Maybe she's annoyed about something. And when I listened to that line about being hung up and not knowing why I asked myself: where would the rest of the letterbox-shaped pictures from this set be now – at your best friend's mum's? What were they of? Of your best friend climbing in and out of his pathetic middle-aged client's yellow Ferrari? Or building a bonfire on bonfire night? Or picking his nose? Or of his cat, Martha, who now lives with his mum? Because only one of these pictures found its way into his special things, in his private drawer, at his place of work. That was one of the great things about the Beatles – they had a song for every occasion.

So you could see where I was heading. It was madness of a kind. A logic that could flow into any shape your imagination could come up with. (Of course the entire set of letterbox pictures could easily have been in Dean's so-called 'private' drawer – his mum just sent the one she thought we'd want. Thanks, Dean's mum!)

It would have been better if Cathy had just lied in the first place about Dean instead of expecting it not to matter. Because the minute one truth is out you start looking for another. You see woods when there aren't any trees. You make the song fit the occasion. You might even know, deep down, why you're doing it. And in a way that's the worst thing.

On the phone he'd seemed almost businesslike. Cordial, you might call it, but with a clipped, corporate 'yep', as though speaking to a client. Or rather not a client – a contact maybe. His London accent had been sanded down and buffed but it was still a long way from the projected Rada tones of the actor who had played him in the film. He was probably ringing from his office, I thought. His own playpen with his name on the door and PR toys on the desk but with a bigger open-plan office just outside. He'd only spoken for a couple of minutes – just long enough to arrange a place and a time – but far in the background there was the dissolved ambient hum of nothing in particular made up of voices and air-conditioning and the tick of running software. He'd introduced himself as Lawrence and mentioned Tanya and the programme, and suggested the Tupelo bar on Frith Street, three o'clock. 'Do you know it?' he asked.

'Yes,' I lied, thinking it was probably the kind of smart place I ought to be thought to be familiar with, but then immediately regretted having stooped to the kind of deceit, however mild, that I felt for some reason associated me too closely with my subject. 'I'll find it,' I added. So. Three o'clock. Frith Street was in Soho. Here was a man who probably wanted the lunchtime crowds out of the way in case he bumped into someone he knew, I thought. He probably worked locally. He was probably a recruitment consultant or a property agent or some cowboy in financial services who had an army of sales serfs cold-calling uninterested housewives fifteen hours a day. But when I walked into the bar, unprepared for the late summer heat in my long reporter's raincoat, carrying a pink plastic bag from Flamingo Sounds and ostentatiously displaying a copy of the *Telegraph*, the man who looked up from his *Standard* and raised a finger in the air as if summoning a waiter or hailing a cab was not wearing the goon suit and humorous Disney tie of my imagination, or sporting a laughable mullet haircut and a ginger beard, but was dressed in long cargo shorts, Camper shoes and a T-shirt that said 'Go Now' in a *faux*-1960s typeface on the front. He peered over a pair of violet, rectangular sunglasses as I approached the table.

'Drink?'

I leaned across to shake his hand. 'What's that you're having?'

Lawrence lifted his empty glass. 'It's just mineral water.'

'I'll have a beer,' I said, shedding my coat and digging through each pocket in turn for my tape recorder. The drinks came. We talked about the astonishing weather. I drained the half-glass of cold suds the waiter had poured and apologised for my thirst, then began bowling Lawrence a few preliminary questions and jotting down his replies in my still excellent shorthand as the tape ran. Lawrence was thirty-seven, he drove into London every day from the country, he had three children – one of each, he said, grinning. I smiled without looking up. He worked in the entertainment business on the creative side. His wife didn't work. He'd had a conventionally happy childhood. He had been to school. He had been to university. He supported a football team. He wouldn't say which one.

Still sweating, I gulped down the second half of my beer and thought about calling the waiter, but the waiter was busy at the other end of the long room talking to two Japanese tourists wearing drape jackets and rock'n'roll quiffs. There was a 1950s studio photograph of Elvis above the bar. I could see the connection but didn't know why . . .

'Tupelo,' Lawrence said, reading my mind. 'It's where Elvis was born. These guys were probably expecting themed karaoke - maybe just a jukebox.'

'Right, so . . .' I began. I paused, slightly irritated by the Japanese tourists and uncomfortably aware of the non-sequitur now sitting on the tip of my tongue, but unable to think of any way of avoiding it, having already exhausted all pleasantries and introductory questions. 'So . . . you go out and pick some girl up and have sex . . .'

He nodded, concentrating on squeezing his slice of lemon into his glass.

'So . . . what do you feel like when you wake up the next day? How do you feel when you think about your wife at home with the kids? How do you feel about lying to her?'

Lawrence crossed his arms behind his head. 'You make it sound like she's stuck in some eighteenth-floor council flat, with crack dealers in the corridor and people pissing in the lifts. Listen, I'm not saying this to brag about money, but . . .'

He was already counting on his fingers. 'We have an au pair, we have a cleaner who comes in every day. We have a pool, we have someone who comes in to look after the pool. We have ponies for the children, and a goat and a donkey and ducks and someone who comes in to look after those. My wife has a circle of her own friends based around our village. She has a nice car, she goes to the gym with her mates, she does two mornings voluntary, helping at the school, she . . .' He waved an arm to indicate everything he had missed out. 'She has a great, fulfilled life. And I have that kind of life too when I'm at home. But it's not enough on its own – I need this . . . this swinging metropolitan life too.'

'But how do you feel about her? Isn't it cowardly to go behind her back like that instead of . . . instead of making a clean break?'

He peered over his glasses without speaking, then lit a cigarette, swept a drape of glossy hair behind his ear and glanced at his reflection in the mirrored panels of the bar counter. The hair was somewhere between late-mod-period Steve Marriott and grown-out Paul Weller, falling long and straight at either side of his face. It was the kind of hair that hung this way or that independently of what your head was doing; the kind of hair I had envied when I was young; the kind of hair that even now I felt conferred a kind of effortless insouciance that springier hair, such as my own, could not be expected to deliver. He didn't look thirty-seven. Was it the hair, or the clothes, or just the way he sat in a chair?

Lawrence shrugged. 'Believe it or not I love her. We still have a sex life together. I love the children. There's no conflict of interest. I'm not looking for love – just recreation. We all know that men are programmed to have sex with loads of women. Some suppress the urge, I surrender to it. It's as simple as that.' He eyed my wedding ring. 'How long have you been married?'

I felt myself redden slightly. 'Fourteen years.'

He scrutinised me for a moment. 'Ever had an affair?'

I smiled and shook my head slowly. 'I think you probably have to be in the market for it, and I'm not. I'm not open to opportunities.'

'OK, let's make this simple – have you ever looked at another woman?'

'I don't really think about it.'

'Come on, you're kidding yourself . . .'

I waited for him to continue, staring at my pad and at my hand holding the pen. I had a sudden recollection of myself and Cathy, years ago when we were students, on the ferry back from Dieppe. She had accused me of ogling some underdressed French girl in the cafeteria. I had denied it and she had laughed, and told me to admit it. It wasn't as if she cared or anything – she just wanted me to tell the truth. But I couldn't admit it. Not because I couldn't go back on what I had already said and feel a fraud and a crypto-womaniser but because it hadn't actually been true. I had just been daydreaming, probably staring right through the girl. Because the fact was, back then, I did only have eyes for Cathy. I didn't ever fancy anyone else. I marvelled at it myself sometimes, but it was true. I thought that was what love meant – to be so crazy about someone that you could be watching some sexy French girl who looks like Debbie Harry with fantastic legs in a short skirt and not even notice. I thought it would be like that for ever, and of course for a long time it was.

'The point is,' Lawrence was saying, 'where does the lie start? Standing too close to someone in the lift? Thinking about what someone's breasts look like? Dreaming about having sex in the stationery cupboard with the girl from accounts? Deciding to look for an opportunity? *Being* in the market? The truth is, by the time you're doing it you've already done it. Morally, you've already made your great leap into the void. And it's not cowardice we're talking about here, it's courage.

Because you have to be prepared to lose everything . . .' He stubbed out his cigarette and blew smoke out of the side of his mouth. 'So where do you stand?'

'Well, we're not really here to talk about me.'

He smiled. 'Matt, we're here to talk about everyone. That's what makes me so interesting, isn't it? What's in the bag?' He nodded towards my Flamingo Sounds pink plastic carrier.

'What? Oh, it's . . .' I was embarrassed for a moment, then pulled out a Cellophane-wrapped album and turned the sleeve towards him. 'I picked it up at lunchtime. It's . . .'

'The Sandpipers – who the fuck are they?'

'They were around in the psychedelic bit of the Sixties. I only bought it for one song.' I ran my finger down the track listing to find it.

'"Yesterday" – Lennon–McCartney.' Lawrence looked up at me. 'And?'

I slid the album back in the bag. 'I collect them.'

'You collect Beatles covers?'

'No, just "Yesterday". I've got loads of them – well, around twenty-nine.'

'*Around* twenty-nine . . .'

I laughed. 'OK, exactly twenty-nine.'

'Fuck, it's worse than I thought.'

'I'm just into the Beatles, that's all. I don't do tons of memorabilia or anything – just this one thing. Though obviously you're bound to pick up a few bits of other paraphernalia here and there. Posters, the odd programme, you know . . .'

'Ever been to The 34?'

'What's that?'

'Sixties club. You'd love it. It's got that kind of stuff hanging up in the toilets.'

'Is that where you go?'

'Sometimes.' He leaned back and caught the waiter's eye, and scribbled out the word 'bill' in the air.

I was still hot, but the moment when I might have risked

another beer seemed to have been and gone. 'Are you frightened of middle age?'

He laughed, just as he had laughed when the interviewer in the programme had asked if he liked fishing. 'Oh, *please* . . . Anyway we don't have middle age any more, do we? It's all late-middle youth now, according to the style writers – you should know. Growing up is what our parents did, right? Look at Jagger, Bowie, Rod Stewart. No one retires from stuff they enjoy doing. What's the average age of a Porsche owner?' He waited for my bemused shrug. 'The answer is forty-eight. We've all got a long way to go. There's nothing wrong with pursuing things for pleasure. I mean, what do you think *you're* up to when you go hunting round junk shops for dodgy versions of "Yesterday"? What do you think that's about? In a sense that's all I'm doing. We're both enthusiasts – it's what men are good at. It's what we do. It's how we avoid staring death in the face.'

I asked him about contraception (he was in favour of it) and Aids (he tried to avoid it) and the kind of women he went for (ones he fancied) and how he would feel if his wife did the same (pause, grin – bad). We talked until the tape clicked about promiscuity *vis à vis* the rock fraternity, returning neatly back via Jagger, Bowie and Rod in this respect, to McCartney (notoriously faithful to the end) and the Beatles – who clearly constituted my only extramarital adventure, he pointed out with a deep chuckle. He looked at his watch and let me pay the bill. We walked out to the street together. I took a card out of my Filofax and said if there was anything he wanted to add . . .

'Fine,' he said. He grinned. 'I won't give you my card, if you don't mind.' I thanked him and we shook hands, but instead of parting we carried on walking together towards Piccadilly Circus until we stopped again at the end of Shaftesbury Avenue and shook hands again. And even now we paused at the steps leading down to the Underground. For a moment I wondered whether he was escorting me to the

Tube to make sure I wouldn't follow him back to his office. But he seemed in no particular hurry, content to kill time for a few minutes with his hands in his pockets, offering his face to the warm sun, while I stood there with my hair clinging slightly to my forehead, my ridiculous long coat draped limply over one arm and the crowd flowing round us on the pavement and ascending doggedly from the heat of the tunnels below.

'So how many covers of "Yesterday" are there?' he was saying, still squinting at the sky.

'I'm not sure exactly – I'm working through a list of about a hundred and sixty at the moment. A lot of them are deleted, so I look in record shops. Every now and then I put an ad in specialist magazines. I've got most of the obvious ones – Val Doonican, Matt Munro, Cilla Black . . .'

'Max Bygraves?'

I laughed out loud. 'Yes! I've got him too – everybody's done it. Plus arrangements for jazz, reggae, strings, disco, folk . . . there's even a Daffy Duck version.'

Lawrence nodded, smiling, looking down at his shoes and then eventually looking up again. He paused. I knew he had to be getting at something. 'OK, which is the rarest one – the one that you'd sell your grandmother for – the one you'd cheat on your wife for?'

I laughed again, though this time it was nerves. 'Bob Dylan recorded a version in 1970 but it was never released – so I suppose that's the rarest. The rest of them can be tracked down, in theory.'

We stood for a moment longer. 'And that's the fun of it, I suppose, isn't it?' Lawrence said. 'You find one, you take it home, you listen to it once and you add it to your collection.'

I nodded. He was right. That was the way it happened.

At the office, I listened to my messages, caught up with the pile of proofs Isobel and Isabel had left, then made a start on transcribing the tape, smiling to myself during some bits, frowning at others.

Come on, you're kidding yourself . . .

It was still warm but getting dark when I stepped off the bus at Crouch End and called in at the supermarket opposite the clock tower for wine and crisps and sugar-free gum with whitening agent. I chose two bunches of flowers from the plastic buckets on display and stood with them uncertainly near the checkout, wondering whether two was enough. Through the window I saw Bev walking her dog on the opposite pavement and I stood to one side until she was out of sight. One out of two British households had pets. Five million had a dog. Five million. I didn't know why I was hiding. There was nothing embarrassing about taking flowers home for your wife of fourteen years. It was symbolic, wasn't it? It meant something.

Dean wouldn't have remembered a girl called Pam: tall, red hair, same age as us (sixteen), surname unrecorded, real leather coat, funny accent (Geordie), pendulous breasts (he wouldn't know that). She was Diane Cookson's cousin, staying for the weekend. It was one of those half-term youth club discos and a gang of us – not Dean – had been smoking No. 6 and drinking Strongbow behind the pavilion in the freezing cold, waiting for the doors to open and talking rubbish. Anyway, to make a short story even shorter, the others scooted off when they heard the music start up, but for some reason I still had the bottle, so we stayed, just me and her, and we got snogging and went to a little hut in the graveyard full of shovels and gardening stuff and she sat on the bench and let me put my hand inside her shirt and then up her skirt. Christ! I thought. Because, I have to say, this was pretty quick for me, plus I'd never got seriously beyond top thigh (outer) before. But I didn't panic or anything, even when it became obvious that my luck was in and we would have to do it standing up (I'd heard this was possible and, yes, although the cider had gone to my head, it hadn't gone anywhere else). Then we heard voices coming up the gravel outside. It was only a bunch of idiots cutting through from Elizabeth Street, but we ducked down below the little window, knees to knees, feeling stupider and stupider breathing in the dark, my absurd, extra-gusset-flared Levi's undone, her knickers half-down, everything cooling off rapidly. These kids stopped by the lamppost near the pavilion, talking and showing off to each other. I couldn't hear what they were saying but I could see the fag smoke coming out of their mouths in the cold when they talked and took it in turns to kick the bottom of the lamppost. When they'd gone, this Pam just started getting herself back into her clothes really quickly as if she'd just woken up and found herself naked at the bus stop. She had to catch up with her mates at the disco, she said. Of course there was never any question of our turning up there together. You didn't do that. But I made her promise to meet me back at the pavilion after the disco finished at ten and she said OK.

What reminded me of this was a set of pictures Dean used to have (red photo album) from the Beatles' first sessions at Abbey Road in 1962. He'd had them for ages before we found out that the photographer had had to snap George from the right side because someone had given him a black eye outside the Cavern (I didn't know this until much later, but apparently the scuffle was caused by fans protesting about Epstein firing Pete Best in favour of Ringo. Astonishing). Anyway, it reminded me of our famous difference of opinion, circa 1975. I know Dean *thought* he knew why I smacked him in the eye about eight miles into a twenty-six-mile midnight sponsored walk we went on in the flurrying snow. It was the night after that disco. He gave me a shove first and I slipped and went down, but it was me who'd been winding him up for hours as we tramped along by wrongly accusing him of duff harmonies on 'If I Fell' and then taunting him about a twiddly bit of solo on 'Something' that I said he could never quite bring off, which was a lie too, and we both knew it. He couldn't for the life of him understand why I was getting at him. The truth was it had nothing to do with that . . .

Rewind. There she was at the disco with Diane Cookson and another girl Dean went out with afterwards for a while . . . Debra. The three of them came up and he asked her name and she said 'Pam', sucking on her straw and looking up at Dean like fucking Lolita. She would have been all over him of course, if she'd had the chance. I could tell. He only danced with her for five minutes ('Jean Genie', 'Blockbuster' – identical riffs, which is why they played them back to back) because Dean was really after Debra and just used Pam to make her a bit jealous. But that was enough. Her eyes followed Dean around all night. I remember, when I finally attracted her attention by barging into her at the Pepsi bar, she said 'oops sorry' to me as if we'd never met. I kidded myself into thinking maybe she just didn't want the others to know about us, which would have been fine because neither did I. In fact I used to hate it when some of our lot would come out of the bushes and straight into the club flushed with triumph, making everyone smell their fingers, and then lead the communal sniggering when the girl in question showed her face at the door. I hated all that grope-and-tell bravado. Though, obviously, I suppose if I'd ever achieved penetration I might have had to put an ad in the paper.

I was at the pavilion at ten. I waited for ages.

Look, Dean. Look at me waiting. Hunched against the cold in my cheap pointy-lapelled jacket, trying to see across the rec in the dark, smoothing down my virgin's moustache with the tip of my finger.

Dean wouldn't have remembered. He wouldn't have given it a second thought. It wasn't his fault. It's not as if he even got off with Pam. It's not as if he wanted to. He never really had to chase anyone: everything came to him ready-wrapped. And that's why I had to hit him so hard. He could have hit me back but he didn't. He just walked on ahead without me.

I saw Caroline with the red jacket in the lift, except this time she was wearing a black one. She thanked me for the piece (filed an over-eager two weeks early), but wondered whether I shouldn't have gone in a bit harder on this Lawrence guy. She wondered whether I should really have been describing such an obvious bastard as 'engaging' and 'witty' and 'charismatic'. I joined her for a second in glancing up at the numbers going on and off between floors as if they were suddenly the most absorbing spectacle in the world. Of course this had me worried. Had this Lawrence guy actually been witty, or was it just that this Lawrence guy laughed at my jokes? Had Caroline been hoping for something that was more my opinion than this Lawrence guy's?

'I don't sound as though I agree with him, do I?' I said, looking mock-worried as if being soft on obvious bastards would make me one too.

'A bit,' she said, laughing. 'Nothing we can't sort out. And it *was* pretty good to get to talk to him.' She grinned and I grinned back.

You can't have a conversation in a lift. They're built for two people to perform a short sketch for a nervous audience. What did she mean, nothing we can't sort out? But our journey was too short for supplementary questions, except maybe unaskable ones about whether it was true about her and Jeremy.

Cathy of course said 'Ha!' when I told her about Lawrence. She said he deserved all he got. What – did she mean loads of money, wit, charm, good looks, as much sex as he can handle and a favourable write-up by her husband in the *Sunday Post*? I'd been hoping for some kind of conjugal rapprochement that night but she literally closed her book, switched the light off and turned over with an impatient yawn, which was usually a sign that the current session of social intercourse was adjourned and the prospect of any other kind of intercourse postponed until there was a K in the month.

Funny, but when you're twenty-one and having a lot of fantastic sex, you don't stop for anything, not even because your girlfriend's got her silly old period. There's no time like the present and, by definition, it's always the present. And let's face it, it's no worse than eating potatoes with the skin on – i.e., not ideal, but better than waiting till the kebab shop is open (trick analogy – the kebab shop is always open). But then later in your relationship, when twice a week seems an absolute feast, and even later still, during those difficult child-rearing years when months drift by without your hypothetical Cathy noticing who that strange bloke is who gets into bed with her every night, a period is not so much a healthy sign of continuing sexual frolics – hurrah, she's not pregnant again! – as one of those chalkmarks you put on the wall of your cell when you're a prisoner of celibacy to show how long it is since you've been inside. Or not.

Alex had been bugging me, trying to get me to go to the gym he sneaks off to a couple of times a week. 'Why would I want to do something like that?' I said. Alex went into his slightly dated Henry Winkler Fonz pose with his thumbs stuck in the air. 'Get in shape, Matts. Why do you think I'm conspicuously successful with women?' he said. 'Anyway, it's more interesting going with someone else – we could play squash.'

Jane pointed out that a) Alex isn't conspicuously successful with women and b) by the way, Alex gets 20 per cent off his annual membership if he introduces new people.

'That's no reason not to do it,' said Alex.

'I'll think about it,' I said, though I'd already mentally filed it under 'not wanted on voyage' along with genital tattoos, rap music and skiing.

'Excellent,' said Alex, who could never be as smart as he looked.

The night after the Lawrence conversation we were having dinner and Cathy suddenly wondered whether we might go skiing. I was so surprised my heart forgot to sink. '*Skiing?*'

'Yes, you know . . .' (Humorous skiing-pole mime from Cathy. Good mood. Sadie looked up from her vegetarian meat-balls like a dog who has just heard one of those silent whistles they used to advertise in the back of Superman comics, along with X-ray specs that could see through women's dresses.)

I kept calm. 'I thought we always said we weren't skiing types.'

'No, that's what *you* always said. I never really knew what a skiing type was . . .'

'Well, someone interested in going skiing.'

Sadie was looking interested. 'Everybody goes skiing, Dad.'

'You might as well say everybody's in favour of hanging,' I said, slightly forgetting that I was in favour of hanging too, for selected people – persistent skiers among them.

'It's quite reasonable actually,' said Cathy. 'Bev is organising it. Romania. You have to get a party of twenty or more. The more you get, the cheaper it is.'

'We could think about it,' I said, mentally filing it under 'not wanted on voyage' along with genital tattoos, rap music and getting 'in shape'.

I didn't want to come right out and say no, with Sadie sitting there being so enthusiastic for the first time since she was seven. I didn't always want to be the one that said no. I wanted to be able to say yes. Or have someone else to say no for me.

My mum rang while we were in the middle of all this. She had her quiet voice on. Dad wasn't well and Vicky had been on the phone in tears. 'What, because of Dad?' I said.

'Never mind,' she said.

I hated it when she did that. Then Cathy's mum rang and kept Sadie on the phone for hours. Not our bill, obviously, but no doubt she was still trying to poison Sadie's mind against her cruel father for dragging her off to the forbidden city. And actually, it seemed to me that Sadie was settling in a bit. She'd had a friend round a few days before to watch a video and leave pizza under the bed. She didn't bother to introduce her, of course. Weird-looking with a bolt or something stuck through her tongue. I wondered whether maybe I should have let Sadie have her navel done if only to head off something worse.

Cathy was OK too by now. She'd got Bev. She'd got her reading group. She hadn't bumped into any high-achieving ex-chums from Oxford who went on to become barristers or futures dealers or forensic scientists instead of getting pregnant.

But skiing was one of those things everyone expects you to have already done. Twenty years ago, people were perfectly happy not to have ever been skiing. These days it's a bit like admitting you've never had anal sex. I was nearly forty. I didn't want to start following herds this late in life. To me it was like people who went on about *Citizen Kane* or *Casablanca* being their No. 1 films of all time. I don't mind anyone old enough to have gone to the cinema to see them when they first came out and thinking they were the best thing since Rudolph Valentino. But isn't something wrong when 80 per cent of twenty-five- to forty-year-old film fans seem to have discovered this for themselves without any prodding from the experts?

I don't know what this says about me, but I managed to hold out against seeing either of those films till I was about thirty-five. I'd just decided to avoid them. They'd been corrupted by too much attention. So if anyone ever said 'Rosebud' or 'We'll always have Paris' or some such bollocks I'd look blank and pretend not to know what they were talking about. Then I'd have to tell them I'd never seen *Casablanca*, just to see the look on their faces. I'm just about old enough to remember the fad for white dinner jackets in the '70s and would-be sophisticated nightclubs called Sam's and Rick's. And those wankers who insisted on repeating all the dialogue (they were the same lot who recite the 'Three Yorkshiremen' sketch from Monty Python and the parrot stuff). I hate all that. Sorry, but I hate seeing unimaginative people having fun. I laughed out loud one rainy Sunday in front of the box when I finally saw that scene for myself from *Casablanca* when they're in the bar and Humphrey Bogart is whistling through his teeth about gin joints and playing it again Sam. It was like being driven mad by listening to 'My Way' for years in pubs and clubs and karaoke bars and then suddenly hearing the Frank Sinatra version for the first time. Aaaaaaargh! You'd just have to turn it off. You'd have to say, please God, not this old rubbish again.

Sexual abstinence. I have to say there was a lot of it about. At this point, Cathy and I had managed to go without since the fourth of April. I remember because on that day in 1964 the Beatles had records at numbers one, two, three, four and five in the American singles chart, a further eleven singles in the top 100, and numbers one and two in the albums chart. McCartney was only six years older than Sadie. The Beatles were practically kids and they stood in triumph with the world kissing their feet. Nothing would ever be the same again. Of course this was no consolation to me. The fourth of April meant four months. And the worst thing was, that wasn't even a record. All I can do is point to the classic irony which boiled down to a) Cathy asking for her tubes to be done when she was in having Ellie, thus theoretically freeing us up to have all kinds of sex at the drop of a hat without hanging around trying to sustain interest while Cathy remembered where she put her cap, and b) never having *any* sex any more because we were too tired or arguing about something. The thing was, on

4 April it wasn't even that difficult to bring about. I'd brought home a bottle of wine and a video (*LA Confidential*) and made a bit of an effort once we were in bed. It was only hard if you'd got used to *not* making an effort. And having long gaps between sex was a bit like being a virgin again – the longer you left it, the harder it was to get on the score sheet. Anyway it worked that time. It was good for the Fabs and it was good for us too. Fourth of April. I can only say it wasn't entirely a coincidence. You have to make an effort on a day like that.

Isabel brought a custard doughnut and a large cappuccino to the comfy chair outside the frock cupboard where I was sitting in front of the TV with an A4 pad resting on my knee, half concentrating on the programme and half thinking about the rumour, which was probably true. I put the tape on pause as she put the coffee down on the desk nearest to me and lingered for a moment pointedly looking at the screen. She was late starting her shift, hence the peace offering, and she was carrying a vintage American comic – *The Archies* – in a plastic wrapper, which meant she'd popped into Forbidden Planet in Soho and couldn't quite get out again.

'Why are you watching last week's *EastEnders*?' she said.

'Oh, you know . . . keeping up with events,' I said, biting into the doughnut and making a meal of licking a glob of custard pus off my thumb.

'So why are you taking notes?'

I sucked at the froth on my coffee in what I imagined was an amusing way until Isabel actually frowned. In the background I could hear Milo whacking his Apple Mac round the side of the head – *fuck* – and then talking quietly to IT.

'I might write a piece,' I said. 'About . . .' I sighed. I couldn't quite be bothered to make something up and didn't really need to, so I trailed off without answering and set the tape going again as if to suggest to her a man distracted by the business in hand rather than one who didn't want to talk to someone. 'Don't you have something to attend to?' She wandered back to the TV desk.

The rumour was that James Thomas had been offered a spanking, overpaid job as chief cultural pronouncer at the *Courier*, which meant that his column and those seven 'Watch It' previews on my pages would be vacant and up for auction to the highest talent. I had not formulated a wizard plan exactly, or at least had not let myself believe so, but was nevertheless following a voice in my head that told me to write seven drop-dead-stunning critiques of last week's TV using exactly the same programmes that James himself had selected, and push them under Jeremy's nose while Jeremy was still pissed off at James's defection. The simplicity of it! And then all Jeremy would have to do, under this admittedly entirely hypothetical scenario – which culminated, in my imagination, with my own face, shot in a favourable light with trademark quizzically raised eyebrow, appearing at the top of the page in place of the present incumbent's owlish, bespectacled mugshot taken in 1986, and perhaps accompanied by the words, chosen by the Deputy Editor himself, 'Introducing our lively new TV columnist' – was simply spend two minutes away from his sex life and notice how my brilliantly trenchant, hilarious and effulgent (yes, *good* word) observations on the people's medium shone out against the limp, quasi-cerebral meanderings that James seemed to trot out these days. OK, perhaps not quasi-cerebral. No one had ever suggested that James's columns were quasi-anything, or limp or meandering – and, in fact, contrariwise, maybe the putative, unturndownable offer from the *Courier* would seem to indicate a man at the height of his powers. I sighed. Still, someone had to get the job and what better opportunity to add another feather to my bow or string to my cap, as either one of the Iso/abels might say, with no irony intended.

From across the floor I heard Alex announce his arrival by blowing his nose loudly and plugging in the hairdryer he kept in his top drawer to let everyone know he had spent his lunchtime doing lengths at the pool at the gym and had now swum back to the office. After a minute the hairdryer noise stopped, and I caught a whiff of chlorine in the air immediately behind him.

'Hey, Mattie, what are you up to? Why are you watching last week's *EastEnders*?'

I hit the pause button. 'God, what's wrong with everyone? I'm the TV Editor – I'm watching a TV programme. Is that so controversial?'

'Absolutely not, old mate,' said Alex, holding his hands up in mock surrender. He sat down on the corner of the desk. 'Did you hear about old JT going to the *Courier*?'

I was about to deny any knowledge of the morning's career gossip, having been detained with the job of unscrambling the other Isobel's satellite listings as deadline loomed, but now today's Isabel was gesturing overefficiently and willingly from across the office, waving my phone in the air. I went to take the call, glancing back to show my annoyance at Alex, who had sunk into the chair I had vacated and set the *EastEnders* tape running again.

I picked up the phone. 'Hello?' I said, still glaring at Alex.

'Is that Matt Lewis?' I didn't recognise the voice. 'It's Lawrence – we met the other week in the Tupelo?'

'Yes, of course – Lawrence. How are things?' I said, immediately feeling slightly foolish at having to use a name we both knew was a fiction and was, it had occurred to me after our meeting, possibly inspired by the master pagan-sensualist serial shagger D.H. himself.

'I wondered if you'd be interesting in meeting up. I might have something for you.'

'What . . . you mean to do with the programme?'

'Mmm, tangentially. Something we touched on. Can you make Tuesday evening?'

'Er . . . probably. Can I get back to you?'

'I'll ring you. I'll call Tuesday morning – OK?'

I put the phone down. Tangentially. Touched on. Nice use. Nice bloke really, if it weren't for the other thing.

On Sunday Cathy said that, actually, she was hoping I would be in on Tuesday to look after Ellie while she went to Bev's to discuss setting up a babysitting circle.

'Tuesday? But Bev hasn't got any babies. You told me she was barren.'

'I said she decided against children for ecological reasons.'

'Oh. Is that why she split from her husband?'

'Could we get back to Tuesday, please?'

'OK. Why can't Sadie babysit?'

Sadie, crosslegged on the sofa, stirred behind a copy of *19*.

'Well, she can sometimes, but if you and I are going to resume our impoverished social life, it'll probably happen on Saturdays when Sadie is out too.'

'No, I mean, why can't Sadie babysit on Tuesday? I've got to meet someone.'

'Who?'

'A contact.'

'Oh. I see. And what kind of contact is it that a deskbound TV listings editor has to meet so desperately on the one night I have to go out?'

'Cathy . . .' I said plaintively, as if to reproach her for reminding me that I had the kind of job that didn't often require me to meet contacts of the Tuesday night kind or any other night kind.

'Sorry, but you're the one who said you were deskbound and that no one's asking you to do any writing, apart from the piece about . . . what was it, the marriage infidelity business?'

'Yes, yes,' I interrupted, 'but, you know, I do get invites to the occasional book launch, film preview etcetera.'

I reached across the table with my fork and speared a left-over roast potato, which I didn't want but was prepared to consume with a show of hungriness in the emergency of not wishing to add to my statement.

Cathy stood up and started to gather the dishes together. 'You can go out if you want. Sadie won't mind babysitting on Tuesday, will you, love?'

We turned to watch Sadie turn a page of her magazine without expression and slowly inspect its contents. 'Suppose so,' she said, without looking up, which meant 'suppose not', I supposed.

I came up via the subway to find myself outside the cinema on Edgware Road, which I knew wasn't right, and by the time I'd hurried back through and come up at the other side, heavy splats of rain were hitting the pavement. It was already gone eight-thirty. I'd decided against taking a cab on the grounds of having spent the last of my cash at Eamonn's with Alex and Milo at lunchtime, and reckoned on using my travelcard to get me to Bond Street, but the Tubes were unexpectedly (to me) on strike and then I'd gone a stop too far on the bus because I was busy trying to find George Place, off Marylebone High Street, in my *A–Z*, which of course I would have checked before leaving the office had it not been for the late bowel-churning panic triggered by someone called Martin at the printers mercifully spotting an upside-down film still of Dustin Hoffman standing on his head that someone called Isobel had asked to be put the right way up and therefore the wrong way up. Looking on the bright side (as it had still been possible to do before the weather took a hand in things), I was now on Park Lane, an area only familiar to me as the second most expensive place to buy hotels on the Monopoly board and therefore no doubt lined with banks and cashpoint machines. But I saw no obvious sign of cashpoints as I hurried haltingly along in what I knew to be the opposite direction, head tilted against the slant of the rain, conspicuously lacking the protection of the long mac I'd carried around London for the past seven weeks, though there were, as expected, plenty of expensive hotels lighting up the dark as far as the eye could see, plus, every now and then, the luxury thick-plate frontage of a showroom crammed with the kind of cream-leather-upholstered drop-top Mercs whose primary function at this moment seemed to be to remind me that I was in the wrong neighbourhood and not just metaphorically. By the time I'd been directed to a NatWest-friendly ATM, taken out £50 and on second thoughts gone back for another ten, I'd lost my bearings again. The only cabs now were ones full of sparkling people on their way to the Royal Opera (or so I imagined, momentarily casting myself in my mind's eye as a sclerotic wretch in period damp rags pleading at the feet of the Duke of Urbino for clemency in the wake of some unspecific crime against court etiquette), and by the time I'd traced a rough arc back to Bond Street and eventually Marylebone High Street and George Place – and discovered that The 34 club wasn't actually at number 34 but at number 2a – I was so wet that my trouser legs were making rasping noises at each other as I walked.

There was an electric-purple neon sign – 34, it said simply – but it illuminated the club foyer from the inside and could only be seen from the street if you stood in front of the building, an arrangement set up possibly to annoy postmen and couriers, I thought. I stood for a moment outside and attempted to slick my dripping hair into a style that might channel the rain away from my face and help give the impression of someone who had, say, simply been caught in the rain walking the few hundred yards from his own convenient mansion block as opposed to someone who had taken a short cut across the Serpentine. As I dithered, a cab hissed up alongside and unloaded a couple in their early twenties – a blonde in a short dress with a tinkling accent who hurried up the steps with a glittery silver jacket over her head, and a guy with a ponytail who paid the cabbie and vaulted up after her in a black cape and patent-leather red boots. I closed my eyes. I could go home. But I steeled myself and squelched up into the lobby. The girl on the desk, who I expected to have me thrown out simply on the grounds of being made up of too many parts water, looked up at me from under a long Mary Quant fringe and gave me a smile so wide I half-glanced back to make sure Tom Cruise wasn't standing behind me.

'I'm meeting someone here at eight-thirty,' I said. 'It's, er, Lawrence . . .' I paused.

Just ask for me, Lawrence had said. But who was he?

'What's the name?'

'Actually, I'm not sure . . .'

'No, no, your name.'

I told her. 'Sorry,' I said. 'I'm a journalist,' I added pointlessly and realised how stupid I must sound, but she took it for a journalist's joke and laughed. 'That explains it.' She found my name in the signing-in book and sent me upstairs. 'Third floor,' she said. I exhaled and felt the steam release from my pores. The fat bass tones of an indistinguishable ballad pulsed through the ceiling and I followed the winding staircase up to a large, dimmed, smoky, retro-1960s lounge, three-quarters full of drinkers crowding the bar and others at the tables set back from a black-and-white geometric floor where more drinkers stood in knots of threes and fours and a waitress picked her way around with a tray of champagne flutes. Scott Walker was crooning 'Make It Easy on Yourself' but the music was nearly lost in the mix of chatter and clatter. A second waitress glided past from an open galley kitchen carrying an armful of plates piled with sandwiches, toasted and quartered, with cocktail sticks holding them together, and trailing an aroma that reminded my stomach that it should have done more eating and less drinking at lunchtime. I glanced around, taking in the kitsch cup-shaped chairs, the mirror set into the wall at the far end etched with James Coburn's face from *Our Man Flint*. Above it was a big purple-neon 34, identical to the one outside. There were a couple of people in Hendrix-style floppy shirts and velvet bellbottoms and a handful of others sporting understated mod ensembles featuring the odd deckchair-striped blazer and two-colour chisel-toed shoes – but no capes. I looked across to where a white baby grand stood beneath the staircase to an upper floor. There was a wineglass and an ashtray on the piano, but no sign of anyone who looked like he could play it. Lawrence was sitting at the table immediately to the side smoking a cigarette and talking earnestly to a girl in a red leather top and matching short skirt. She looked annoyed with him, I thought, as if he had let her down in some way and now had to charm her, cajole, be persuasive, touch her hair, smooth her back to normal. I felt my blood rush slightly. There was still a chance to turn and flee. But then Lawrence noticed me.

'Hey, Matt.' He stood up and shook my hand. The girl shot a glance at him and stood up, pulling her skirt down at the hem before slipping away, unintroduced. 'Come and sit down, man. Get dry. What happened to you?'

I smiled. 'I got wet.'

'Wine?' Lawrence was on his feet shouting to the waitress to bring a glass. 'What do you think?' he was saying above the noise. 'There's another bar upstairs with a dancefloor – it gets busier later.'

I nodded. 'So, what was the—' I began, but someone had turned up the volume and Eddie Floyd was booming over the sound system. Lawrence was mouthing the lyrics and drumming the tabletop expertly with crisp beats, abruptly shifting the focus of his attention beyond the tone and range of probing inquiries into his sex life, and diverting me into speculation with a pang of pre-emptive envy as to whether Lawrence had ever been in a proper band, perhaps with gigs at the Marquee and a healthy following and a Transit van with girls in the back. I took a gulp of my wine. You couldn't disturb someone when they were tucking into one of their favourite records, and maybe this wasn't the place anyway to talk discreetly about whatever Lawrence had on his mind. On the other hand, I couldn't exactly enquire after his wife and the kids and the ducks or ask whether he'd had a good day at the office.

But none of that seemed to come into play and in any case Lawrence was happy to spend the next twenty minutes enthusing about the Small Faces while I managed to add two glasses of red wine to the two pints and two halves of Guinness I'd absorbed at lunchtime. We talked about the phasing effects on 'Itchycoo Park' which I reckoned they'd obviously overdosed on after listening to 'Lucy in the Sky'. I let Lawrence refill my glass while I nibbled my way through the dish of olives and added my thoughts to Lawrence's take on late '60s studio techniques and the impact of Townshend's brute realism on British lyric-writing of the period. 'But weren't the Kinks doing that, more or less?' I was saying, searching my mind in vain for a for-instance, and only coming up with 'Waterloo Sunset', which though brilliant in its way was more English whimsy than gritty whatsitcalled . . .

'Yes, kind of, but if you think about the opening of "I Can't Explain" . . .' Lawrence was saying, but the act of thinking about the opening of 'I Can't Explain' suddenly seemed irretrievably incompatible with the house red gurgling through my veins and 'Like a Rolling Stone' blaring away in the background. Another bottle of wine arrived and at some point, possibly while I'd been loitering in the toilet looking at the framed posters of the Beatles and Manfred Mann and the Troggs, I noticed we had been joined by a couple, who Lawrence eventually introduced as Graham (droopy ginger moustache) and Clarice or Alice or even possibly Gladys and another girl who reminded me slightly of the waitress in *Twin Peaks*, except skinnier and understandably not quite as fanciable out of her gingham dress and white ankle socks – what was she called?

'Who was the waitress in *Twin Peaks*?' I asked, hearing my voice slur as the music stopped, and I wondered for a moment whether I was shouting, but no one seemed to notice or care or both. The bar wasn't so full now and the piano player had arrived from nowhere and was working his way softly through a medley of easy-listening hits.

'What people don't seem to realise,' Lawrence was saying, holding a bottle of champagne in his left hand and trailing a small cigar in the air with the other, 'is that women do it all the time too – we just don't notice it happening unless we know what to look for.' He put his arm round me. 'It's whatever hits the pleasure centres – sex is like just another extreme sport, right Matt?' The piano player segued from 'This Guy's in Love With You' into a slowed-down mellow jazz version of 'I'm a Believer'.

'Sorry, I wasn't quite . . . hundred per cent attention span,' I said.

'Ah, that reminds me.' Lawrence jammed the cigar into the corner of his mouth and leaned across to fish in the pocket of his designer anorak. 'Present for you, Matt. I knew there was some reason . . .'

He handed me a Jiffy bag. Inside was a CD in a plain white cover. I turned it on its side, read the spine and took out the disc. '"Yesterday" – Dylan session, Colombia Studio B, New York, fifth of January 1970 . . . Are you kidding?' I blinked up from the disc to Lawrence and back again. 'That's impossible!'

'Yes, isn't it?' He stared at me, grinning. His hair was hanging down like Steve Marriott's or Paul Weller's and he looked jubilant.

I looked at the CD again. 'I'm amazed. What can I say?'

'It's a bootleg, of course.'

I shook my head. 'Fantastic. I didn't even know there was one.'

'There wasn't until a week ago. And there's only one copy.'

Lawrence smiled at my expression. 'Contacts, mate,' he said, raising his glass.

I was still shaking my head. 'Brilliant, thanks.'

'I think this calls for more champagne,' said Graham, calling for more champagne.

'Matt's a Beatles expert,' Lawrence said, sitting back, closing his eyes.

'Did he tell you about this club?' Graham was saying.

'No, what's that? What club?'

'This club – The 34 . . .'

'Oh, we love the Beatles,' Clarice or Alice was saying. 'I love "Let It Be" and what is it – "Hey Jude". I love "Hey Jude". Hey *Jude* . . .' she started to sing. The girl who didn't much look like the waitress from *Twin Peaks* joined in.

'Hang on a minute.' Lawrence leaned back and called to the pianist. 'Michael, how about some Beatles songs?'

Michael wound down a homage to Burt Bacharach with a flourish of jazz shapes, and looked doubtful. 'I could probably manage "Yellow Submarine" or "Let It Be" – what were you thinking of?'

'I was thinking of "Eight Days a Week",' Lawrence said, grinning at me.

'Can you do it in B flat?' I heard myself shouting. 'B flat to . . . C seven to E flat and then G minor on the—'

'Whoah!' Michael held his hands up. 'Do you play?'

I felt my heart roar. 'I can play some Beatles tunes.'

Michael beamed me a generous smile and stood up to make room for me. 'Let's rock,' he said, with a sweep of his arm towards the piano.

I took the stool and tentatively poked out a sequence of fat chords. Then I ploughed into 'Eight Days', dispensing with an intro and concentrating on a vocal capable of masking the effect of my wooden left hand, which as usual was hopping rather than rolling through the bass figure, and finding myself gurning and actually shouting a cringe-making 'Yeah!' when

Lawrence unexpectedly came cruising in to carry the harmonies on the bridge and middle eight. There was clapping and whistling, and feeling the combined heat of triumph and drink, I pounded on through 'Lady Madonna' followed by a soulful 'Fool on the Hill' and an imperfect but joyous 'Hey Jude' in which I, in deference to a rousing accompaniment from my new, interesting friends, was happy to repeat the same two verses four times, by now unashamedly employing the full disguise of McCartney voice, McCartney mouth and McCartney eyebrows, as if it was only yesterday and not a year and seven weeks ago that I last managed to get to the end of a Beatles song. There was a swelling cacophony as the whole room seemed to join in on the na, na, na na-na-na-naaaa section followed by applause and whooping on my climactic, sustained, rumbling, majestic F major (because this was not an occasion for fade-outs). Lawrence had his arm round me as the cheers died down, leading me back to the table. 'Solid man,' Lawrence was saying. 'Excellent.' A couple of faggish-looking Bowie refugees from the wrong decade joined our table, then someone who worked at the BBC. I was suddenly in the chair, the puckish god of a small universe built for my talents, delightedly fielding my favourite trivia questions, reciting obscure lyrics, identifying with wit and judicious use of examples the distinguishing marks of a Lennon composition as contrasted with a McCartney, parroting album track listings and singles chronology including B-sides, detailing guest appearances, even recounting the tragic story of Dennis Brain, the best French horn player in the world. I was glowing in the fucking dark. 'So you never felt like teaming up with anyone – form a band or something?' someone was saying. 'Well, you know how it is,' I said, moving on to the question of Jimmy Nichol who stood in for Ringo on the Australian leg of the 1964 world tour for the not especially princely sum of £500 plus a gold watch, and then moving on further to Lawrence's question of whether to move on upstairs. 'I must organise a cab at some point,' I said, closing one eye to yawn. Lawrence laughed. 'I'll give you something for that.' Upstairs was purple and black with a teeming floor and mirrorballs sweeping white spots across the room and dancers moving in an exaggerated 1960s fashion to a spiky organ riff from the Doors. At one end, matching go-go dancers in fur bikinis writhed energetically in two cages flanking the DJ's stage, their moving bodies bathed in yellow then red by the low-tech lights humming and flashing to the music . . . 'Hello, I Love You'.

'Alicia, right?' I was saying, pointing my finger. 'Clar-*icia*,' she said, as if for the fourth time, pretending to be indignant. 'Come on, let's do the mashed potato.' Jesus. I looked behind me but Graham had vanished with Lawrence, and I felt myself pulled by the arm towards the scrum of dancers. In real life, I hated 'dancing', which I felt was as undignified as running for a bus or slipping on a patch of ice and somehow always boiled down to a choice between non-committal shuffling and self-expression of the kind best kept out of the public arena. But here nobody knew me, and anyway this was pretend dancing, where all you had to do was imagine yourself in a crazy party scene from *Room at the Top* or an early episode of *The Saint* where everyone wore a white nylon rollneck sweater and jerked their shoulders around to an unidentifiable twanging soundtrack. It was post-*Austin Powers* ironic dancing and couldn't harm your reputation. The skinny version of the waitress out of *Twin Peaks* had weaved her way in to make a threesome, tick-tocking her head from side to side like a metronome and looking into my eyes like a pantomime temptress. I tick-tocked back. I was moving dangerously to the brink of attempting Travolta's forked-fingers routine from *Pulp Fiction* when Lawrence appeared, easing me to one side and speaking into my ear. 'Matt, I don't know if you'd be interested in some coke . . .'

I had to stop to think, the drink thudding behind my eyes. Do I what? It did seem the oddest question. I knew it was not odd in the circumstances, only odd for me, and I wondered, even as I laughed nervously at its absurdity and shook my head in time to the descending chords of 'Blackberry Way' that came ringing over the sound system, whether the only reason I had never done (done?) drugs was that I had genuinely never been offered any. The absurdity wasn't just in the fact that I had never said yes before, but that I had never said no either. But the answer had to be no. Because even though I had never been asked for an answer, you surely couldn't get to being almost forty years of age without knowing what the answer even *was*.

I turned and edged back through the crowd of dancers but Claricia and her friend were making their way out to the toilets. I retreated to the bar and found my drink. After a few minutes I saw Lawrence talking to the girl in the red leather ensemble who had been with him earlier. Lawrence was holding one of her hands in two of his. Then he was kissing her and she had one arm around his neck.

'Hi.' Claricia's friend was back, standing beside me, topping up my glass from a full bottle, her eyes liquid and beaming.

'What was your name again?' I asked above the noise.

'Penelope.'

I nodded. 'Do you work round here?' I said, stepping over my first thought about whether she came here often, which I wanted to know but was not so drunk that I didn't not know I couldn't ask, so to speak.

She shrugged and smiled. 'Publicity,' she said. 'Here, I've brought us an apple to share.' She opened her fist to reveal a pale heart-shaped tablet.

'What is it?'

'E,' she said. 'It'll keep you awake. These are very good actually.' She snapped it with her fingernail. 'Take it,' she said. This wasn't asking. It wasn't Do you smoke, or play the violin, or like rollmop herrings? It was Everybody Does This. She was in her twenties, and your twenties were a place where everybody *did* do this, and here I was, dithering on the steps of this place wondering whether it was OK to go in. *Social Trends* fact number 1,001: 71 per cent of over-thirty-fives had never taken an illegal drug. Only 1 per cent had tried ecstasy. I looked at her, then put the half-hearted fragment on my tongue and washed it down. E. There. Too late. I swept the room with my eyes looking for monsters to emerge out of the walls. Nothing happened. But then it did. I giddied up. We danced for an hour and another hour. I wasn't drunk now. The drunkenness had gone and in its place something else. It was, like, I thought, how if you turn the big light on, you can't see the little light from your torch any more. It was like that and I told Penelope, because that seemed quite astonishing and certainly worth passing on to everyone else. I was part of the crowd and the irony of my dancing melted into non-irony and then into euphoria. It was hot but there was no better place to be than among these people in this place. We danced and laughed and talked. I hugged her and she laughed, watching me. Talk, talk, talk, talk. The Beatles, Cathy, Cathy's mother, Ellie, Sadie, Sadie's boyfriend, Sadie's dog, Dean, the *Echo*, the *Post*, the old world, the new. The time went nowhere and at one point I swear I spotted the ragged figure of Milo stalk across my line of vision, nodding at people, grinning. I loved Milo and tried to get to him. I wanted to put my arm around him and tell him how great everything was and to make him come and dance, but the DJ put 'Penny Lane' on and by the time the pretty nurse had finished selling poppies from a tray, Milo had gone and Penelope was saying, 'Come on, Matt, we need to make a move – there's a cab outside.' I looked at my watch. It was gone two. Shit. Right. A waitress came with a bill to pay for the upstairs drinks. 'Haven't you got a credit card?' she was saying. 'Yes, yes, absolutely . . .' because that wasn't a problem. Then I had my arm round Penelope in the cab, singing 'Penny Lane', except it was coming out as 'Denny Laine', and I was laughing at the same time and trying to explain to Penny – Penelope, I mean – that Denny Laine played guitar with McCartney in Wings, so wasn't that odd? Penny Lane, Denny Laine, Dennis Brain. I laughed. I saw London flashing by and asked, 'So, how long have you known Lawrence? What does he do? Who is he? What does he mean? Is that his real name? I asked because I hadn't put my hand on her leg or kissed her, so I was still a journalist pursuing my enquiries, and even as I felt a great warming towards Penelope, there was still the germ, or iota or scintilla (good word) of a chance right there in the back of my head somewhere that I might still make my excuses and leave. But she shrugged and said of course it was his real name but she didn't know that much about him, and I didn't leave. You couldn't just walk out on a girl. I paid the cab out of my cash and we went up to her place and she kissed me on the cheek in the lift and we kissed some more on the lips, though not for long and it seemed more friendly than anything. It was a block among other joined-on blocks of lowish-rise redbrick flats with long walkways and a central area below like a version of a massive council development but without the urine and the graffiti. There was a big pond and a beautiful fountain down there. She opened the door and turned on the heating and opened the fridge. There were two bottles of champagne. We went to the bedroom. It was like a hotel. She switched on the TV and dimmed the light and kicked off her shoes while I uncorked the bottle. We cheered when Mott the Hoople came on and danced together. 'Pen-el-o-pee,' I said. 'That's my favourite name.' Then there was a band playing that I had never heard of. It was MTV, Penelope said. Rod Stewart came on and we both sang 'Maggie May', then 'Livin' Thing' by ELO, which I knew to be awful rubbish but that was buried deep in my critical faculties somewhere and not where it counted, in my heart, and it sounded great and you could sing along to it, and I remembered reading how Wizzard and ELO had made an entire career out of copying the cellos on 'Strawberry Fields' and 'I Am the

Walrus' and I told Penelope about it for what seemed like a long time. 'Did anybody ever tell you you look like the waitress out of *Twin Peaks*?'

'Mädchen Amick?'

'That's her! That's *her*!'

She laughed out loud. 'Do you think so? Really?' She dashed to the mirror and stopped smiling to look at herself properly. *Twin Peaks* was something that I and Cathy had been glued to for weeks and weeks and weeks. Cathy. Mmm. Mädchen Amick. 'Damn fine cup of coffee,' I said. We both burst out laughing and danced some more and then flopped on the bed and talked. I saw the champagne on the table, uncorked but untouched. Green with cold, dewy drips on the neck of the bottle. Neither of us wanted any. 'I've had it,' she said. She pulled off her shirt without undoing the buttons, momentarily showing a long white torso and ribcage, then she shucked off her skirt and tights in one awkward wriggling movement. I noticed with a disinterested forensic eye that she was wearing a scarlet bra and white knickers and had red marks round her waist where her tights had been too tight. She got under the duvet and I took my trousers off and threw my shirt into the corner. It was strange that neither of us was embarrassed, but then it wasn't really. It seemed if not the right thing to do then not the wrong thing either. I looked at her. She smiled and yawned and rolled over turning her back to me. Her bra strap was twisted. I lay beside her and snuggled in and put my nose into the hollow of her neck in the warm soft hair where I'd never been before with anyone else. She smelled nice. It was odd. I didn't have an erection but I supposed that if she turned to face me, the something that I'd expected inevitably to happen might start to happen and the rest would happen inevitably after that. Not that I had expected it to happen right at the start when I'd come in out of the rain at The 34 club, or even when we were dancing. None of this was desire. But maybe it would be now that I had taken the trouble to come all this way and stay out so late and spend so much money.

'Better not,' she said at one point, which was fair enough though I dimly wondered why not. We talked more. Turn off your mind, relax and float downstream . . . Lennon borrowed that from Timothy Leary, I thought and said at the same time. Penelope didn't answer. Timothy Leary. He was a psychedelic guru, I said, and oddly enough was once married to Uma Thurman's mother though he wasn't Uma Thurman's father. We didn't sleep a wink and yet I seemed to wake suddenly with her next to me. She had blonde hair but slightly unattractive black bristles up her nostrils. There was a dried trail of saliva at the corner of her mouth and I looked at my watch quickly. It was 5.05.

She turned over at the same moment, hugging the duvet to her chin, shivering slightly. 'We'd better go,' she said at last, as if she was the one who had just looked at her watch. She blinked at me, not as a friend, not as a lover. She climbed out of bed and started gathering her clothes. I pulled myself up on one elbow. I didn't feel a thing. Not foolish. Not bad. Not tired.

'Can you ring a cab – Hammersmith,' she said.

I was puzzled. 'Don't you live here?'

Time had gone by so quickly I couldn't believe it. She shook her head, more it seemed in exasperation at my obvious puzzlement than in answer to my question, and she took her clothes to the bathroom while I retrieved my trousers and found a phone on the floor in the hall with a card from a minicab firm.

'Where are we?' I shouted.

'Barbican – the address is on the back of the card.' It was. Who would need a card with their own address on it? The Barbican. Lawrence? I remembered they'd said the Barbican in the TV programme. A flat in the Barbican it was that he had, they said.

I ordered two cabs and we left together, pushing the key through the door and going down to wait out in the cold. It wasn't raining. We made small talk about what kind of work we had to do that day (a book launch, my TV pages) and she said how tired we'd be later on. I didn't ask whether this was Lawrence's flat because suddenly I didn't want to hear the answer. My jaw physically ached with talking. Her cab came. I wondered if she'd kiss me and she did, quickly, on the cheek. I wondered if she'd look back and wave from the cab but she didn't.

When Cathy woke up and came down to find me sitting in the kitchen eating the cold leftovers of last night's risotto from the pan I told her I'd got drunk, forgotten about the Tube strike and been up all night with a contact. Which wasn't a complete lie. But I'd never felt so bad in my life.

This is the absolute truth. I dreamed I was talking to Alex. (I know dreams are all about texture and nuance but I make no apologies about recalling this one with syntax and verbs.) We were in a gym, and I started telling him about this friend of mine – George his name was, I said – who'd been on a walking tour of somewhere recently. The Yorkshire Dales, I said. George's wife wasn't interested in walking, I said, so she'd taken their children – two boys, twins possibly – up to her mother's in Leeds, leaving George on his own. George had taken a few days off from his job, which was in the entertainment business, I added. Anyway, it had been drizzling all day as George tramped across the moors consulting his compass and looking at his map and eating Kendal mint cake and talking to the sheep, and it was getting dark when he came upon this rustic inn rising out of the mist with the yellow of its lamps glowing in the windows and the clinking of glasses and laughter reaching him down the winding path. So he comes in out of the cold and gets out of his wet anorak and puts his rucksack in the corner, and asks the cheery landlord if they've got a room for the night, which is no problem. So he orders a pint of ale and a hearty bowl of warming mutton broth with a hunk of home-baked bread, which he wolfs down hungrily in front of a roaring fire while the landlord's wife sorts out his room. Then George gets talking to this girl, who's wearing a big jumper and has tumbling, red pre-Raphaelite hair and only a hint of pale make-up. She's on her own too, hiking back to college in Manchester, so they have a few drinks together. It's a bit strange for him because he's in his late thirties – thirty-nine if memory serves – and she must only be about twenty or something because she's only a student. But of course she's fascinated by what he does for a living, which sounds exciting and glamorous, especially after he tells her how he met Rod Stewart at a party once and talked about Rod's early blues days before the Faces. Anyway this girl, Alice, is studying literature and is about to take her finals, which is less interesting for him, obviously, but he acts as though he cares and he asks her what books she's doing and impresses her with his 'reading' of *Sons and Lovers* by D. H Lawrence, which he remembers from a brilliant essay he'd written at Cambridge, because he did English too and got a double first and was in the rowing team. To cut a long story short, they have too much to drink and end up in Alice's room. Which is odd in a way because a) they haven't snogged or anything and b) he doesn't actually fancy her that much, and besides he's supposed to be happily married and all that. But still something makes him go along with events and they go up. It's hot in her room and she struggles a bit to pull her baggy jumper over her head, providing an interesting glimpse of substantial breast movement under her T-shirt while she does it. Anyway, this friend of mine – George – lies on the bed with this girl and they talk for a while, and he puts his nose in her hair and loves the new smell and then he kisses her, which she seems to quite like. But just as he's getting this stonking hard-on, she pulls away and says better not. So they talk more and cuddle a bit, and he carries on for a while trying to persuade her with extra nuzzling and whispering in her ear, which again she doesn't seem to mind, but then she falls into a drunken sleep and he eventually stumbles off to find his own room.

'So . . .' Alex said (unaccustomed as he is to spending so long without speaking himself), 'is there any higher moral purpose to this story?'

'Well,' I said, 'look at it from this man's point of view. He feels terrible, right? Anyone would. He's cheated on his wife and yet he hasn't cheated on her. Plus, he feels a bit like he's been led up the garden path for a shag by this girl and then ended up without the expected shag. So funnily enough, he feels a bit cheated himself.'

'Hang on though,' Alex said, 'he hasn't actually cheated on his wife – nothing happened. He didn't have sex with her. Where's the cheat?'

I got exasperated at this point. 'Because, you fool, he has reached the point of no return. He has stepped over the mark he has drawn for himself and which he has never before allowed himself to cross. He's made the decision to do it and that's enough. All that remains is the formal exchange of bodily fluids. Don't you see, in his heart, he has been unfaithful to his wife, so of course he has to hate himself for it. And of course it would have been better if he had shagged her.'

Alex looks at me. 'How so?'

'Because . . .'

Anyway, the thing is, as I explain gently, is that this bloke – George – doesn't know whether to be more depressed about being emotionally prepared to betray his wife's trust after twelve years of marriage or the fact that this girl wouldn't have sex with him. What was her problem? Did she suddenly decide he was too old? (He's only thirty-nine, for God's sake.) Too married? (He didn't mention it.) Too bald? (Receding gently, though not to the naked eye, and anyway it didn't do Jack Nicholson any harm.) Too fat? (Had I mentioned that this man took his clothes off? He did, though not by any means all of them. I'd read recently that once you've hit forty, you're 47 per cent more likely to be embarrassed by your unyouthful body during new sexual encounters. Not that the man in my story *was* forty.) But, Alex was now wondering, why does this George care so much if he didn't fancy her in the first place? Because, I say, he has turned out to be a failure twice in a few short hours, and that's why it's eating away at him so much.

Of course, I point out, one thing that emerges from this story is how you can't underestimate the beneficial effect of artificial stimulants on the libido in the absence of proper desire. Someone eminent (but not so eminent that I can remember who) once pointed out how you could stand on a street corner all day and never spot a single woman you'd really like to have sex with. So obviously it helps if you've had a few drinks. Everyone remembers the *Simpsons* episode when they visit the beer theme park where you can buy novelty specs that let you see the world through the eyes of a drunk and transform hideous old hags into Uma Thurman. Spot on. I suppose it works the other way round too, hence George and the student. The girl's beer goggles must have fallen off, but George's stayed on. And when he woke up in the morning and found her gone, he felt a sense of loss that he couldn't put his finger on. It's not that he still wanted to have sex with her. He just wanted to talk things over, have the continental breakfast together, explain that he didn't make a habit of this kind of thing, laugh about it, part on cordial terms in which both partners recognise the folly of their ways with genuinely no hard feelings. Because, I say, there's nothing more terrible than being alone with your thoughts when you know in your heart that you've behaved like a complete cunt.

In the morning Cathy said her piece and made a show of not wearing her wedding ring, which meant we were still on speaking terms but not as husband and wife. Plus she had a go at me for getting through too much money, so of course I had to explain again that in this kind of job, you had to be able to keep up socially, otherwise everyone would think you were a wuss. And that I was actually earning about ten grand more than at the *Echo*. And that if she was really concerned, she'd stop Sadie spending so much time on the phone to her ex-friends in Leeds.

And at the office . . .

They knew. Not everything of course, because they couldn't know everything. They could only know everything if. But that was paranoia. Did ecstasy make you paranoid, or was that cocaine? Even so, Alex knew something, or seemed to know, and if he knew, you could bet everyone else did. As soon as I arrived that morning, I could see Alex clocking me as I made my way down the editorial floor in that annoying, smirking way he had, with his feet up on the desk and a green Berol in his mouth; grinning as I nodded good morning and took off my raincoat and draped it over the chair, sat down, logged on, rubbed my eyes, yawned, unfolded a newspaper and waited for whatever class-A cretinism he was lying so openly in wait with. It was weird how he seemed that touch more dangerous for having so recently featured in my dream.

'So how's the social life, Matso?' he said at last.

I stared at a headline about pensions management and left a beat of nonchalance before turning with mock weariness in his chair to face him. 'Meaning what?'

'Oh nothing, just wondered.' Alex smiled and winked at Jane, who shook her head irritably and turned back to her work. 'I hear you've been burning the candle a bit.'

'Not particularly.' I looked at him and Alex pursed his lips. He couldn't know. Hang on . . . Milo. I wondered for a second whether I might have just imagined that bit. No. 'All right, spit it out, what has Milo been saying?'

'Milo? Why Milo?'

'Because I saw him in a club, and no doubt this is what all this rubbish is about. I was out with a contact if you really have to know. I am over twenty-one.'

'What's her name?' Alex cackled and prodded his keyboard.

'Oh, come on . . .'

'Just pulling your leg, old mate, just pulling your leg.'

Jane had looked up again and I shook my head slowly in what I hoped looked like a pitying way.

But that was all. I spent the rest of the morning doing the right thing, burying myself in my proofs, drinking coffee, calling the printers to complain about something, pretending to listen to Isobel moaning about yesterday's Tube strike. At some point I even found myself agreeing to go to the gym tomorrow with Alex for a free no-obligation induction and debut game of squash. I was actually feeling quite on top of things, or at least equal to the job of appearing lively and interesting. 'OK, Isobel,' I said, 'how would you like the chance to make amends for those grotesque satellite listings last week.'

She looked up from her proof. 'I thought you agreed the satellite listings could have happened to anybody.'

'In theory,' I said. 'Like, in theory, every horse could win the Derby. Anyway, all you have to do is recommend a decent West End musical to take my wife to – nothing too Andrew Lloyd Webber, but on the other hand nothing so pretentious that it's going to send the entire audience to sleep – and then get me a couple of free tickets for it, via your network of luvvie contacts.'

Isobel issued a sigh dramatic enough to headline at Glyndebourne itself, opened the *Standard* and started to leaf through the entertainments pages. 'There's Brecht on at the Barbican. *Threepenny Opera*. Or . . .'

The Barbican. I glanced back at Alex. Not a flicker. He couldn't hear anything. And he didn't know anything, of course. No one knew. Except the girl, Penelope, with a key to

Lawrence's flat. Lawrence, O Lawrence, O Lawrence. I wondered for a moment if Penelope was one of Lawrence's cast-offs. I shook off a small wave of depression.

'Or how about Gershwin? *Porgy and Bess* is on. I could probably—'

'Right, excellent, perfect. That's a kind of classical-music musical, isn't it?'

'Well, yes – or opera, as people sometimes call it. But it's American. It's not Wagner or anything long and tedious.'

'Perfect again. So if you wouldn't mind . . .'

And then an hour later I was standing next to Jeremy McVie in the toilets. In an ideal world I would have asked whether Jeremy had had a chance to look through those TV columns I had sent to his office with a short memo affixed – as Jeremy himself had suggested when I'd buttonholed him in the lift. But there were some things you could talk about with your boss in the lift that you couldn't talk about when you were standing next to him holding your penis, even though Jeremy seemed genial enough and asked how it was all going as he was zipping up, and I said fine, at which Jeremy followed up with a little light joshing regarding the Dustin Hoffman upside-down-picture fiasco, which gave me something to worry about while we washed our hands together in the ensuing silence. Still, the fact was that Jeremy hadn't come back and turned me down flat, so there was every chance, I figured. James Thomas was being forced to work out his notice, so there was no rush. Jeremy was a busy man, not given to hasty decisions. No point pressuring him into saying yes, because then a person like Jeremy would have to take the easy route and say no. So I'd give him another week. Cool.

'By the way, nice piece about the chap with the wife,' Jeremy said. 'What a shit, eh?'

'Sorry? Oh right, the man with the wife, yes . . .'

'You know we expanded it into a big feature, don't you?'

I brightened. 'I didn't know that.'

I expected Jeremy to say more but he strode off, fluffing his hair with his hand as he passed the mirror.

A big feature! But what was that about him being a shit?

I stopped at features on the way back to my desk. Caroline was out of the office but the sub on 'Manners' dug out the proofs for me and laid them across the desk – huge banner headline: 'THE NEW CADS'. Wow. A five-pager. 'Infidels' it said at the top and had a block of pictures featuring rock stars and footballers and their women plus a meaty wraparound article about how the habits of skirt-chasing stars were spreading to any self-made Flash Harry with a bit of cash. There were portraits of embittered wives, now divorced and telling all, who had been left behind to get hooked on antidepressants and alcohol and look after the kids and the classical-cum-ranch-style Essex homestead and a cross-reference to the opinion pages of the main news section. My interview with Lawrence was plastered across the opening spread. 'Oh Christ,' I murmured, as my eyes took in the strapline over the copy. I could hardly believe it: 'Lawrence thinks he's the biggest bastard in town – but he could be the saddest too. Matthew Lewis meets a man who can't get enough extra-marital SEX. What IS his problem?' Oh God. I scanned down the rest of the page quickly and felt slightly queasy. All the quotes were there, but every few paragraphs someone – Caroline? Jeremy? – had used Lawrence's own words to give him a trashing. My own attempts to bring light and shade, a subtle touch of objectivity, to allow my subject the chance to air his character and philosophy, had been given a malicious spin.

'Everything OK?'

'Well, I was just thinking, er . . .'

'Steve.'

'Steve, right. When does this page have to go to press?' I asked. 'I just need to tweak it a bit. Could I do some quick changes on screen?'

Steve looked doubtful. 'I dunno. This section should have gone by now. If you tell me what you want to change . . .'

'Actually, it's quite complicated – I think I'd be better doing it myself. Ten minutes tops, I promise.'

'Well . . . OK. If you give me a shout when you're done. I'll just pop out for a fag.'

I slid into his seat and scrolled down the story, restoring some of my own copy and ditching bits of Caroline's. It wouldn't be a good idea to touch it too much. And maybe I had been wrong. Maybe it had been too flattering. It wasn't now, that was for sure. I started adding in a few cosmetic touches, removing a few unsightly adjectives. Five minutes later Steve was waiting at my elbow. I swivelled round in the chair and pointed at the screen. 'Steve, do you think we could just change this standfirst to say "but is he happy?" rather than "is he the saddest?"'

But Steve was now looking uncomfortable about the whole thing. 'No way, I'm sorry, I can't,' he said, 'all the heads have been cleared. If Caroline thinks it's fine, I think it's fine. If you want to talk to her, she should be back around three.'

'But won't the page have gone by then?'

He gave a thin smile. 'Well, that *is* the idea.'

I went sighing back to my desk to hear a message from Cathy saying that Sadie had been escorted home by a policewoman.

Excellent.

'I can't believe you'd do such a stupid thing,' I heard myself saying. Sadie was sitting on the couch wrapped in her dressing-gown, her knees pulled up to her chin, a tissue crumpled in her fist, her eyes puffy from crying.

'They're not bringing charges against Sadie, Matt,' Cathy said softly. I noticed she was wearing her wedding ring again. 'It was the other two girls . . .'

'She shouldn't have been there. She should have been at school. Why wasn't she at school?'

I was doing what Cathy was always telling me not to do. I was speaking to Sadie through her. I'd never had any trouble getting cross with Sadie when she was little ('Daddy says no! Pick that up! Go to your room!'). I could do that over my newspaper. But I'd never been able to get heavy with her, which meant getting cross in a more rational, sustained manner – it was something I discovered you had to master when a child hit puberty. But I always pitched it the wrong way. I could never find a language capable of penetrating the gloomy fog of adolescence, and I became inarticulate and splut-tery and angrier than I needed to be in my search for it, and that added to the problem by making me seem unreasonable. I could do calm refusal. But I was artless when it came to giving her a hard time.

Cathy didn't say anything, but looked back at Sadie. Sadie stared at her toes. I tried again. 'Don't even think about going to Gran's next weekend. I want to know where you are *every* minute of the day.' I sounded absurd even to myself. Of course, Cathy had already dealt with all this before I'd even got on the Tube to come home, but I couldn't just not say any-thing, having left the office early to deal with it.

'Well *you* stay out all night,' Sadie shouted, bursting again into breathy sobs. 'Mum doesn't know where *you* are . . .'

Cathy touched her shoulder.

'*I* am not out stealing perfume from Selfridges,' I said.

'I didn't steal anything.' Sadie pulled away from Cathy and threw herself face down into the cushions. 'I didn't, I didn't . . .'

I looked hopelessly at Cathy and retreated into the kitchen, leaving Cathy to take Sadie up to bed. She came back down after about twenty minutes.

'What does the school say?'

Cathy looked tired. 'Well . . . because there were no charges against Sadie, Mrs Leech seems pretty reasonable about it. There'll be some kind of punishment for bunking off. Nothing too draconian. We had a chat. It happens all the time, Matt, with girls this age. It was the same at my school. It's mainly a girl's thing. Make-up, jewellery. Anyway, she wants Sadie to stay off school until Monday. Give her a couple of days to sort herself out.'

I nodded. 'Do you think she'll be OK?'

Cathy nodded. 'Hope so.'

I took Cathy in my arms for a second, and put my cheek on her forehead. 'I think we should just put this one behind us.'

'I'd booked a table for us all at the Goose on Friday for your birthday. Bev was going to sit for us.'

I brightened. 'Hey, we can still do that.'

Funny, I'd almost forgotten about my birthday, even though it was so momentous. Forty. No fuss. Small family celebration. No flowers please.

Putting Sadie behind us wasn't easy. She took to her room, which was OK until I needed to call King's Cross and she happened to have our only working phone in there. I knocked gently on the door frame. 'Sade?' I tapped again. 'Sadie?' It wasn't as if I was about to barge in or anything. 'Sade, you in there?' I knew she was in there. I was just being courteous. 'I need the phone, Sade.' No answer. 'I need to call the station? About the Tubes?' I waited patiently. No answer. So obviously, in the end, I had to push the door open a fraction and stick my head in. She was lying there on the bed facing the wall. I could see the phone, off the hook on the floor. All of a sudden, obviously she sensed me standing there, or the door creaked, and she leapt up screeching at me. 'Leave me alone!' she yelled. 'Get out!' she yelled. I was shocked. I still hadn't physically set foot in the room. But now that she was trying to shut the door on me I felt obliged to put my foot in the way.

'Hang on, wait a minute,' I started to say, but she was screaming and somehow I went from being understanding and gentle and reasonable to shouting too, and Cathy and the yapping dog came thundering up the stairs wondering who was on fire.

'I just want the phone,' I said, my foot still in the door. 'She's going berserk.' Of course by now Sadie wasn't berserk, just sobbing away on the bed, where she'd thrown herself. Jesus.

Cathy glared at me as though I'd been an insensitive, cruel pig in every way known to social workers and marched past me (Sadie didn't budge), unplugged the phone and plonked it into my hands. 'Happy?' she snapped. Now it was Cathy who was waiting to shut the door on me, wondering how long I was going to be standing there making things worse. But it was bound to get worse.

On Friday, security rang from downstairs saying there was a Ruth Appleton in reception, which meant absolutely nothing to me, and I descended the four floors in the lift half-wondering if I'd left something at the gym yesterday other than my dignity, or whether Cathy had maybe arranged a birthday strippergram, which I had to admit would have required a radical shift in thinking this late in life. At first I didn't recognise the smart-looking woman in the heels and the sharp chalk-blue business suit (which seemed to be asking to be rained on in the middle of October, I thought) sitting on the leather couch showing her legs, until she turned and saw me and smiled and revealed herself as Ruth Appleton. Or rather as just Ruth. *That* Ruth.

'Well, well . . .' I said, coming towards her, wondering whether a friendly-cum-businesslike peck on the cheek was the thing, but the turnstiles would make that awkward and I was already settling for her over-firm handshake. 'Hello, how are you?' I said. 'What brings you down here?' I stopped myself saying that I hadn't recognised her or that it had never occurred to me that she had a surname, because then it would probably make her feel a bit too much like the Ruth who didn't normally dress like someone's remarkably short-skirted attorney-at-law on *Ally McBeal*, too much like the newish girl Ruth, whom I knew little more than slightly at the *Echo*, who had been at my farewell drinks, who worked in lowly listings, and over whom my male colleagues might have cast a drooling eye as she passed carrying a tray in the canteen, and whom I had myself engaged in dumb fellow journalists' banter when we had occasionally found ourselves between floors in the lift or at the coffee machine. Loved my stuff too, she'd said once. *So* funny. Something like that anyway.

'I hope you don't mind,' she said. 'I was in London and I remembered you said I ought to look you up. So here I am,' she smiled, 'looking you up.'

I glanced at the big clock over the reception desk. 'Why don't you come through – I'll buy you a coffee, show you around if you like.'

And why not? Me, the old hand, the avuncular guide; she the young, wide-eyed aspirant – how old? Twenty-four, twenty-five? There wasn't much to show her, of course – desks, terminals, more desks. 'Photocopier,' I said as we passed the photocopier. She laughed. I pointed out James Thomas from a distance. 'Star columnist,' I said. 'Just been poached by the *Courier*. Might be a nice opportunity there for someone with the right background,' I added, pursing my lips humorously. I introduced her to Isobel and Isabel, whom I described drolly as my crack subbing team, and briefly to Jane and Milo, who were disputing the toss of something at the pigeon-holes. Alex gave her what he no doubt thought was a winning smile, raising a salute as we skirted quickly past. We had coffee in the Coffee Stop on the third floor where we bumped into Jeremy, who pretended to be interested and charmed, even when she told him she worked at the *Yorkshire Echo* and had moved on from listings to my old desk, doing general features and interviews, which was news to me. 'Well, keep it up,' Jeremy said, winking. 'We're always on the lookout for new talent – isn't that right, Matt?' I raised my eyebrows modestly at what I took to be an allusion to my own elevation from the provincials. Ruth raised her own eyebrow of admiration for me as Jeremy strode off.

That's right, I thought, first names with the deputy. 'Bit of a bullshitter, old Jeremy,' I whispered, leaning towards her as if someone might hear.

'Oh . . . isn't he the one who gave you the job?'

'Well, yes, technically. He's OK, I suppose.'

'Seems a nice chap.'

I looked inscrutable, as though there was some insider knowledge I was reluctant to divulge. 'So, where are you staying?'

'Ivory Gardens – the *Echo*'s paying for it, so . . .'

'You're here for the paper?' I tried to look interested rather than impressed.

She licked cappuccino froth from her spoon before she answered. 'Oh, it's not much. Brad Pitt was doing interviews at St Martin's Lane first thing this morning. Polly and the new bloke who does entertainment were both off with the flu, so I got the job.'

'Hey. In at the deep end. The usual scrum, was it?' I said.

'Well, yes but . . . actually I did get five minutes to myself with him.'

Blimey. I nodded to indicate a very decent effort. 'Well done. How did you swing that?' I sipped my coffee.

'I just asked his minder.'

I walked her to the automatic doors. 'Sure you won't let me buy you lunch?' she said. 'Celebrate my five minutes with Brad?'

'I'd love to but I'm afraid I have . . . other fish to fry,' I said, smiling ironically as if to own up to a cliché amusingly intended, though I realised that to the wrong ears it could sound like a very banal thing to say indeed.

She offered me a businesslike hand. 'Well, if you change

your mind, you'll find me feeding the pigeons in Trafalgar Square.'

I laughed, opting for unironic now. 'As bad as that? Tell you what – we'll do it next time. Give me a call.'

Lunch was pasta and a glass of wine with Caroline. I didn't tell her it was my birthday in case it got back to Alex, who was still only thirty-four and would want to commemorate the occasion by going on about how the over-forties are more susceptible to genital warts and subscribing to *Reader's Digest*, before insisting on dragging me to Eamonn's after work, which would make me late for dinner with Cathy and Sadie. Sadie had still been in bed when I left, and didn't seem to have got round to buying me a card, which was slightly hurtful but I guessed that was the point. Cathy had surprised me with a can of Beatles 'Air' plus an authenticated square of used hotel towel in a glass case, both souvenirs from the 1964 American tour which she'd spotted advertised in one of my memorabilia mags, which was fantastically thoughtful since all I'd asked for was a shirt from Paul Smith, and then she'd come down and made me a boiled-egg-and-Marmite-soldier breakfast, which was sweet and thoughtful again and made me feel slightly depressed for reasons to do with what I wished hadn't happened at The 34. 'Don't worry about Sadie,' she'd said as I dipped and crunched.

'The point is,' Caroline was saying, scowling slightly, talking out of the corner of her mouth and showing me more of her seafood rigatoni than anyone would reasonably want to see, 'you have to let us edit. You must know that.' She had her red editor's jacket on, munching away, tucking in.

I sighed. 'Yes, OK, I just thought it was a little over the top, that's all, and you weren't around, and the page was about to go. Maybe I shouldn't have done it, but I do think you might have discussed it with me if you were completely rewriting it, or at least let me see a proof before it went to press.'

'Oh, come on. It wasn't a rewrite. We just tweaked it a bit. Well, all right, maybe I could have sent you a proof. It's just that when Jeremy started to get excited about it because of all this current government froth about families and divorce et cetera, it sort of drifted out of my arena. Anyway, I'm glad we've cleared the air a bit. You might want to do some more stuff for me . . .' She smiled and sent her tongue on a brief clean-up operation round her gums.

'Yes, no problem.'

When I got back to the office, there was a yellow Post-it on my screen. Isabel's scrawl. I read it and went slightly cold. Cathy. It was a Leeds number. 'What's this?'

'Your wife's rung twice – she's at her mother's,' said Isabel, not looking up.

'At her mother's? Did she say anything?'

'Just said to ring.'

My mouth was suddenly dry. I called the number and Cathy's mother answered. 'Oh, Matt . . . I know it looks bad but try not to be angry with her, dear. She's very upset. I did warn you that something like this . . .'

'What do you mean? Let me talk to her.'

'Well, I think perhaps you should speak to Catherine first.'

'What? What are you talking about?'

'Just a moment, Matt . . .' I could hear Cathy now at her mother's side, taking the phone. 'Hello, Matt? Sorry, I've been trying to get you. Look, Sadie's here. She caught the train up this morning.'

Fuck. 'How? Why?'

'I don't know. I thought she was still in her room. She must have set off at dawn. By the time I got back from the library, Mum was on the phone, frantic, so I whizzed straight up here in the car. Sadie's OK but she's really upset.'

'*She's* really upset? For God's sake, Cathy. If it's that fucking boy again . . .'

I could sense Cathy waiting for me to calm down; almost as

if she thought I was making a show of blowing up for her benefit but had misjudged by a degree or so. 'She went to look for him at that pizza place where she and her school-friends used to hang out sometimes. It turned out he was with one of the other girls in her crowd. I think she probably must have known.'

I gave her one of my philosophical sighs.

'Look, we'll be back tomorrow afternoon,' she said. 'Can you cancel the Goose? Sorry Matt – maybe we can reschedule it.'

'Yes, fine.' I was back to calm now. 'So, how is she?'

'Inconsolable. But sorry too, I think, which is a good sign. She keeps apologising and saying how she's let us down. Bit on the dramatic side, of course. In a way I think maybe this had to happen for her to make a cleaner break. I've told her she can still keep in touch with her friends up here and they can come and visit. I think she just feels humiliated by this boy, Matt.'

'Well you can hardly blame the boy.'

'Ha. Funny, I had a feeling you'd say that. Anyway, happy birthday. What will you do?'

'Oh, I don't know. Probably just go for a couple of pints with Alex and Milo.' I could hear Ellie talking baby in the background.

'Listen,' she said. 'Don't forget to feed Kite in the morning. I've left a key with Bev. She's going to walk the dogs this afternoon.' I put the phone down and rubbed my eyes. There was a ripple of applause from sport as Amy passed my desk pushing a huge trolley with piles of clothes on it. She smiled and made a weary expression for me and I smiled back. I watched her unlock the frock cupboard, then picked the phone up again and dialled 192.

What was it then? I hadn't gone out that night with the explicit intention of sleeping with Ruth. You couldn't say that. I had just stepped out in front of her and she'd hit me. Bam. She could have swerved; I could have stepped back on to the pavement. What would you call that – misadventure? What would the jury say – that I was looking for an accident to happen? Well?

I lay unmoving, submerged to the neck in my hot, comforting bath, though it was well past midday by then and I knew I should be tutting over Isobel's proofs and eating pre-lunch doughnuts and congratulating myself on reaching forty without doing anything terrible, which now I could never do. I lay back and soaped my willy, which was of course a name for something you urinated out of, not committed adultery with. A willy didn't stand up; it dangled, and was a symbol of comedy. Cock, yes. Dick, maybe. Prick, definitely. Not willy. I watched, warming, steaming, as it floated there, more pleased with itself than I could allow myself to be, this something with a consciousness or at least a conscience quite apart from my own (as every schoolboy knew, and every woman treated with a knowing scepticism, as though it were some story put about to vindicate wayward sexual ambitions); but here it was, responding now to a stray image of Ruth that flitted through my mind, stirring in the warm water. Up periscope. An angled vision of those alien, excellent breasts jigging as she'd leaned forward on her elbows across the white duvet cover, me behind (her idea), her moaning as if on cue (as if, rather thoughtfully, for my benefit), pushing back against my stomach, me sucking in breaths of concentration, trying to keep going for a decent interval (the first time had understandably been a bit brief), my hands on the roundness of her buttocks, the gold of my wedding ring against her skin – the ring I had decided not to take off because I felt, even as I eased myself in and out of Ruth in so satisfactorily manly a manner, that that would be a betrayal too far. I uttered a long, soft moan now myself, half at the thought of Ruth and her body and half at the awfulness of that self-deceit and what I had been prepared to do to inspire it. I sighed and closed my eyes and tried not to think, but then I thought of Bev, which was a problem, and my . . . my penis (good word) eventually sank beneath the suds. I reached across to the portable stereo perched on the toilet lid and hit play again. It was weird to think of Bob Dylan echoing across the decades and bouncing off the goldfish tiles just for me. Just for some English love rat lying in his bath, lying to himself. The quality was poor, the guitar lacked Dylan's distinctive changes and right-hand technique, there was no harmonica, the vocal was almost comically nasal. You could see why he junked it. But it was a gift you had to be grateful for, even though in years to come I knew what it would remind me of.

I hauled myself out of the bath, pulled out the plug and stood sideways in front of the mirror and looked. I sucked in my stomach. I wondered if Ruth's journey north and Cathy's back south would cross and, if so, where. Leicester? Doncaster? Could you see the motorway from the railway? I put my hands over my face. I had to get to the office. Not to do any work necessarily, just to be not here when Cathy and Sadie and the baby got home. I felt like some low, unskilled thief who had left fingerprints all over the house. I could imagine Cathy walking in, recoiling humorously at the garlic on my breath from my welcome-back kiss, and asking about last night. She would find a pubic hair on my lapel, or sperm on my shoe. There would be something.

I'd had to come home this morning, of course, sweating inside my long coat on the half-empty Tube in the rush hour, though not *part* of the rush hour, going up the line with everybody else coming down. If I'd gone into the office, Alex would have had too much fun speculating all morning as to why I was wearing the same green shirt I'd worn yesterday or why I had come to work smelling of sexual intercourse instead of having a shower like normal people, which would be a good question and could only be explained by having to leave the scene of a crime in a hurry. But then not going into work had meant ringing Cathy from a phone-box at King's Cross and telling her I was calling from the office, which had set my blood pumping again the minute she spoke.

'Hi, I tried to ring you last night,' she said. 'Did you have a good time? Did you go out with Alex and Milo?' I could see her face, and felt not just guilt but sheer dread too at kicking off with this unnecessary, stupid lie. Why couldn't I have just rung from home and said I was too hungover to go into work?

'Yes,' I said, 'I didn't get back till late. What time did you ring?'

'We left it late. About twelve I suppose. Ellie was still up, needless to say, and Sadie wanted to wish you a happy birthday.'

'That's nice. How are things? With Sadie.'

'Well, you know. She said she'd try again this morning. Maybe you'd already left for the office.'

'Yes, sorry, actually, I did leave early this morning. I thought I'd make a start on some . . . well, just some boring stuff at work.'

'What's that noise? It's a terrible line.'

'Oh, you know what it's like here. Madhouse.'

'How's Kite – she missing us?'

It took a moment for my mind to register. Fuck . . .

'Yes,' I said. 'No problem.'

But when I got home and saw Bev suddenly there like a ghost in the kitchen, I could have died of fright. She had one knee on the floor spooning Pedigree Chum into a bowl, the dog already with its nose in it, chomping away like a real animal. Bev looked up at me. 'Don't tell me,' she said.

'Christ, sorry, I completely forgot. I've just come all the way back.' Guilt thudded through me with every beat of my heart. My eyes went to the dog and then back to her, as if I FUCKED RUTH was written all over my face and all she had to do was reach for her reading glasses. I couldn't move.

'From work?' She looked at me again, as if I was mad. I

nodded. 'Oh well, not to worry. I heard the poor baby scratching at the door as I was coming back from the library.' She gazed indulgently at Kite with her head still in the bowl, noisily wolfing down the mess of meat and minerals and marrowbone jelly. 'I did knock,' Bev said. 'Cathy gave me the key.'

'No, no, that's fine. You saved my life. I'm sorry, I just . . .'

Could she tell? Was it obvious I hadn't been here? I looked around, and fingered the front of yesterday's shirt. 'It was my birthday last night. I didn't get home till gone midnight and then I completely forgot this morning because I was in such a rush and late for the office.' I forced a grin. 'Feel free not to tell Cathy if you don't want.' I said it as if it didn't matter, but I felt my hand checking my jacket sidepocket for a protruding foil packet containing one unused condom, though I knew I'd dropped it in a rubbish bin outside King's Cross an hour ago.

Bev had given me a wry smile and shook her head. 'Happy birthday for yesterday. There were some cards for you on the mat, by the way. They're on the table.' I wondered whether the postman had come before or after I was supposed to have left the house late and wondered whether Bev was wondering the same thing. I wondered whether Bev had been upstairs to see if my bed had been slept in, or if the hot water had been switched on, or whether I had used my toothbrush. 'Aren't you going to open them?' she said.

And then at last Bev had picked up her shopping and books from the library and gone, Kite following her to the door, wagging her tail.

I towelled my hair, found a white, nothing-to-hide shirt and stared in the bedroom mirror as I buttoned it, smiling to myself, though I had no right to smile now or ever again. I was smiling at how Ruth had almost shrieked with excitement. 'You didn't tell me it was your birthday!' How she had given me an impulsive peck on the cheek, and grabbed my arm in a jocular-affectionate way for a few moments as we walked along towards Gray's Inn Road.

'I was trying to keep it quiet,' I said.

'You don't look forty,' she said, which might have been an untruth, but one I could warm to, and even the fact that I had offered up my maturity to be openly contrasted against her own youth betokened a kind of innocence of intent, did it not? I'd thought so at the time. She had changed out of her chalk-blue outfit and was wearing a plain mac with a black jumper and black trousers, which I found myself slightly disappointed about, though I didn't get as far as allowing myself to wonder why. I was wearing one of my work suits from the Next catalogue, dark grey with the legs tapered to make up for my small feet, black Chelsea boots and the pale green shirt with a speck of Caroline's seafood sauce on the collar. It would be easier, I'd said, for me to pick her up at the hotel. 'We could get a cab from there into Covent Garden if you like.' But that hadn't happened. We'd had a couple of drinks at the Ivory Gardens 'tropical' bar and I had casually mentioned a French place that I was pretty sure was somewhere in the area – though, of course, I was only pretty sure because I'd picked it out from the listings in *Time Out* that afternoon and checked it for its proximity to the Ivory Gardens in my *A–Z*. 'It's my birthday today,' I'd said, as we walked along.

If Ruth had done the right thing, having sex could have been ruled out from the start. I, at least, had done it by the book. I had explained that my wife had had to dash with the children up to Leeds (I had, not unreasonably, spared Ruth the details, saying something about Cathy's mother being quite ill, though not so close to death that it would make a chap feel bad about going out and rolling around naked in a hotel room with someone who wasn't his wife's mother's daughter), and so I had suddenly found myself at a loose end on my birthday and immediately thought of Ruth, and her with only the pigeons for company. Of course mentioning Cathy's absence might have sounded as much an invitation as a statement of unavailability, but that was hardly my fault, was it? Well?

And so we'd found the restaurant (Chez Georges, small but not too intimate), ordered the house white, talked about the regeneration of the city of Leeds, and about regional papers versus the nationals and pay differentials and benefits, and she'd looked into my eyes with her own starry ones when I'd modestly recounted how I was plucked from the *Echo* to come to London, though I'd never been particularly ambitious, I said, it had just kind of happened. Of course, she already knew all this. The waitress came back and Ruth gaily ordered oysters as a starter, saying she'd never had oysters before. 'Oh, everyone owes it to themselves to try oysters at least once,' I said, with my head in the menu and opting myself for the lobster bisque, a choice that hinted towards enough sophistication to discourage any suspicion that I had never eaten oysters before either and wasn't going to start now. She had been a big fan of my stuff at the *Echo*, she said, peeling bits of soft wax off the candle. She didn't ask why she hadn't seen my byline at the *Post*, but returned to the general sound notion of being able to forge ahead without even trying. 'You can't hold talent back,' she said. We drank to that, and to Ruth's coup with Brad. She hoped it would do her some good, and I hoped so too. I told her about the difficulties of setting up in London with a family, and she nodded and lit a cigarette and said it must be tricky, and didn't seem to notice that I asked nothing about her own domestic circumstances, which I found myself unaccountably not wanting to know about. We didn't have pudding, but lingered over coffee and more wine. She let me pay for dinner, leaving me with the vague thought that it was she who had offered to buy me lunch, which I assumed was on exes but it probably wouldn't have been, knowing the *Echo*. Maybe I could bill this to the *Post*. Though, better not.

'What now?' she'd said, and I had looked at my watch and shrugged, as though possibilities were expanding rather than converging. It was ten to eleven. 'If I walked you back to your hotel, we could have a nightcap or something.' I looked at her, my mouth suddenly drying up so much that I had to avoid literally licking my lips.

Was it at this point that I really decided to hell with it? To hell with everything I'd always believed in about marriage, though obviously not to hell with *my* marriage in particular, which this was nothing to do with, and was as good and healthy as any after fourteen years. Or was it later, halfway through our nightcap – our third bottle of house white of the evening (though we had been happy to leave our second at dinner still half-full, as if somehow it had served its purpose) – when under other less equivocal circumstances I would be hurrying towards King's Cross cursing my lack of physical fitness and wondering whether the last northbound Piccadilly line had gone?

But we were murmuring quietly now in the lowlights of the lounge, sitting side by side on a small, comfortable, cream sofa, our trousered legs touching occasionally every time we laughed at something, and I remembered Ruth's untrousered legs at my farewell drinks in Leeds next to mine a lifetime ago, and again in reception that morning, crossed, long, slim and promising. And so, when she said, 'You can stay if you like,' and took a sip of wine, looking at me over the rim of her glass, the shocking thrill of it left me able only to raise my eyebrows in reply, even though I might have guessed long ago the way the evening was pointing, and had in fact bought a packet of three non-flavoured condoms from the machine in the hotel toilets, an astonishing act of boldness, which in itself had set my heart pounding in case the door should burst open and someone should step in to remind me that I hadn't bought condoms since 1980, on which occasion, like numerous others before, I hadn't needed to use them. So I couldn't say no, because 'no' wouldn't get me what I really wanted at this moment, and Lawrence was right, it wasn't weakness in the face of temptation but having the moral stamina to follow the trajectory of a sudden desire, and though this scenario would doubtless in due course seem little, sordid and regrettable, right now it seemed grand, wicked and impulsive, which were all good words and in the circumstances the due course of things could go fuck itself. Sex was stronger than drugs. Sex was addictive before you'd even had any.

'Shall we . . .' I'd said, making an upward sign with the browns of my eyes, though wondering if going straight to her room rather than affecting an interest in finishing the wine, which again seemed to have served its purpose of giving us a purpose while we decided whether we were going to have sex together or not, would constitute indecent haste. Then there had been the strange walk down the carpeted lounge steps, not together, not apart. I wondered if anyone was watching. The night porter. Someone who might step forward to challenge me ('Excuse me, sir . . .'), and reveal my status as a non-guest about to enter the guest-only zone of upstairs in the lady's chamber. I had yawned, as if nothing more compelling than legitimate fatigue was drawing us towards the lift doors. I wondered what would happen. I imagined her saying, 'Are you sure you want to go through with this?', but there was nothing to talk about when the doors closed, just a satirical re-enactment of the scene from *Fatal Attraction* where Michael Douglas and crazy Glenn Close reject the imminent comforts of a respectable room with bed and start pressing their eager hot bodies against each other and insinuating their eager thick tongues in each other's mouths (in this case her first, then me) the moment they leave the ground floor. I caught myself viewing with an odd disbelief this badly lit performance in the mirror over her left shoulder, watching myself and this beautiful, desirable woman I was about to have sex with, writhing in a public place, and realising that this was it, and that there was no going back. We tumbled into her room on cue and collapsed on to one of the twin beds, my right hand travelling enthusiastically between her outer thigh and the fleecy hillock of her breast. I vaguely wondered whether this kind of wrestling match was still the thing or whether customs had moved on and she would have to throw me out at the last minute for being too 1979. It was what you did on the sofa in your parents' front room back in the days when you could only *dream* of a bed and a minibar and free Kleenex.

I had imagined (when had I imagined this?) . . . I had imagined watching her unbuttoning her chalk-blue suit jacket and unbuttoning her white shirt underneath, and stripping naked in slow motion with the light from a neon sign flickering on her skin, because that's how films told you to imagine it when someone was dressed like someone's short-skirted attorney-at-law in *Ally McBeal*. But tonight she was wearing black trousers with tights underneath and had sensibly gone to the bathroom to sort herself out, leaving me to get undressed and into bed with studied composure. Then she'd come skipping in to join me. And she *had* been naked and beautiful, so that much was right. 'Happy birthday,' she said afterwards, and lit a cigarette. I had given up smoking when Sadie was born, when I was about Ruth's age, but I'd never wanted one since as much as I wanted one then.

'Hang on a minute,' she said. She lit one and passed it to me.

I had woken Ruth briefly to say goodbye, but she turned over and was asleep again when I'd left, her hair covering her face. I'd crossed the hotel lobby, avoiding the eye of the woman on the desk, and stepped into the street, my stupid heart pumping with its own wild laughter, my head full of terrors.

fool

A day went by. Then two. An e-mail arrived at the office that leapt off the screen at me with a loud bloop, setting my heart thudding (*hi. enjoyed our evening vv much. R xxx*). I glanced about like a bad shoplifter, as though the entire features staff might at this moment be reading over my shoulder with a view to frogmarching me off to the fashion editor's office where they would force me to turn out the bulging pockets of my faithless heart and record the contents for a series of colour spreads to run over four weeks supported by a seven-figure TV promotion and a competition to win my share of the divorce settlement. I shot off a smart, giddy reply ('Me too. Let's do it all again next week,' I wrote, feeling the sting of disgrace as I did so but also the visceral rush of excitement; knowing Ruth was safely in Leeds interviewing local folk musicians but thrilling at the notion that sprang into my mind of her boarding the next train south and setting herself up as the *Echo*'s London showbiz correspondent in an expenses-paid luxury sex parlour located in an area so convenient for lunchtime visits that I would be powerless to resist). I smiled stupidly to myself, and dithered stupidly over my work and stupidly praised Isobel and Isabel cheerfully for theirs, but at other, saner, rational moments was buffeted by terrifying misgivings that set my heart clattering all over again, though for reasons that had nothing to do with breasts and panting and labouring pelvises and everything to do with shame and ignominy and being caught and having my nose rubbed in the disgrace of my own doings.

But the deeper the ache of regret and desire, the more nothing came of anything. I was almost narcotically animated at supper with Cathy and Sadie, laughing out loud at Kite's doggy antics as she sniffed round everyone's feet under the table and gobbled up Ellie's jettisoned chicken dippers. Even the official inquiry into the offence of leaving a starving animal to be rescued by a neighbour (Bev had, of course, spilled the beans and complicated things dangerously by remembering that I had been late for work the morning I had told Cathy on the phone that I'd gone in early) proved an interrogation marked more by weary resignation than suspicion, and was certainly no more penetrating than those that routinely followed, say, a failure to bring home an emergency loaf of bread or a rash decision to stop off for a quick half at Eamonn's when I was supposed to be at home by seven-thirty to look after Ellie on Cathy's book-group evenings. After all, wasn't it reasonable to tell Bev I'd been late for work rather than confess that the balance of my mind had been temporarily disturbed owing to the abscondment of my eldest daughter? Cathy had rolled her eyes in exasperated submission.

It seemed odd, but it was precisely on these occasions, in the warm bosom of Crouch End, that I felt least vulnerable to the horrors of sudden disclosure. It was the reassuring physical presence of my family itself that stood against the tremors of shame and fear that disturbed my daydreaming hours, and even the thought balloons that materialised uninvited above my head containing pornographic images downloaded from an evening at the Ivory Gardens went unremarked amid Cathy's deadpan account of an afternoon at the launderette when the washing machine broke down and Sadie's newfound enthusiasm for loitering at the bowling alley with her schoolfriends in the new yellow leather jacket that had been purchased with her father's surprisingly ungrudging concurrence and groaning Visa card from an expensive shop on the Broadway. I began to relax. Nothing bad could happen while I was here. No one was going through my pockets, or viewing with disbelief a time-dated security film of myself entering and leaving a hotel on consecutive days, the first with an unknown woman, the second with an irrepressible expression of triumph on my face, or discovering some undealt-with anomaly in the inventory of my underwear drawer that would make a nonsense of my alibi on the day of the twenty-eighth.

'Can I go to Glastonbury next year, Dad?' Sadie said, slinging her arm over my shoulder with exaggerated affection. 'We'll see,' I answered, smiling, addressing Cathy's querying eyebrows with a broad wink. 'I might go myself!' I added. How we laughed.

At the office I checked my e-tray hourly, though I well knew my computer would tell me when I had mail. My heart fell a little when nothing came, though I knew it was better that way and that it was tantamount to tempting fate to dare to be dismayed at another day passing without the chance of someone getting hurt. The news bulletins led with the story of a fourteen-year-old boy missing for two days after failing to turn up at school. The class teacher had yawned and put an X where he usually put a tick, because that's what you did for absentees, but it meant the boy was missing seven hours before anyone knew he was missing, which was the worse kind of setback, said the police, because the longer a case like this went on, the harder it was to find a trail. Clues dried up, people's memories for crucial details evaporated, public appeals fell on ears deafened by competing events. The boy's disappearance was completely out of character, said his parents. You could tell by the language of the media and the expressions on the faces of those employed to man the helplines and the incident rooms that no one expected to find him alive. The truth was that real criminals got away with murder every day. You only had to listen to the news to know that. I awoke in the early hours to Ellie's cries and held her close to me long after she'd dropped back off to sleep, there, rocking her gently in the half-light from the landing, lost in her warm infant smells and softness. Tears sprang to my eyes but they were for no one but my stupid self.

On Sunday, Cathy brought a cup of tea out to the garden where I was clipping furiously at the undergrowth with the shears I'd borrowed from Jonathan next door. 'Someone called Lawrence rang this morning,' she said.

I felt my neck redden as I stopped clipping, as I stared now at the bushes with what I hoped would pass for a preoccupied air. 'Mmm?' I said. I glanced sideways at Cathy, but instead of waiting for her to repeat what was already ringing insistently in my head I returned to the offending evergreenery and began snipping, this time with judicious darting movements – once, twice, here, there – as if I had come to the sudden conclusion that the most efficient way through jungle was via the application of topiary skills.

'Lawrence?' she said, more loudly. 'Telephone call. This morning, when you were in bed?' She stood expectantly at the edge of my vision as I peered into the tangle of branches, shears poised.

'He rang here?' I said, still not looking.

'Yes. Lawrence. *Here*. Where else do we answer your phone

calls?' She put the mug on a fence post. 'Cup of tea for you. *Tea*.'

'OK, thanks,' I said abruptly, because abruptness might make her go away shaking her head and give me a moment's grace to calm my welling thoughts and pull from their depths plausible answers to the awkward questions I imagined similarly welling in Cathy's mind. In the meantime I gathered up an armful of brushwood and half carried it, half dragged it, huffing and puffing absurdly as I went, the branches scraping my averted face, to a wheelie bin in the corner of the garden. 'I don't know what we're going to do with all this rubbish,' I muttered.

Cathy followed me, eating a biscuit. 'Well, don't you want to know what he said?'

'Oh, right, sorry. What did he say?' I said, still not facing her.

'He just said . . .' She finished munching a mouthful of biscuit. 'Who *is* he, anyway?'

I stood on the chair I had brought out from the kitchen and grunted ostentatiously as I tried to cram the branches down into the bin with my foot. I looked up at last, forcing a fake grimace. 'Who – Lawrence?' I panted, squinting at her.

'Yes, Lawrence. Who *is* Lawrence?'

'Oh, just someone I know from . . .' I stopped. 'Why did you say it like that?'

'I don't know. He just seemed odd.'

I relaxed a little. 'What do you mean?'

She gestured vaguely with the biscuit. 'Well, he was just a bit matey. A bit, you know – overfamiliar. Not that there's anything wrong in that, but . . . well, I assumed he was someone from your office and that it must be something important.'

I went to scoop up another heap of clippings. 'So what did he say?'

Cathy followed me back to the bin. 'Well, Sadie answered, and he kept her talking for a while or vice versa. Then when I spoke to him and told him you were still in bed, he said not to bother you and that he'd catch you later. But then he asked how *I* was, and how the family was settling in and how nice it was that Sadie seemed to be enjoying school, which was news to me. Then we had this ridiculous conversation about your ridiculous obsession with the Beatles and your TV pages and whether I saw *Dangerous Liaisons* on Premier last night, and I said no, we didn't have satellite, and he said it was funny that the TV editor didn't have satellite, then he told me that Uma Thurman was in it, and did I know by any chance that Uma Thurman's mother was married to Timothy O'Leary, who I thought was a football manager but who apparently knew the Beatles in the Sixties.' She paused. 'You know – all kinds of rubbish like that. And because he was talking to me as if I ought to *know* who he was, obviously I couldn't simply come out and *ask* who he was. So in the end I just let him rabbit on like a . . .' She gave a little wave of her hand, impatiently wafting away the unfinished end of her sentence, like she always did.

I crinkled my brow, to suggest that I was as baffled as she was, and moistened my lip with my tongue, a classic sign, we both knew, that someone had something to hide. 'Don't worry. I'll give him a ring on Monday. It's probably to do with this production thing.' I picked up the shears and scowled hard into the prickly foliage, as if looking for the one arterial stem whose removal would end all domestic horticultural labours everywhere for ever with one clinical stroke. 'We've just had some production things to sort out,' I said. 'Not very interesting.' I snipped once, sending a handful of leaves fluttering to the ground.

'So, you *do* work with him?'

'What? Oh, yes – well, no. He's more on the print side.' I smiled at her quickly, searching her expression for traces of a correct answer. Or at least not an incorrect one. 'They're all a bit chatty down there. I don't actually *know* him.' I allowed myself a smile. 'Not very well.'

'But he asked if you got home OK the other week.'

'Ah yes, that's ri-i-ght.' I was nodding, pulling my eyebrows together, remembering. 'I bumped into him the other week when I was out late with . . .' I clicked the air impatiently with my shears, trying to clear an imaginary jammed leaf.

'With your contact?'

'That's right. Yes. I'd forgotten about that. Bumping into him, I mean.'

Cathy shrugged. 'Anyway, that was it. He just said to say he rang. He didn't leave his number. Which makes me wonder why he rang on a Sunday morning, when decent people are up changing babies' nappies and idle husbands are still in bed.' She raised an eyebrow now, inviting my jocularly defensive response but getting none.

'Thanks,' I said, finding nothing else in my head to say that wouldn't damn me to hellfire.

She shrugged and turned to go back into the house. 'Don't mention it.'

'Love you,' I called after her cheerfully, which after fourteen years of marriage had become less a statement of a fact we both still took for granted than an emergency way of signalling that all was well when the usual connections between us petered out unexpectedly.

'Love you,' she called back wearily.

I hung around for a moment longer then followed her into the house. The *Post* was still intact on the hall table. Cathy never read a newspaper until the evening, when none of the news was news any more. I located the 'Manners' supplement between 'Finance' and 'Sport', took it out and stuffed it deep into my gardening bin, feeling simultaneously terrified and ridiculous as I did it. But that's what this was about. And though under normal circumstances I would have taken some pride in pushing the first piece I'd ever written for a national newspaper under Cathy's nose, there was no point pushing two twos under her nose and expecting her to come up with anything but four. She'd be looking high and low for it later but wasn't the newsagent forever losing the supplements?

On Monday, I rang Tanya's production company. 'She's not with us any more, I'm afraid,' said the woman who picked up the phone.

'She's the producer on *Cheating Hearts*,' I said.

'Yes, I know who she is,' the woman said, 'but she doesn't work here any more.'

'That was a bit sudden, wasn't it?' I asked.

'She's gone freelance, I believe.'

'Well, is there anyone else I could speak to about *Cheating Hearts*? I'm trying to contact one of the people featured in the programme running this Thursday. I wrote a piece for the *Sunday Post* – you might have seen it yesterday?'

'I'm sorry, I really can't help,' the woman said. 'You'd need to speak to Tanya about that.'

'Do you have a contact number for her?'

'No.'

I didn't know what I wanted to say to Lawrence. But not antagonising him would be a start. I could understand him being pissed off about the interview, but I couldn't have him ringing the house. I couldn't have him ringing up and trying to make someone else's wife wonder what the fuck was going on because obviously something was. That morning I had actually found myself standing on tiptoe in the hall, running my hand along the high windowsill where the phone line came in. I had actually, momentarily, nursed a strong impulse to rip it out, as I might well have done had it not been for the unappealing prospect of trying to convince Cathy that the dog was to blame or in fact of coming up with *any* explanation that didn't entertain the possibility of poltergeists. I consoled myself with the thought that, if Lawrence had really wanted to tell Cathy exactly where he had come across the interesting snippet about Uma Thurman's mother's late ex-husband's connection to the opening line of a 1966 Beatles album track, he would have done so yesterday. He was obviously just playing games. I would wait.

Milo was passing behind my chair on the way back from the coffee machine humming a Stones song. I leaned back and stopped him to chat, guiding the conversation in a gentle arc from what turned out to be Milo's favourite Jagger–Richards single (predictably, 'Paint It Black'), via the 1960s generally and eventually into the vicinity of The 34 club, where I had spotted Milo that night, though Milo had to be reminded that he'd seen me too, partly because he'd been a bit hammered but mainly because he didn't track my social life with as much prurient interest as Alex. 'Are you a member?' I asked casually.

'Yeah. Well, you know, kind of . . .' Milo said, looking up and studying the ceiling tiles as he answered. 'They generally let me in.'

'I'd really love to go back there one night,' I said, sensing that what Milo would really love to do was go back to his desk, drink his coffee and crash his computer.

'Sure. We'll have to arrange it some time. Couple of weeks maybe, yeah?'

The afternoon and evening news led with the missing boy, who had been found alive and well. He had gone to Bournemouth to see a girl he'd met on the Net. I caught up with the story on the Tube on the way home, in the late edition of the *Standard*. It occurred to me that what happened to the boy wasn't out of character at all. It was just a part of his character that had never been switched on; a part that had never really been exposed to the world before. Sex was like a butterfly coming out of its shell for the first time and thinking, blimey, I didn't know I could do *that*. Nevertheless, the lost lamb was returned to the fold. The boy's parents were jubilant, the media turned its guns on negligent schools and the hidden evils of chatroom culture *vis à vis* impressionable young adults, and I had to admit, to my shame, that to see such a gratifying outcome as an unfavourable omen for myself was the mark of a man with too much on his mind.

By the evening of my rescheduled birthday dinner at the Goose, I had already survived sitting with Cathy through *Cheating Hearts*, yawning and fidgeting and wondering aloud whether maybe we ought to get an early night while Cathy shook her head with irritation as Lawrence expounded his philosophy on love, sex and marriage, though she seemed happy not to link this hateful 'Lawrence' with the millions of other Lawrences who had no reason not to use their own voices and may or may not have legitimate business on Sunday mornings with her own husband. My stomach registered a nauseous blip of recognition as the interior of The 34 club rolled on to the screen revealing a laughing waitress in black, the angle of an open-plan staircase and the *Our Man Flint* James Coburn mirror and flash of neon purple 34, as the camera circuited the lounge, finally coming to rest in a corner to catch moodily the dark, indistinct reflection of Lawrence's profile in what I realised was the white baby grand piano. 'I think you can be a better husband and father by not completely giving yourself up to one single emotional focus,' the voiceover was saying.

'My God, did you ever hear such pathetic, self-serving rubbish,' said Cathy though a mouthful of digestive, glancing crossly at me as if to demand strong opinions consistent with hers.

I shook my head in sympathy with Cathy's disbelief. 'Of course, we don't have to watch it,' I said, ostentatiously stretching both arms to the ceiling and yawning again. But we did have to watch it, if obliged only by the dark forces of my bad luck, which had manifested themselves at breakfast time, when Cathy had been on her knees in the living room, setting the video for some daytime black-and-white musical of historical interest and had spotted *Cheating Hearts* in my

TV listings, cross-referenced to the interview I had written up in the supplement. 'Hey, I haven't read your piece!' she cried through a mouthful of toast. 'Where's the "Manners" bit?'

'I don't know. I was looking for it the other day – it wasn't there,' I said. 'That newsagent's hopeless. I'll try and bring one in from the office if I remember.'

'Oh, but we must watch the programme – then I can read your interview and see how your man comes out of it.'

'I was pretty tough on him,' I said, though only yesterday afternoon I had spent two hours out of the office furtively exploring the residential upper walkways of the Barbican, trying to work out, in the confusing perspective of daylight, first, the level on which Lawrence's flat was located, with only the relative position of the fountains in the communal space below as a guide, and, second, to identify which of the three most likely front doors was the correct one based on the reliability of my memory for colour, as perceived in the dark, via chemically altered retinas. In desperation I knocked on all three doors and when I got no reply from any I even more pathetically posted a scribbled note through each one, pleading with Lawrence to *please* call me at the office. That's how tough I could be.

But again, here at the Goose, where Sadie, in purple eye make-up, was already excitedly rehearsing what in her mind had now become the firm promise of Glastonbury amid the warm natter and clatter of N8's coolest and possibly most expensive grown-up eaterie (according to Sadie's school chums, whose own parents brought them here), I retired from the heat of my proliferating torments into the succouring (perfect word) embrace of the familiar. 'It's brilliant, Dad – over a hundred thousand turned up last year. Everyone from school went.'

I buttered and bit into my bread roll with the enthusiasm of someone put on the earth by God to be lively and expansive.

'Well, let me tell you something truly astonishing, Sade. When the Beatles . . .'

'*Daaaaad*, not the Beatles again. You're living in the past. Mum, make him stop.' She was laughing out loud now, not merely playing up to the cheerful attentiveness of her parents, but seizing the stage in a manner that was alert to the goodwill of a wider audience of admirers, displaying that happy exhibitionism that comes so naturally to teenage girls when they're not locking themselves in their rooms.

Cathy smiled. I sighed, gazing at the ceiling with hammy indulgence and enjoying for a moment the warm feeling of Cathy enjoying the warm feeling of Sadie enjoying warm feelings with her father, as if the strains of the past weeks were past for good. I hoped they were, but then hope was all you had once the coin was up in the air.

'*When* the Beatles were touring Australia . . .' I continued, as Sadie squealed, and clapped her hands over her ears, 'they used to get crowds of three hundred thousand or more just outside the *hotel*. Imagine. Tell that to Oasis.'

'What? The Oasis CDs are *yours*, Dad, not mine – remember?' she squealed.

'Yes, but I bought them for you.'

'Yes, but only because you want me to like the Beatles. And anyway, *you* weren't even there in Australia so it doesn't count. Auntie Vicky says the Beatles were her generation. You were too young to remember them properly – and now look at you.' She punched my arm. 'I can't believe you're forty, Dad.'

'That's because I keep myself looking so trim and healthy.'

'I didn't say you don't *look* forty. I said I can't *believe* you're forty because that's *so* ancient. Anyway why are you suddenly having poached salmon, Dad – and *salad*?' she shrieked. 'You never eat salad. Why aren't you having chips?'

I smiled benignly. 'I'm turning a new leaf, and it's called baby spinach,' I said, pleased with my joke, which slipped by like one fish among many.

Cathy leaned across the table towards Sadie, cupping her hand in a stage whisper. 'He's keeping himself fit for Penelope,' she said. Sadie laughed out loud.

'What?' My eyes darted from Cathy to Sadie, and I felt my stomach weaken. I took a gulp of wine and eyed the two of them wryly. 'Okaaay,' I said, an elastic grin springing to my lips, my head tilted in the attitude of the kind of dad who was game enough to be the butt of goofy jokes. 'Come on, out with it . . .'

'Well, this Penelope woman, of course, who's on the answering machine,' Cathy said, sawing into her fillet steak. 'Don't tell us you didn't get the message . . .'

'She sounds *very* sexy – *Matth-yew*,' said Sadie in a breathy voice.

Cathy smiled.

I borrowed an expression from the pantomime book of frowns. 'Penelope?' I turned the name in my mouth like an obscure foreign word. 'Odd. What did she want?' I said, taking care to frame my question in a way that suggested I didn't *think* I knew who she was but that the right clue might well jog my famously poor memory.

Cathy shrugged and winked at Sadie. 'You'll have to find out for yourself.' I untensed my body enough to offer a shrug of surrender in the face of superior witmanship, and Sadie burst out laughing again.

The rest of the evening I worked at keeping up an unprecedented level of good humour. Penelope's name came up again when they ribbed me loudly for not touching the Goose's recommended three-citrus tart I had rashly ordered in a sudden desire to dispel the idea that I had abandoned my customary dietary habits in the suspected pursuit of a perfect body, but now realised I could no more wolf down than the oversized plate it came on. I poured more wine for myself and made a fuss of opening the gift-wrapped box Sadie produced containing a violin bass tie-pin I had seen in the Beatles shop near

Carnaby Street and had duly dropped hints about. 'Sorry I missed your real birthday,' she said, pecking me quickly on the cheek. 'And sorry about your clock.'

'What clock?'

'Your Yellow Submarine clock. I had to borrow it when I went to Leeds.' She looked at Cathy, who grimaced and sucked air in through her teeth.

'And now it's not working.'

I sighed. 'Don't worry,' I said, then yawned. 'Sorry,' I said. 'Tired.'

'Must be your age,' Sadie said happily, snatching my untouched after-dinner chocolate from under my saucer.

In the taxi I pretended to doze off, allowing mother and daughter to fill the journey home with chatter about CDs, clothes, skiing and eventually mock GCSEs, on which, Cathy reminded her, so much of the other stuff depended. When they got back, I waited until Cathy and Sadie were busy laughing their heads off in the kitchen with Bev before running the tape on the answerphone. I listened with eyes closed, my face folding into a pained expression as a message rang out in the barely credible, breathy tones of a matinee siren from the innocent years of British film comedy. *Hiiii . . . this is Penelope, at Mädchen's Music, calling for Matth-yew. Just to say we received your note with regard to the supplier of the um . . . rare Bob Dylan import you were interested in, and that we'll be in touch again soon. Byyye . . .*

'Coffee, *Matth-yew*?' Sadie was in the doorway smiling, Cathy and Bev at her shoulder watching. I raised my chin in acknowledgement, grinning hard in return, my eyebrows springing up with nervous levity.

Much later, I went to sleep thinking, alternately, of Penelope and Ruth, but in the night I had an erotic dream about Cathy, a dream in which I suddenly discovered to my puzzlement that I had never married Cathy at all, and that she was still free to roam, free to send me into a frenzy of doubt by not telling the truth, free to show favour in unspecified sexual ways to the other men who figured vaguely in the background while withholding such favours from myself, even as we lay together on a bed that didn't belong to either of us. In the dream there was nothing of the familiar left about her, just an exotic *aching* from somewhere in the past, a desperate urgency to tell her how much I loved her, had to marry her, to have her quickly for ever before someone else did. I awoke, part of me back there still in the dream, hanging on to these anxious feelings for Cathy, and I edged sideways until I was hugging the curve of her sleeping body, eventually bringing her to consciousness with nuzzling kisses to the downy nape of her neck and shoulders. She didn't seem surprised, as if my dream had been piped down as background music to her own (as it might with the perfect husband and wife), and she manoeuvred herself round to face me, to let me kiss her and to get my fingers tangled clumsily in her hair, until we found ourselves, strangely and unexpectedly, having long, slow, tingling sex in the small, ticking quiet of the room, noiseless as if afraid to break the illusion of unusualness, but smoothly practised and efficient in our movements; not fully alert, but aware of the ritual of blessing our new home with a splendid, if belated, act of conjugal union. 'That was nice,' she murmured afterwards, as if it was something we still did three times a day. She was asleep again, leaving me alone, glowing now like a burglar in the dark of someone else's house, making a vow to go straight if only the bad man would leave me alone, my eyes closed tight against the sudden invasion of thoughts from the planet of fatal, sexually transmitted diseases that I knew would now occupy whatever hours were left until the first rude cock-crow of Ellie's early morning call.

The bad man rang first thing Monday morning at the office, asked me how I was, blew his nose down the phone, apologised for his terrible cold and invited me to The 34. 'How about the thirteenth?' he shouted. 'Next Tuesday. It's a Sixties charity pop quiz. They're lining up Tony Blackburn to compère. You should come along. It'll be fantastic. What do you say?'

I looked at my watch distractedly, as though next week was this lunchtime. 'I don't know . . .'

'It's two hundred a table – but, hey, we might win a grand. Plus, there's bound to be a few pop celebs there wanting to show off, which means you do yourself a bit of good by getting a couple of diary stories for your paper, right? And, Matt, Lady Penelope will be there.'

'Listen, Lawrence, about these phone calls . . .'

'Oh, come on, it was just a bit of fun. After all, you did stitch me up a bit.' He paused. 'Very cruel, some of it, I thought. Very hurtful . . .'

'Yes, I wanted to talk to you about that . . .'

'Excellent. Next Tuesday, then. Eight o'clock start?'

I did need to straighten things out with Lawrence. But I wanted to go back to The 34, too, if only to come away with a different memory of it – a memory without all the things that still made me feel like a complete jerk whenever it came back to haunt me. I wanted to see Penelope, but only to show her that, actually, I didn't want to have sex with her, and to suggest – perhaps in the casual course of sloshing back wine and gabbling on about '60s pop or *EastEnders* – that the fact I had once vaguely pursued that outcome was in sober truth a matter of indifference to me, and that even happily married men got into scrapes sometimes. Ideally, I would like to have been the one who had said 'better not', as she had so casually done – the one for whom choices like this were nothing but a whim of the moment because such moments were ten a penny, but it was too late for that. I could, though, make things right in some way. Recover something. I didn't know what or why. What would you call that if you were a psychiatrist? It wasn't like revisiting the scene of some horrific accident or getting back on the horse that broke your neck. It was more like being stuck in the enchanted forest trying to retrace your steps through the spooky trees in search of the fork in the path where you turned right instead of left. It was like wishing you'd never seen the gingerbread house, because once you'd got the taste for it, the rule was you had to shag the next woman you saw called Ruth. That was how the magic worked. And then it was up to you to break the spell.

And where did I stand on lying at this point? I only ask because when I got home from work the following Thursday, Cathy was swishing about in the living room wearing an ambitious new haircut and asking what I thought. Well, she didn't actually *ask* what I thought, but I couldn't just not say anything. I didn't know what I thought really. It was one of those severe fringed jobs that slope down at an angle from the back of the neck and are designed for women in shampoo adverts who have to swish their heads for a living and need their hair to perform miracles twenty-four hours a day, seven days a week. Plus she'd had highlights put in, which meant it was more or less exactly the same colour as it was before except she got an alarming red halo if she stood near a standard lamp. Anyway, she was obviously really pleased with herself and had obviously thought long and hard without getting round to mentioning it to me, in case I tried to put her off. 'I've finally come to the decision that you can't have long, straggly, wild hair all your life,' she said, looking this way and that in the mirror, making her new hair swish this way and that. 'I think this is a bit more mature.'

So, understandably, I'm there, nodding, enthusiastic, supportive. 'It really *suits* you,' I said, though it had been no secret between us for the past fourteen years that, actually, I'm rather partial to the long, straggly, wild, less-mature look in a married woman. And what was the point of having it cut this late in life? Surely one of the few advantages of being a member of the downtrodden sex is having hair that doesn't start falling out the minute you hit twenty-seven. Admittedly I was partly in shock, but what else could I have said? With a normal haircut you can just say it's fine, which is just a way of putting it on the record that you've noticed it. But with a statement haircut, you have to respond with a statement of your own.

The average passerby might think that this was not a very fair example of a lie, because I wouldn't have wanted to hurt Cathy's feelings, right? OK. Take a more hypothetical scenario: imagine it's a typical Wednesday back then and Cathy wasn't expecting me home till gone midnight because Wednesday is my big press day and it always takes for ever, but the system on this particular Wednesday miraculously doesn't crash taking all my clean pages with it, and both my subs have been taking competence pills and don't have to do everything eight times before they get it right, and we end up finishing at the unearthly hour of 7.30. The question is, do I head off to Eamonn's with the rest of the team or do I rush home to spend some windfall quality time with my loved ones? OK, let's skip the trick question. When I finally roll in at 1.30, I don't really have to explain myself because that's what time I always roll in on Wednesdays. But tonight, for some reason, I can't resist waking Cathy with a bit of weary huffing and puffing as I sit on the bed trying to get my socks off and telling her what hell it was out there tonight and how the people in IT are morons.

Why don't I tell her the truth? Well, obviously because I don't want earache for the rest of the week. But, when you think about it, the only reason she'd get all miffed and uncommunicative – which wouldn't have been entirely out of character – is the idea that I would rather go and get drunk than come home to watch her fall asleep on the couch in front of Busby Berkeley or whatever ancient musical entertainment she has already decided to amuse herself with on an evening when I'm meant to be elsewhere. So, you see, here I am sparing her feelings again, even though in this instance her feelings are misguided, because obviously if it had come to it – I mean, if I'd been taken to the fiery abyss at gunpoint and forced to choose between *always* going to the pub or *always* going home to Cathy – she would have won, if that's the right word, and she knew it. Eamonn's was full of men who wished they had a Cathy of their own to go home to every night, though it struck me that if they had one for long enough they would hardly be human if they weren't curious enough to be occasionally lured into the world of Eamonn's to see how they might have ended up. So no, I didn't want to go to the pub every night. But I admit I did like to keep my options open when the god of beery opportunities threw one in my path.

I know what you're going to say. You're going to say, the trouble is, you could follow this logic for ever. Where do you draw the line? After all, who wouldn't forgive you for lying about your reasons for getting home late on Wednesday night if the alternative is having to tell your wife that you were standing up in a shop doorway having sex with a woman you met on the Tube? Would she really be happy to know that? Can you spare her that anguish? The truth is, it was all the same lie. So you can see why I felt a bit uneasy about the new hair.

If Dean had been alive I would almost certainly have told him everything. (I think everybody tells someone at some point. Telling yourself doesn't count if you can't bring yourself to tell the truth.) On the other hand, if he'd been alive, as I said, probably none of this would have happened. Or maybe it would. To be honest I can't remember who I was blaming at this stage. Certainly, for my own well-being, I couldn't afford to rule anybody out. It surely couldn't be just my fault.

The good thing was I was getting on very well with Sadie. The key, I had decided, was to be more laid-back and enjoy the spectacle of domestic life instead of going mad trying to be in control of everything. But I was now beginning to realise that what I was really doing was just *sitting* back – nodding, smiling, making jokes – while Cathy got lumbered with having to control everything. How much easier it was to say yes to everything and let Cathy make all the doubtful clucking noises. I had become a responsible parent in appearance only. I turned up for things, I was upbeat, I took part, but, to be honest, anyone at around the same height and weight could have stood in for me. Cathy looked at me in a strange way but she hadn't worked it out. I was like the BBC's political correspondent standing in my trenchcoat outside No. 10 Downing Street filing my report in the pouring rain. Did I really need to be there? Couldn't I read my press release and wire-copy in the warmth of a studio like everyone else? Was I a complete fraud whose credentials were based on my geographical proximity to events? Was that a real microphone in my hand? The point was, of course, you don't actually have to be an insider to look like one. The audience may never catch on. And I have to tell you, it does free your mind for other things.

The less good thing was that Mum was on the phone to say that Vicky and Richard had split up. Fuck! 'How? When?' I said. Weeks ago, she said. She hadn't wanted to mention it, and didn't really want to mention it now by the sound of it, though she seemed happy enough to mention it at great length to Cathy, as usual. Dad was even more upset, because it was their last chance of having a grandson, she said, though if Dad thought about it for two seconds he would have worked out that Vicky was pushing forty-six and probably gave up that idea long ago. 'What about Richard?' I said, but by now Mum was listening through gritted ears. 'You'd better ask Vicky about that,' she said.

Lawrence was unexpectedly brilliant on the American stuff – Stax, Motown, Atlantic – while I cleaned up on the Beatles section by playing our joker and collecting two points for every track listed in order on the White Album (which technically is called *The Beatles*, of course, but I didn't want to seem a pedant) plus a bonus of twenty for getting them all, and another ten for getting them in the right order. Graham with the droopy ginger moustache nodded irritatingly in agreement at all the answers ('Yeah, of course, that was him!) as though they were permanently adhered to the tip of his tongue, while Claricia happily flaunted her entire ignorance of the period by keeping everyone's glass brimming and excitedly hugging Lawrence's arm every time he snatched the sheet of paper and feverishly scribbled down an answer. I alone among the three hundred competitors knew which song from which 1937 Disney film inspired the tune for 'Do You Want to Know a Secret'. Penelope was absent, which I found a relief to start with and a disappointment once we were into our third bottle of house white, the traditional point at which yesterday's embarrassments could be uninhibitedly traded in for tomorrow's. We celebrated coming third – not bad, we agreed, for a team of four – by cracking open our prize of a magnum of Moët at the usual spot near the unattended piano.

'What happened to Tony Blackburn?' I said.

'They couldn't get him.'

'So who was this guy again that nobody's heard of?'

'Everybody's heard of him. He's a household name, mate,' said Lawrence.

'Not in my household he's not.'

'I bet your little Sadie's heard of him.' Lawrence winked and took a sip of champagne. 'Did she tell you I spoke to her? Just briefly, of course.' Lawrence kept sipping. 'Just said hello. Asked what bands she liked. Told her I could get her some free CDs. I could if you like. What do you think?'

'Lawrence . . .' I began, impatiently.

'Mmm?'

'How did you get my number?'

'You're in the book. Journos are *never* in the book, mate, but you're open to everyone. You ought to watch that.'

'And what about you? Are you in the book?'

Lawrence looked at me, smiling indulgently.

I shook my head morosely. 'Nothing happened, you know.'

Lawrence patted me on the back. 'Matt, Matt . . . I'm hardly in a position to comment on whatever hanky-panky married men might get up to in their spare time, even those who aren't – what was it you called it – in the *market*?' He grinned and sipped his champagne.

'Oh, come on . . .'

'Anyway, I'm sorry to hear nothing happened. Maybe next time, eh?'

We ended up at the piano singing. 'This Boy', 'Baby's in Black'. Lawrence's choices. I had to admit he *was* good. 'I used to play a bit with my brother,' said Lawrence. 'Guitar. Just for fun really. Nothing special.'

'A brother? Revelations! What does he play?'

Lawrence took a sip of wine. 'He used to play keyboards. He's dead now.'

I stared at him. 'Blimey. Really? Wow. Sorry . . .'

'Got killed in a motorcycle accident. Long time ago now.' Lawrence fished for his cigarettes in his pocket, shook one out of the packet into his mouth and lit it. 'I'd rather not talk about it, to be honest,' he said, blowing out smoke wearily. 'Bit gloomy.'

I was suddenly hit by the thought of Dean, fag in his mouth, tuning his old black-and-white Lennon Rickenbacker in the kitchen in Headingley. I shook the image off, and the sudden urge to mention him. I wondered how gloomy it was to be still wondering what Dean would have thought. But Dean didn't belong here. He was dead to this new world.

There were no drugs, no dancing, just a lot of good music and slurred talk. Lawrence had his arm around me, telling me not to worry, relax, it was great to see me. Graham, eager to join the circle of people who knew stuff that other people wanted to know, told me how The 34 club was named after the Beatle flat in Montagu Square owned by Ringo, who rented it out to Paul as an *ad hoc* mini-recording studio and dosshouse. 'Number 34,' he said. 'Everyone used to hang out there – John and Yoko used to get fucked up there, Hendrix threw paint all over the walls when he was on acid, William Burroughs would turn up and do experimental things on tape. It was just a typical Sixties pop-star crash pad – bean bags, silk purple wallpaper, happening music, pot-smoking, nothing in the fridge. Very peace and love . . .'

'Didn't Paulie work on "Eleanor Rigby" there?' Lawrence said.

'Actually, now I come to think of it, I've heard of this place . . .' I said. 'Where is it again?'

Graham stroked his moustache. 'Ten minutes' walk towards Edgware Road? There's nothing there now. Not even a blue plaque. It's just a basement flat.'

I checked my watch. I could go there. I would go there. Just to have a look. There would be still be time to catch the Tube. It was easy to find, Graham said. I got up to go, a map of three streets in my head. But on the way out, I saw Penelope checking in her coat. She was with the girl in the red leather skirt and top who I had seen with Lawrence on the first night here. Tonight she was dressed down in standard black office fatigues, as if she'd come out straight from work. The two of them were laughing and seemed happily drunk. Penelope was wearing a silk dress printed with red cherries. She was smoothing it down with her hands. I waited till I caught her glance and her look of uncertain recognition. Then I smiled and raised my eyebrows at her. 'Well, *hello* . . .' she said, laughing as she came to kiss me at both sides with a loud, ironic *mwaah* for each. 'How are you?' Her eyes were lit up with some earlier intoxicating mischief. 'You're not leaving already, are you?' She lingered briefly, her hands light on my shoulders, pouting amusingly.

I gave her what I hoped was a casual, regretful smile. 'Got to go. Train to catch. See you next time maybe?'

'It's a date,' she said. The faint scent of her stayed with me as she pulled away and gave a little promiscuous wave, before following her friend into the crowded bar. I paused for a moment just to see if I might be tempted to change my mind and stay, but I didn't. Outside I felt a rush of elation. Why was that? Because we had touched base with the mutual status of something other than strangers in a bed belonging to neither of us? Because I had now said my 'better not' and there wasn't anything left to explain or talk over? Or was it that to be looking forward to a hypothetical next time at The 34 club with acquaintances who were cool enough to offer a kind of robust intimacy and fellowship without strings seemed suddenly more promising and alive than the prospect of trying to extract personal meaning from a block of flats in Montagu Square? I strode off to the Tube at Bond Street and got home at half-past midnight. Surprisingly, Cathy was still up, in her dressing-gown and sitting on the rug in front of a low fire in the flickering darkness. She turned to face me as I came in and I saw her expression, anxious and solicitous beneath her new, incongruously bobbing fringe.

'What's wrong?' I said.

'Your mum rang. They think your dad's had a stroke.'

I couldn't say what it was exactly, but I just felt like I was waiting for something to go wrong. Maybe for Cathy to pause suddenly and say, hang on a minute, something's not quite right about this . . . I wanted to be mistaken, but I had the feeling that all it would take was the addition or removal of one small detail for the picture to change. But into what? I couldn't be more specific. It was just a feeling. It was like the old Coca-Cola T-shirt that you suddenly realise spells Cocaine, or . . . No, I'll tell you what it was like. It was like the *Help!* sleeve showing the Beatles wearing those black capes and hats with their arms in the air, each of them signalling a letter in semaphore to spell out the album title. You'd know it anywhere. But then you look at the cover as reshot for the American edition and . . . hang on, you say. When you look closer, you realise that although individually all four of them are still doing the same thing with their arms, there's only George, there in his top hat, who's standing in the right spot. The others are all over the place. See? Compare and contrast. That's what was driving me mad. I was just waiting for Cathy to take a closer look at things and say, HPEL? What the fuck does that mean?

Vicky was sitting in Dad's armchair and staring out of the window at the grey afternoon, red-eyed and puffy-faced, a cup of tea resting in its saucer on her plumped-up thighs. She was wearing a crumpled white *Cats* sweatshirt and overtight black Lycra leggings. She had taken up smoking, and was smoking a cigarette now, though no one had been allowed to smoke in the house for years because of Dad's cough, and Mum had had to bring an extra saucer to use as an ashtray. She looked terrible. Mum glanced at her and then back at me with an unintentionally comic flash of her eyes that meant *say something*. I sighed and stared for a moment at the long shelf of albums belonging to my father – orchestral, brass bands, but mostly works for the horn by the mighty Dennis Brain. Mum's modest collection of Tom Joneses and Shirley Basseys were hidden away, like second-class citizens, in the sideboard.

'So . . . have you actually seen Richard?' I said.

Vicky left a long pause, still looking out of the window. I was about to ask again a little louder when she replied. 'Oh, I've seen him all right,' she said, her voice even and just about controlled. I waited for her to say something else but she just closed her eyes, her lips pressed together against some hidden thought I couldn't guess at, the cigarette smoke rising in a twirl from her lap. I didn't know what to say. I'd never seen her like this before. She was supposed to be the tough, practical one. She was the one who had gone her own way, dropped out of university, rucksacked it to Thailand and Australia and God knows where, pissed Mum and Dad off, come back, finished university, proved them wrong without malice, made a decent career in pharmaceuticals doing something unfathomable, got married to Richard, who did something even more unfathomable. Two incomes, no kids. She was a proper grown-up. When I imagined her at work she wore a white coat with pens in the pocket; she waggled test tubes over Bunsen burners, or looked down microscopes shaking her head and saying 'Can't be'. That was how I saw her. She was the one who gave out advice, whether you wanted it or not. She was my big sister who had given me the Beatles and then laughed at me for keeping them so long. She would speak to Cathy like an adult but together they referred to me in the third person, laughing, while Richard pulled me away into the garden where he bent my ear about golf or rugby as we strolled around the dead leaves drinking high-density home brew. ('It takes a scientist to make beer properly,' Richard would say, raising his glass to the sky, and turning it in his fat hand to admire its clarity and colour.) I wasn't the person to put my arm round Vicky now and tell her what the world was like. I didn't know. All I knew for certain was that there was nothing I could say that she hadn't already thought of. I went over and sat on the arm of her chair and exhaled down my nostrils in a way that I hoped suggested fellow-feeling in the face of something that might happen to anyone – like catching the flu or being delayed by a train. Because I was sorry about what had happened. I put my hand on her shoulder. 'Sorry about what's happened.'

'You don't know what's happened,' she said.

'I'm willing to listen.'

'For God's sake, Matt,' she snapped, which took me by surprise because this was not her way of handling things, and struck me as the most serious thing I'd heard her say in my life, certainly to me. 'There's no bloody point coming over all concerned now, in the middle of all this, with Dad. You're *so* busy with your smart new job in bloody London to notice or to ring. You hardly *ever* ring Mum . . .'

She clattered her cup and saucer on the glass-topped coffee table and swept out of the room, leaving me stranded on the chair arm. 'What was that about?' I said.

Mum shook her head. 'She blames herself for your dad.'

'Sounds more like she's blaming me. Anyway, that's stupid, blaming herself. Isn't it?'

'I've told her it's stupid. Though he was upset when he heard what happened . . .'

'When *what* happened?'

Mum stared out of the window. After a moment we heard the door slam in the hall, the sound of footsteps disappearing down the path and the clang of the gate. 'Richard left her,' she said.

'What, you mean for another woman?' I said, trying and failing to keep the astonishment out of my voice.

Mum pressed her lips together, like Vicky had done, looking for a moment exactly like Vicky, just as I had caught a glimpse of myself in my father's expression when the three of us had traipsed into the yellowed ward at St James's at lunchtime and he'd looked up in surprise as if we were the last people he expected to see. It had seemed shocking to find Dad here in new pyjamas among strangers, sitting upright tucking into soup and minced beef and mash and . . . well, not looking sick at all, I thought, but in fact looking better than he had for ages, chuckling gently about things as we chatted, and nodding, maybe not quite with it, a slower churn in his recollections, but visibly happier, casting round at his surroundings with fresh eyes, as if losing a chunk of whatever he had lost had rid him of some kind of burden too. I smiled, not really listening to him, trying to think of the right things to say.

'His memory's a bit fuzzy,' Mum had said. 'But he seems

chirpy enough. Don't you?' she said, angling her tinted permed head towards him.

'Oh yes,' he said, catching each pair of eyes in turn.

'So how's the job, Matt?' he'd said at one point, which seemed to me to come not from today and this hospital ward, but a familiar casual enquiry from his armchair at home, delivered in a low monotone from behind a lowered newspaper, like a sudden blip of memory thrown up into the present from the past, perhaps even from when I had been at the *Echo* and still lived in Headingley.

'Oh fine, Dad. Cathy and Sadie send their love.'

'And how's our little Sadie?'

'Growing up, Dad,' I said, wondering now whether he was talking about Ellie and had got their names mixed up, or worse, was back there somewhere in the days when Sadie was a baby. I looked at him. What was in there? What secrets from another time when Dad had a pencil moustache and his hair was thick and stood on end like George Orwell's and he played the French horn and women found him attractive? What women had he slept with before Mum? Or after? What did he think about?

Vicky sat throughout the visit holding Dad's hand, the one with a bandage and a drip inserted, breaking into a smile whenever one was called for, easily filling the silences, sternly addressing her father with jocular disapproval about imagined indiscretions involving the nursing staff, bedpans and a comic conceit involving Dad leaping out of bed to switch the TV over to watch the racing from Goodwood behind everyone's back, baffling the nurses and infuriating his mute, toothless, bedridden fellow patients with his youthful guile, agility and spirit. Dad laughed, as if to publicly recognise the absurdity of his leaping anywhere under any circumstances, as if to reassure us all that he still knew a joke when he heard one, before falling to reflection, abandoning himself to some passing thought, his watery eyes fixed on the bed-tray with its empty tea cup, plate, bowl and licked yoghurt spoon. 'He's never eaten so well,' Mum said.

At seven a taxi parped dully outside and I picked up my coat. Vicky turned in the chair. 'You're not thinking of going *out*?'

I felt myself shuffling on the spot. 'Well, I've just arranged to see a few people from the *Echo*.' I looked at my mother. 'Dad seems to be OK. I thought . . .'

'Off you go and enjoy yourself,' she said, shooing me with a tea towel, as I knew she would.

Vicky stared at me, her mouth tightening at the edges. 'Oh yes, you go off and enjoy yourself, by all means,' she said, nodding hard. 'I'm sure you will.'

I turned to her for a second. On another occasion I supposed I might have stayed and had the argument, or returned her fire with a short burst of sarcasm of my own, but – at this precise moment – there was really no point. I didn't feel stung or upset, or angered, or saddened by Vicky's hostility. She may even have been right. The simple fact was, I hadn't allowed myself to consider whether going out tonight was the thing to do. The fact was – at this precise moment – if you could slice me longways and examine the full inventory of my feelings, there would be nothing stirring in my head or heart that might place me emotionally within these four walls. All I felt now was a compulsion for the alternative element, a swimmer pushing up towards the light, about to break the surface with a satisfying *plip* and to taste the air of my evening plans. I hurried down the path, closing the gate gently behind me, climbed into the back of the black-and-white taxi and waited for it to glide off. I closed my eyes.

I could have got in the front. Most people in Leeds would have done. But I was a Londoner now and Londoners took black cabs, and black cabs didn't have front passenger seats, and, unlike here, you could hail one in the street and be chauffeured around properly, not have to sit there like someone who was being offered a lift and being done a favour. It was absurd, but I got a small hit of satisfaction playing the kind of somebody who would have the sophistication to get in the back and not the front, and I wondered if the driver sensed it too. Certainly I thought I detected an air of élan (yes) – professional pride, even – in the way the driver had responded to my studiedly careless instructions with a clipped 'yes sir' (they didn't do 'guv' up here); the way he had manoeuvred smoothly and quickly into the traffic flow on the ring road, settling on an optimum cruising speed, adjusting the radio dial, re-angling his mirror, tilting his seat forward a fraction and back again, as if to impress a sophisticated passenger with a customised environment. I didn't know the hotel, but the driver did and didn't mind telling me. It was part of a big complex near to the stadium itself, he told me. 'You get a lot of businessmen and sport and charity shows,' he was saying, enumerating the drops he had made there, many of them fares from the station or the airport, sometimes TV personalities. He offered the name of someone I had only vaguely heard of. 'Oh really?' I said, checking my watch, though there was really no hurry. On one occasion, the driver said, losing his straight back and talking over his shoulder now, it had been Spanish football officials up for a European game. Feyenoord, he said. Feyenoord were Dutch, he added. I nodded. The driver asked whether I had business at the hotel. I said I was just meeting someone for a drink. The driver nodded and had nothing to say about that. I sensed his disappointment. As a journalist I could appreciate something that just wasn't worth passing on. There was no currency in meeting someone for a drink.

It was some kind of classic car auction, Ruth had said, though she was on her mobile when I'd caught her, and in traffic, and in a hurry, and had to keep it brief, the point being that she was pencilled in to talk to two footballers about their involvement for charity and there was some kind of reception and it might go on for an hour or so, but after that, maybe . . .

'Maybe?' I gurned down the phone, dismissing my first instincts about the terseness in her voice purely as the understandable distractedness of someone in charge of a vehicle, and I kept my eye fixed on the closed sitting-room door, though Vicky was safely out walking off whatever was boiling up inside her and I had left Mum humming in the kitchen ironing Dad's shirts, because that meant he'd be coming back and if it kept her happy and focused she should hold *on* to that thought, as I had found myself saying, with Oprah-style crassness, to my mother's grateful bewilderment.

'Maybe?'

Ruth sounded harassed. 'Well, you might have to hang around . . . but I could meet you in the *bar* there.' She was shouting now. 'There's nothing else for *miles*.'

As I stepped into the hotel lobby I was surprised at the old-tech pegboard sign indicating the auction in the underground arena, decided not to follow it and took instead the chromed, mirrored lift to the mezzanine where I spent an hour sipping Staropramen, eating honeyed cashews from the dish on the bar and reading sport and court reports in the *Echo*. Eventually there was a growing murmur as people started streaming into the lobby from somewhere – the basement, I guessed – holding catalogues or bulky press kits, coats draped over their arms, standing in groups to talk, some waving goodbye to others, shouting final rounded comments as sales and ad people tend to do, exiting the stage like comedians, leaving their audience wanting more, I thought. I folded my newspaper. PRs and their guests, corporate people, fundraisers, press, hired glamour. Taxis began to pull forward from the rank outside. A gleaming, old sports car, cobalt blue, came through into the horseshoe forecourt, engine roaring in celebration as it came to a halt, attracting a small group of admirers. One man was patting the neat curve of the wing. A girl got in, blonde model hair illuminated by the hotel lights. Skirt hitched up, legs together. The car moved off round the horseshoe, its horn sounding in the night. Others were coming up into the mezzanine now, freshening the bar with the cold air of their chatter. Then I saw Ruth's head arrive at the top of the escalator followed quickly by the rest of her – tall, clad in office jacket and trousers, hair gripped in a ponytail by a scrunchie at the back, a white mac over her arm, not as I still remembered her from London, red-lipsticked and crisp as a Friday-night fiver, but as any number of the pale, flat-heeled, casually acerbic women journalists tucked under the wings of the third floor of the *Echo* building. She grinned when she saw me and came over, a reporter's totebag slung over one shoulder. 'Well,' she said. 'Look at you. Is it all coming flooding back?' She waved at the surroundings as if to suggest – what? Local papers? Provincial glitz? I wasn't sure what, but I was happy to take it as a prompt for whatever touch of modesty was incumbent upon someone who had gone up in the world but had graciously popped back to look over the old territory.

'On a deadline?' I asked, an innocent enough question from one hack to another, though at the same time I knew it was one that could be read two ways.

'Yes,' she said quickly. She smiled mysteriously, or at least I took her failure to answer more fully as a mystery, designed, perhaps, to discourage any thoughts I might have of a prolonged dalliance; to suggest even that London had been pleasure and this was the daily grind; to suggest that I couldn't just parachute into the middle of a motor auction attended by minor celebrities and think the story started with me turning up.

'I *have* got time for a drink though,' she said, nodding at the bar. 'If you're in the chair . . .'

'Oh yes, sorry,' I said, one hand fumbling for my wallet stuffed with two tenners and receipts from the newsagent's near the Tube, the other raised towards the bow-tied barman. But the barman had turned away and was leaning forward to serve another customer who in turn had turned, hand cupped to his ear, to read the lips of someone barking a drinks order across the rows of heads. Waiting, I felt my spirits dip, here in this crowd of nodding faces lit up by the sudden current of out-of-hours gaiety, suspended in the middling air of not working and not going home yet. It was a place where competition, far from evaporating with the fall of the old corporate barometer, began instead to revolve on the social. I had been here a hundred times – not in this exact place, but this gathering of interchangeable characters – that's what Ruth meant. But why my sudden mood swing? *In the chair.* I grimaced inwardly. Did she really say that? That was one of theirs. These people here. If you listened you could hear it all the time. 'Hey, *tell* me about it,' someone behind me was saying. That was another. I felt suddenly depressed. I didn't know why I should be so irritated by what was no more than an overfamiliar phrase, an off-the-peg expression you might hear a million times in the course of a working day passed among the commercial classes like tokens of belonging. *Good to have you on board.* No one ever said 'good to have you on board' without at some later point talking about rugby or car engines or bonuses and targets or the imagined sexual proclivities of female subordinates or the best way by car from Hull to Birkenhead.

But Ruth. To hear these words pop up in Ruth's mouth, a woman who I was fully preparing myself to like for herself as a bright and possibly even brainy person, and not just for sex in a hotel (or just possibly elsewhere), sounded like a dispiriting vote for golfy comradeship of the chummiest, least admirable kind. And it wasn't just that she was like one of them; it was the fact that the idea of *them* now seemed much stranger to me after being away from it all. Matey banter had never bothered me before in the slightest – perhaps I had been one of them too, or at least, like Ruth, had been perfectly happy to slip in and out of *them* mode according to the demands of the occasion. But now, it struck me how so much had changed in the months since I'd been gone, or maybe how much I had changed. How, that afternoon, I had, to my shame, caught my newly metropolitan sensibilities wincing unconsciously at the exotic clangour of northern accents at the hospital. How weird it had seemed to hear them all at once, to hear them like an outsider might hear them. The nurses, the visitors, the woman who took my father's lunch tray away, the uniformed man on the desk joking loudly with his partner. And now these people. Of course they weren't murderers or arsonists or even shoplifters. And too literal and unwily in their thinking to be paedophiles. Adulterers, yes. *Playing away*. That was one of theirs too. They had words for everything.

I looked for a table but there were none free and Ruth sat up on the tall bar stool I had vacated, stirring the ice in her gin and tonic with her finger, one long leg swinging gently against the metal crossrail. 'So?' she said.

'Sorry, what I meant was . . . I mean, obviously I *know* you've got a deadline, but are you free tonight, or is this just a quick—'

'Quick what?' she said, smiling tight-lipped and archly, her eyebrows up so far as to instantly usurp in my head all thoughts turning on the idiosyncrasies of language and class and triggering instead an immediate pounding of the old heart tom-toms. She tugged gently at my tie now, as if forgiving me for something, as if letting me off some hook. 'I'm as free as you are.'

I looked at her as I took a gulp of my beer. 'How was the auction?' I said.

'Oh, you know. The usual. Well, quite promising actually. I managed to set up a couple of good interviews.'

'*Excellent*,' I heard myself say with too much enthusiasm. 'Who with?'

'I was thinking of pitching them as freelance pieces.' She looked at me, trying to gauge my reaction. 'What do you think?' A champagne cork popped across the room followed by a muted cheer.

'What – you mean for the nationals?'

She nodded.

'Well, not a bad idea,' I said, nodding too. 'Though, as you probably know, it can be tricky to get *established* with the nationals. Features editors tend to use people they're familiar with. Plus, interviews are hard to place unless you get an exclusive with someone who never talks, like . . . like the Queen or someone. And the thing is, in the usual run of things, we'd get access, you see. When I say "we" I mean at the *Post*. Our own people would do interviews. But then it depends who—'

She punched my shoulder. 'You're just trying to put me off.' She looked irritated but I couldn't tell if she was serious.

'No, no, I'm just saying. It can be tricky.' I smiled, trying to coax her back on to neutral ground.

She pursed her lips at me. 'It helps if you know people, I suppose.'

'Well, yes, there is that. I could give you a couple of names if you like . . .'

'Well if it's not *too* much trouble.' She smiled excitedly and pecked me quickly on the cheek. She drained her gin and tonic and unearthed what I could see was a brand-new contacts book from her bag. She scribbled down the numbers I gave her.

'Your round I think,' I said, feeling safe enough for banter of my own. 'If you're in the chair.' I smiled.

'What? What are you smiling about?' She peered at me, as if trying to see the joke. I just shook my head and laughed mysteriously, as she had done earlier.

'You're mad you are,' she said, turning to the bar.

Someone veered into view and touched my arm. 'Matt?'

It took a second or two to take in the incongruous suit and tie, the open, clean-shaven face – in fact, not just clean-shaven but *clean*. He was holding a glass of champagne. 'Tony?' I put my hand in Tony's outstretched palm and shook automatically, my mind clunking shut on me. I saw Ruth ordering the drinks and I took a step away from her, taking Tony with me. 'Tony, how's it going? You're looking very stylish.' I flashed a dry grin. Stylish wasn't the right word. Mercantile was the right word. He looked like he ought to be knocking on someone's door with a catalogue containing pictures of double-glazed white conservatories attached to Edwardian mansions.

'Yeah, you know I bought Dean's place . . .'

'The garage? No, I didn't know.'

He nodded. 'Yeah, me and my partner.' He pointed back into the crowd, though no one stood out as Tony's obvious partner.

'Well, blimey. That's fantastic. Excellent.' I didn't know what else to say. I thought suddenly about Dean's old grimy office gathering dust, and the last unreplied-to couple of e-mails floating about in cyberspace waiting for ever to be picked up, and I felt my throat seize up. I took a sip of beer. 'So . . . what are you doing here?'

Tony nodded towards the escalators. 'Classic performance motor auction this afternoon, you know, back down there in the arena?'

'Of course, right.' I just couldn't stop nodding. 'Did you buy anything?'

'We put a car in. Just finished it in time, as it happens. Made eight grand, near as damn it.' He licked his top lip. 'Less a couple of ton for charity, of course.' He jerked his thumb towards the hotel entrance. 'Did you see the old blue Aston outside, fifteen-twenty minutes ago? 'Sixty-three DB5 . . . Ha!'

'Actually . . .'

'Should have seen it when we bought it. One door stoved in, other one missing, no lights, electrics eaten away. Sound engine though, once I'd stripped and cleaned it. Been stuck in someone's garage for years. Big farmhouse clearance outside York. Husband deceased. The woman didn't even seem to know she had it. Or didn't care. First thing I did was get it back to Leeds from outside York, put it up on the ramp.' Tony indicated upwards with his hands and glanced up at the ceiling, bending slightly at the knee. 'Sills riddled to fuck. Big welding job. Lovely motor though. Lovely engine. All leather interior, walnut dash. Andy did a lovely paint job on it. Cobalt. Fantastic. Andy's my partner. Great bodyman. No one can touch him. I'm engines, he's bodies. Eight grand straight profit.' He lowered his voice, as if imparting a confidence. 'Mind you, it took us fucking *months* to get her on the road.'

I was nodding, glancing back, aware of Ruth, Ruth, Ruth. 'Right, right,' I said. 'Hence the champagne, right?'

'Absolutely.' Tony held the glass out for inspection then took an appreciative sip. 'So, what brings you here then – down from London?' Down? I watched Tony's eye stray to a position over my shoulder to where Ruth was still no doubt sitting, possibly reading the newspaper I had left on the bar, waiting, not interrupting, but not hiding either. I wondered how long Tony had been watching us. Was it before or after Ruth had tugged on my tie, or pecked me on the cheek, or got irritated with me? Having a woman looking irritated was worse than a kiss. A kiss could be innocent, but irritation suggested some kind of intimate history. 'Yes, my dad's not been well,' I said. 'Just a flying visit. And now I'm killing time, just meeting a few old people from the *Echo* for a drink.'

'What, here?'

'No, well . . .' I turned and together we glanced at Ruth sitting on the stool, idly tapping the heel of her shoe against the crossrail, reading the paper, smoking a cigarette. She looked up and smiled politely. I grinned and turned back to Tony. 'Oh, that's Ruth. She was covering the auction – we're just having a quick one, then meeting the others in town later.'

'Ah, *right* . . .' Tony winked. I felt the blood rush to my neck. Tony was joking, but he said he wouldn't keep me, and after a few minutes of asking after Cathy and how things were going up in London (I didn't correct Tony on his sense of north and south) he winked again and made his way to a distant group of fellow champagne swillers, laughing and raising a toast to hard-earned good fortune.

'Sorry about that,' I said, stepping back to the bar. 'Former acquaintance. Man from the motor trade.'

'Good to see you haven't forgotten your old friends,' Ruth said, finishing her drink.

We took a taxi to a big Harvester that Ruth knew on the ring road, where we ate steak and chips and drank a bottle of red wine, talked about football and journalists' salaries and films neither of us had seen but had managed to read about. I wondered who else she came here with. Fellow scribblers in scruffy suits and beer-spotted ties? Boyfriend? She'd never mentioned one and I hadn't asked. She had never mentioned Cathy or my domestic life in London, though she knew I was married. It was difficult, not having discussed it on that first evening, to bring it up now. Plus, I would feel like a cheap philanderer to bring it up myself. Naturally I would prefer Ruth not to care that I was married. To be cold and callous about it. That way I would be free to be at least casual about it, even though I might hate myself in the privacy of my own bath the next day. But the more Ruth decided not to acknowledge any difficulty, the more I felt vulnerable to the charge of sleeping with her under false pretences. It wasn't as if I thought she was the sort of woman who would expect me to leave my wife and family, but she might be the sort who would expect me to do the decent thing and declare my hand. To let her know that my intentions were strictly dishonourable.

Ruth's flat was in the city centre overlooking the river, ten minutes' walk from the office and, coincidentally, I discovered when we arrived some time after midnight, the next block but one to where Dean had lived. I wondered for a moment if Tony had bought that too, but I had drunk too much to dwell on it too deeply. I fell instead to thinking about all the e-mails I used to send Dean in which Tony's name might routinely crop up in connection with some of his notorious timekeeping, youthful cock-ups or personal habits. I allowed myself the amusing thought that, even if Tony had kept Dean's old Toshiba, and even if he did know an e-mail from a G-clamp (which even Tony must by now), he would never in a million years guess Dean's password, which Dean had proudly made up from the first letters of the second line from 'Come Together'. Gus. Grooving Up Slowly. Dean hadn't been able to come up with any suitable first lines. 'Hey, what about *tapir*?' I had said half an hour later, looking up triumphantly from my singles and B-sides manual. 'It's like an acrostic.

'What?'

'Look – "Ticket to Ride", "All You Need Is Love", "Paperback Writer", "I Feel Fine", "Revolution!" T-a-p-i-r – *tapir*. Great password.'

Dean had looked at me, puzzled. 'Yeah, but what's a fucking tapir, when it's at home?'

Ruth switched on the lamp, grinning at me, shedding her bag and coat. 'Sorry about the mess,' she said. She pulled the rubber band out of her hair and shook it loose, showing an inch of smooth, bare stomach as she reached up to fiddle with it. 'Do you want coffee?' The bedroom door was open and I could see Ruth's sex-filled chalk-blue suit peeping out of the wardrobe. I went into the kitchen where she was shaking the last granules out of a jar of instant into mugs, and put my arms round her waist, nuzzling my face in her hair. She moved her head from side to side like a cat being stroked, then put the jar down and turned to face me, arching her back against the draining board. 'We could skip the Gold Blend moment if you want,' she said. And that was more like it.

It was gone six when I crept back into my mother's house. Vicky was sitting at the kitchen table, haggard, wrapped in

Dad's dressing-gown, drinking coffee and smoking a cigarette. I returned her pointed silence with a yawn that was intended to suggest a weary, even rueful, acknowledgement of whatever juvenile pranks I had ill-advisedly allowed myself to be drawn into by my former workmates, all strapping, beery men to a fault, with no women in sight. But still I felt her eyes on me as I stood with exaggerated weariness at the sink and filled a glass with water and glugged it down, more as a prophylactic against my sister's scepticism than against the likelihood of feeling like shite when I finally crawled out of bed for lunch. Because the truth was I had never felt more alive, and even though I now caught the backdraft of Vicky's hurt and loneliness as she sniffed ostentatiously behind me and struck another match, I padded quietly upstairs with a heart too full of revels to admit anyone with bad news to communicate.

'So what's happening?'

Cathy ignored me.

'Who's the one sitting down with the fishing net and the big hat?'

She patted the back of my hand. 'Matt, *shhh*, I'm trying to listen.'

'But what's happening?'

'It's probably better that you don't know – just sit back and enjoy the music.'

'Who's the guy with the limp?'

'Porgy.'

'Porgy's a *man*?'

'Of course he's a man. Now shut up.'

I didn't really care too much about what was happening. It wasn't really my kind of thing, but it was Cathy's and I was happy to tag along and seem interested, even to the point of being annoying. At least I hadn't fallen asleep yet. I'd been pleasantly surprised when one of the women had started singing 'Summertime' – I'd even been tempted to join in with a spot of bluesy caterwauling under my breath, until Cathy intervened with an elbow to the ribs. And now one of the drunks who had been shooting craps had enlivened the proceedings by killing someone with an iron hook, so it wasn't all bad. At the interval Cathy went off humming to the Ladies while I hurried down to pick up the drinks we'd ordered from the bar. I reached the bottom of the steps and froze. Penelope was standing there. She was alone, chatting to the barman as he moved behind the counter setting out rows of glasses, pouring champagne. I took a step back, taking cover among the people shuffling out, before moving into the alcove where the usher had been standing. Penelope had her hair piled up, with blonde wisps hanging down. She was wearing lots of make-up and a black evening number with the back cut out. I watched her as she waited, one painted fingernail tapping the bar, half-smiling, not looking like a regular opera-lover, but as if she was on duty. She was wearing a badge of some kind. Did she work here? After a minute or so, the barman handed her the tray, and she started picking her way through the crowd. I moved forward. She was with a small group of Japanese standing at the rail. I remembered she was in PR or marketing or something. These were clients, out for some corporate hospitality with their wives or girlfriends. Penelope was being charming and hostessy, smiling and cocking her head to one side when one of her men or women spoke. She was about a foot taller than any of them.

'I thought you were getting the drinks,' Cathy said, arriving suddenly and prodding me in the arm.

'Yes, I'm just . . .'

She locked on to my stare. 'Who are you staring at?' Cathy peered across in the direction of Penelope's group. 'Who's the blonde?'

'Oh, it's probably better that you don't know,' I grinned, immediately cursing my inability to resist teasing Cathy with her own words. She eyed me with mock suspicion until I shrugged. 'What? How should I know who she is? Come on.'

Our drinks were standing at the end of the bar on a damp ticket. I steered Cathy to a spot obscured by a figure of a leaping dancer made from chicken wire and old ballet shoes, where we could safely drink our gin and tonics and Cathy could recount the troubled history of *Porgy* and why she thought this production was artistically if not technically more satisfying than the one screened by BBC2 back somewhere in the annals of history. 'Black people weren't coming to see it,' she was saying. 'They didn't like the idea of being depicted as prostitutes and murderers.'

'Not to mention fishermen,' I said, to show I was listening, and to tease out a theatrically impatient smile from Cathy.

The bell went and we trailed back to our seats. I busied myself leafing through the programme. Cathy touched my arm. 'Look, she's staring at us.'

'Who?'

'*There* – that woman from out in the bar.' I followed Cathy's line of vision to what looked like a corporate box about twenty feet away, where Penelope was leaning over the side and waving towards me.

'Look, it's you. She's waving at you . . .'

I stared hard at the lighting rig high above Penelope's head. 'No, I don't think so,' I said. 'Must be someone else.' The lights went down.

'I think it's us,' Cathy said.

'Shh, it's starting,' I hissed.

Cathy stared at me quizzically, then turned her attention to the stage.

I waited for the first gloomy baritone to shuffle out of the wings and open his mouth to sing, then I rose to my feet. 'Just off for a wee,' I said. Cathy tutted loudly but didn't look at me. I made my way behind the back row of seats and out into the corridor, following its curve until I reached a series of doors leading to the corporate boxes, each labelled with a sponsor's logo – Bio-Tuc, *e*-scope, Sumiyoto . . . That would be it. A uniformed usher appeared and hovered near the wall, his hands folded in front of him. I looked at my watch, as if I was waiting for someone, unlikely as that seemed, though I could have lost my ticket and forgotten where I was sitting or . . .

The Sumiyoto door swung open and Penelope stuck her head out. 'Hey Matt, how are you? Didn't you see me waving?'

'Yes. But I'm, like, with my *wife* if you don't mind?'

Penelope laughed. 'So? We don't have to tell her anything.' She laughed again.

The usher glanced at us, as a prelude to asking us to keep our voices down. I felt myself redden. 'Shhh. For goodness sake. Oh God . . .' My heart stopped. Over the usher's shoulder I could see Cathy just rounding the curve of the corridor.

'I'd better get back,' Penelope was saying. 'Clients.' She was pointing at the Sumiyoto ID pinned to her dress.

'It's her, she's coming. Do *not* say a word . . .'

Penelope looked up. 'Oh for goodness sake, relax – she must know you have to speak to other women occasionally. Tell her you used to work with me or something. I'll see you around, OK?' She vanished, flashing a smile at me and a bigger one at Cathy, who was wearing a lost expression that I had never seen before. I sauntered towards her grinning a shaky grin, jerking my thumb at the door clicking closed behind me. 'Guess who that was?'

Cathy was breathing hard, almost as if she'd been running. Her eyes searched my face, like someone expecting bad news from casualty. 'I've no idea,' she said. 'Someone you don't know, apparently.'

'What are you doing here anyway?' I said.

'What are *you* doing here – the Gents are that way.'

'Ah yes . . .'

'What?'

My thumb jerked up again in the direction of the Sumiyoto door. 'That's because, she – *Helen* – saw me coming out and called me over. You were right. She was waving at us.'

'Well who *is* she? Why the big mystery?'

'No big mystery. She's a PR. She's the PR from the firm who got us the tickets. She just wanted to introduce herself and make sure we were OK.' I heard myself say these words and wanted to kiss myself. It was so simple. 'She's called Helen. Apparently. Well?'

Cathy sighed and stared at the floor, thinking. Then she sighed again and mustered a goofy look. 'Sorry.'

I went off to the Gents, splashed a gallon of cold water on my face and went back to rejoin Cathy. I watched the rest of the show but took none of it in. I glanced at her profile from time to time in the half dark, trying to read her mood.

When the lights went up, Penelope caught my eye and I returned her wave. Cathy smiled too and nodded. 'What's the name of the PR company she works for?' she said as we made our way out.

'Why?'

'I just want to know, if that's OK with you.'

'It's . . . Tapir. Yes, t-a-p-i-r, that's it. They're Moroccan, I think.' I looked at my watch. 'Do you fancy a pizza or something?'

'No, we've got to get back. We promised Bev we wouldn't be too late. Isn't a tapir South American?'

'What? I don't know – is it important?'

Cathy shrugged. 'I thought we might want to send her a card, telling them how much we enjoyed it.'

I ushered Cathy quickly towards the exit. 'Are you kidding? They're a PR company. It's their job to give journalists free tickets to things. We're meant to spread the word. We're supposed to be opinion-formers.'

'I don't think that's any reason not to thank someone. I'll bet that poor woman goes weeks without being thanked for anything. What kind of a job is that?'

I laughed. 'I'm telling you it doesn't matter. It's how the corporate world works.' Cathy was looking over her shoulder, and I had the feeling that she might just head back towards Penelope's box and thank her in person.

'Maybe we could just . . .' Cathy was saying.

'No, no, *no*,' I said. 'You can't just barge in. She's with a bunch of clients from Sumiyoto – it would be embarrassing. The Japanese get embarrassed very easily.'

'I suppose so.' We walked down the stairs and out into the street. 'I've been trying to think who she reminds me of. Who was the one from *Twin Peaks*? The one who worked in the diner . . .' I felt Cathy's arm link mine.

'You've got me there,' I said.

When we got home, Kite came yapping round, whipping our legs with her tail, and Bev stood up yawning to greet us. 'Hi, good show?'

'Brilliant – but Matt says we're not supposed to say so. Was everything OK here?'

'Ellie's fine. But . . .' Bev started to half whisper, her eyes raised to the ceiling to indicate upstairs. 'Actually, Sadie came back with a couple of friends earlier. Don't worry, everything's cool. It's just that I think they might have been smoking. I thought you ought to know.'

'Smoking? Oh God.'

I draped my coat across a chair. 'Keep calm everyone, it's not the end of the world. No one's set fire to the house. Didn't you ever used to smoke behind the bike sheds?'

'Actually,' Bev said, 'I meant *smoking* – you know, dope.'

'What?' said Cathy. She swept out of the room and was halfway up the stairs, me and the dog following, Kite wagging her tail and sniffing at the sweetish scent hanging in the air. Cathy tapped on the door. Sadie opened it, looking sleepy. She looked expectantly at Cathy and then at me. 'Hi, did you have a good time?'

'Fine. And you?' Cathy peered over her shoulder into the room. The curtains were open and the sash window was up.

'Yes, why, what's wrong?'

'We were just wondering about that smell.'

'What? Oh, it's just incense. Ryan and Jade came round. And Paul.'

'And Paul . . .'

'Yes, why? What is it?'

'So you haven't been smoking in your room?'

'No, of course not.' Sadie moistened her top lip with her tongue. 'Oh. Well, all right, Paul smoked a joint, if that's OK. In fact, it was only half of one now I come to think about it.' She folded her arms defensively. I was beginning to feel awkward standing at her bedroom door like this, as though we were boring neighbours who had come round to complain about the music, but that the music had already been turned down, the guests had gone and the host was about to go to bed.

'Well, to be absolutely honest, Sadie,' Cathy was saying, 'I'm not sure it *is* OK.' She looked at me. 'Matt?'

'No, absolutely – not absolutely OK,' I said, switching on my newly acquired reasonable-parent persona. I smiled. 'It's pretty late. Perhaps it'd be a better idea to talk about it in the morning.'

Sadie brightened. 'OK, 'night then.' She kissed her mother on the cheek and retreated into her room.

Bev was putting her coat on when we went down to the kitchen. Kite had retreated to her basket.

'At least she was honest about it,' I said, busily unplugging the kettle and even more busily gushing water into it.

'Hang on,' Cathy said. 'Have I missed something? Don't we care whether our daughter is doing drugs?'

'It's not *doing* drugs, honey. Lots of people use drugs at different times of their lives,' I said. 'Kids are bound to take an interest at some point. And it's not as if smoking dope is dangerous or anything. She's not shooting crack in some rat-infested squat in . . . in Broadwater Farm. She's not a heroin addict. She's just, you know – expressing herself. Yes, of course we need to talk about it with her. But we also have to allow her some space. We have to learn to keep everything in perspective.'

'So that's what the opinion-formers are saying?' Cathy said.

I added milk to the coffees and stirred enthusiastically. 'What you have to remember is, everybody uses drugs these days.'

'Well *I* don't. *You* don't. Do you?' She looked at me, the same wave of something flitting across her expression that I'd seen at the theatre, as if she was trying not to read something in my face that she'd never seen before and was fearful of seeing now. She turned quickly to Bev. 'What do you think, Bev?'

'I think Matt's probably right. You can't stop her doing whatever all the other kids are doing. But, you know – Sadie might not *want* to do it. Not everyone does. But you can't expect her to disapprove either. She won't want to withdraw. She won't want to look uncool in front of her friends. Especially new friends.'

Cathy looked at us both and sighed. 'But she's fifteen years old.'

Bev smiled and put her hand on Cathy's shoulder. 'Now isn't that exactly how Sadie would see it?'

I suppose it was a classic giveaway, though it's still funny how the minute you get to a certain age you can't do anything remotely out of the ordinary without someone accusing you of having a midlife crisis. Admittedly, Cathy didn't actually *say* anything, so I suppose it was just nervousness that made me drivel on uncontrollably about how being forty didn't mean you had to close yourself off to new experiences or be afraid to adapt your lifestyle to the rapidly evolving leisure pursuits of the twenty-first century. I even suggested that she herself might benefit from a spot of rollerblading, for example, or snowboarding, and that I obviously wouldn't stand in her way, not if her driving was anything to go by, as I joked to her – in vain as it happened, because she just carried on watching me in that kind of ironic, amused silence, as I bent double on the carpet, trying to thread the laces of my stiff new Adidas trainers. I didn't even think about why I was doing this. I hoped I just wanted to get in shape for healthy lifestyle reasons. I had no plans to continue with the other thing. It wasn't something I wanted to do on a permanent basis. I knew I had drifted slightly, but I hadn't been anywhere near the falls. I wasn't Lawrence.

Astonishingly, Sadie loved the trainers, which seemed to irk Cathy even more, though the decision to go for electric blue with gold stripes was more Alex's than mine. I did point out to him that they were horrible, but he was adamant that you had to have the kit. It was a matter of confidence, he said. There was no point turning up in Dunlop plimsolls, he said, though in fact there would have been no danger of my turning up in anything more sporting than the 1989 Doc Martens I used to do my hopeless gardening and even worse decorating in. My big worry, needless to say, was that the gym would be full of overtanned, baby-oiled bodybuilders hulking about looking like pumped-up leather sofas, but in fact when Alex finally dragged me down there for my induction session, practically everybody looked worryingly like me, which wasn't exactly a brilliant advert for the place. Ah, said Alex, that was because Bunters was aimed at office workers, adding – in a way that sounded too much like a bit of well-rehearsed sales spiel (because, remember, he got some kind of reduced rate for introducing me), that we weren't talking about people who think the body is a *temple* – more a chapel of rest. Ho, ho. No, he says, we're talking about ordinary potbellied lunchtime punters whose primary aim is to stop eating themselves to death two or three times a week. The kind of people who are perfectly happy to cripple themselves for, say, three or four sessions – enough to lose a few pounds and tone their 'abs' or 'glutes' a bit – and then, once they can get back into their favourite trousers, they kid themselves that it's possible to stay that way just by doing a few sit-ups and going for a swim once in a while. It didn't sound too promising to me.

'But what about the expense?' I said. 'What if you give up after two sessions?' (This thing was not cheap.)

'Well isn't that the whole point?' Alex replied triumphantly, slapping me between the shoulderblades. Because, as Alex had it, the more ruinous it was to your domestic finances, the more frequently you were likely to turn up to try to justify the cost. I could see Jane and Milo shaking their heads pityingly out of the corner of my eye as I marched off behind him with my obviously brand-new Nike gym bag slung over my shoulder. It wasn't too far from the office – a brisk ten-minute walk, which seemed much longer, of course, with Alex barking on – but pretty soon I was signing the register and exchanging strained rictuses with this Arnold Schwarzenegger type called Carl behind the counter, who turned out to be my Inductor or possibly Instructor spelled wrong (he wore a badge). The trick was, Alex said in my ear, to take it pretty easy the first time out, by which I assumed he meant I should give up after the rowing machine. But no, you had to try everything, laughed Carl. This turned out, at one point, to involve trying to lift ton weights using only one foot, after which he strapped me into something resembling a giant pair of wings made of lead, which I was then supposed to try and flap.

I didn't feel any healthier by the time we escaped back into the changing rooms, though admittedly I was a lot sweatier. Until then, I hadn't even thought about the showers. I had this theory that if you suffered from a thinning scalp – and, no, I'm not saying this was a big problem for me – you weren't doing it any favours by bombarding it with high-pressure jets of water. Informal research (mine) showed that you could lose up to sixty-five hairs in a shower, whereas you might only recover thirty-one maximum after a gentle shampoo in the bath. But

Bunters didn't have baths and it was too late for a swim, which was just as well because I would have been obliged to drown at this stage, unless there was some stroke you could do when your muscles were in spasm. I might not have guessed it, but Alex was in his element here. Alex was one of those blokes who obviously just *loves* to be naked in public. In any male locker-room gathering there's always one person who feels compelled to conduct lengthy conversations in the nude. They might have a quick shower first, as a kind of necessary pretext to being stark bollock naked, but people like Alex are oblivious of the unspoken agreement that normal people adhere to regarding the modest deployment of a towel. Don't get me wrong. I'm not particularly susceptible to unfavourable comparisons. This wasn't a size thing. Anyway, everybody knows that genitals taper away when viewed from above and therefore seem bigger to other people who may or may not be taking an interest. My own instinct is to stick to classic English procedure, namely: a) tie towel round waist and pretend to be busy looking for a sock; b) when no one is looking, perform dance, first on one foot, then on the other, until you've managed to roll your underpants up your damp legs and over your damp backside; c) insouciantly remove towel and make big deal of drying armpits, eventually hair. Naturally, Alex thoroughly towelled his hair first – in fact he *only* towelled his hair – thereby displaying as much artificially flexed and tautened naked flesh as he could for as long as possible to whoever might have been in the neighbourhood. This took him ages, roughing this side of his head and then the other, then the old double-action rub to the nape of his neck holding each end of the towel. He'd got the driest hair in town, and all the time he was rabbiting on, standing with his knees pushed back and his knob thrust forward like one of those models you see in naturist magazines pictured in the bar sharing a joke with family and friends after a game of volleyball. And it still wasn't over. Alex was thwacking his twisted knot of towel at the locker door as he talked on and on, occasionally using two hands like one of those models you see in naturist magazines practising their golf swing. The Alexes of this world always have a very small towel, which is a throwback from their bullying days at school when, in addition to showing everyone how much pubic hair had been acquired by the age of fourteen, they could snap it at someone's passing bare arse with optimum sting. Eventually, Alex started pulling his shirt on. Not his underwear, you notice. He didn't want to put his dick away *quite* yet. Mine had been tucked away for twenty minutes by now. I was on the point of suggesting that he could put his trousers on on the way back to the office – I was sure he'd be pretty cool about having his dong dangling all the way down City Road. And all the time he was talking about the best way to get to that last tuft of bristle under your nose when you're shaving and the best way to cut toenails, according to an article he'd read in *GQ*. How you should always weigh yourself *after* you've had your morning crap, but *before* you put your deodorant on.

Vanity, health and efficiency. The terrible thing was that I was listening to all this. Alex's plan to defeat the ageing process struck a chord. In addition to weight and hair, I was getting slightly obsessed about losing my mind, in particular my memory. I recall trying to remember somebody's name in bed. Someone I used to work with when I first started at the *Echo* years ago. I mean it didn't matter in the slightest really – her face just slipped through my mind when I was remembering those days when I was half asleep. Jane someone. It was definitely Jane. Then I went through the alphabet hoping her surname would suddenly spring out at me. Something Scottish, I thought. Then I went through every other member of our old features team at that time and found I could recall every single name except hers. Even quite tricky ones like Rufus Mbwayah, who was from Swaziland or somewhere. I could picture their names as bylines, but not hers, even though I could remember some of the stories she'd done in detail. The more I thought about her, the more I found myself excavating more and more about her life. I remembered that she was a terrible driver and that she had a Fiat Uno. Her husband was a solicitor and *his* first name was Meredith. I suppose you would remember that. They lived out of town because they both had a horse and needed a big place with a paddock. I mean, listen to this – I'd got her entire life story there under the duvet with me. She had a child – a little girl who she sometimes used to bring into work – though I couldn't remember her name, which was a relief, in a way. She was always on a diet of some kind (Jane, not the little girl), and kept a bag of uninteresting snacks like celery and bayoneted carrots in a bag on her desk to stop her eating chocolate – and, yes, I can even remember it was Toffee Crisp she used to have because I helped her do a competition on the wrapper once. But what *was* her name? What? What? It kept me awake for ages worrying about it. Cathy used to say that if you couldn't sleep, it was usually because something was on your mind.

Anyway, I made the mistake of telling Alex about this, if only to put the brakes on his rambling seminar about personal hygiene. 'Hang on,' he said, stopping us suddenly in the middle of the road. He'd got his hand holding my shoulder as if there was a chance that I might float off into the blaring traffic. 'Have you got a juicer?' he said.

'What?' I said. 'You mean like a lemon squeezer?'

'No, no, a proper juicer. You can make juice out of any fruit or even any old fresh veg you have hanging about in the fridge. Fantastically good for cell-regeneration. Cleans out your blood. Cleans out your mind. Halts the onset of dementia. Improves your memory. You'll be amazed. You've *got* to have one.'

'So what's in it for you?' I said.

He ignored me and made me copy down the name of an Italian kitchenware shop near Wigmore Street (where Paul McCartney unaccountably used to live with Jane Asher and her mum and dad) who stocked the best and most stylish designer juicers in the world, which incidentally only cost hundreds of pounds. I said thanks anyway and that I was sure such a crucial purchase would get the wholehearted support of Cathy, who at the time was going mentally ill over our household budget. For example: 'What's this?' she would demand, pouncing on something at random from our bank statement.

'Forty-one pounds?'

'I can see that. What is it for?'

'Well, look – B2's. Isn't that your haircut?'

'Oh, yes,' she'd say grudgingly with no sign of an apology. But then she'd scour it for ages until she'd found something that I had spent. Eamonn's or somewhere, on the odd occasion I ran out of cash and had to do something socially in an emergency. 'Look at this!' she'd shriek. 'You seem to live in this place. Don't you ever do any work?'

I pointed out, to her evident surprise, that the average professional male spends thirty-six minutes a day in a place of refreshment (one of Milo's helpful statistics), so it was hardly news if some of it turned up on a bank statement occasionally. The truth is, she'd got it into her head that I was spending tons of money on clothes, eating out, gyms, prostitutes. She might have been right (except the last one) but she wasn't very systematic at gathering evidence. The trouble was, neither of us could be bothered to monitor income against outgoings. 'OK,' I said, 'you be in charge of the finances. I don't mind.'

'Right,' she said.

Actually, it wasn't such a big deal. Sadie had got herself a Saturday job on Oxford Street (not Selfridges, for obvious reasons), which would help pay for her phone calls and black lipstick, and I mentioned to Cathy that I might be considered for the 'Watch It' columns and 'Weekender' when James Thomas went to the *Courier*. That would mean more money, a better profile on the paper and maybe the odd spot of lucrative freelance coming my way. I had tried to catch Jeremy only that morning. 'Must have a word at some point,' he said. Which sounded promising, I thought.

By the way it was O'Connel. Julie. Not Jane and not Scottish.

Mind you, I could forget important things too.

'Hi, this is Ruth . . .'

I quickly put the phone down, unable for a second to do anything other than stare at my own hand still resting on the receiver. I felt my mouth dry up, and I went to the kitchen and opened a can of the new Japanese beer Cathy had found for me at a special importing off-licence in Muswell Hill. This was what Cathy was like. I'd had the beer once or twice at the Japanese near the office and had mentioned it in passing. Shinkansen it was called – like the bullet train, Cathy said. She absorbed details and carried them around in her head for ever. She only had to meet someone once and she'd remember the names of all their children and where they'd just been on holiday and who'd caught chicken pox last Bonfire Night and who'd been having trouble with head of finance or had the sale of their house fall through because it needed underpinning or damp-proofing. She knew my extended family of cousins and aunties and uncles better than I did, and they all adored her even though she hardly saw them. She was someone who took an interest. She could always think of the right Christmas presents to buy because she remembered what kind of dull things my uncles and cousins found riveting and what kind of unreadable books they read. They were always remarking on how thoughtful and serene she was and, by implication I supposed, how lucky I – vague, thoughtless, feckless Matt – was to have tricked her into marrying me.

I took the beer up to my little den in the loft and pulled out an album at random from the shelf. *Beatles for Sal*e. I slumped back in my shabby leather swivel chair and read the sleeve notes and track listings. I could have recited them from memory, but I read them anyway, legs crossed, swivelling slowly to this side then that, sipping beer. At last I slid the album out of the sleeve, set it on the Pye turntable, listened to the first two tracks without really listening and switched it off again, watching the disc revolve until it stopped. Then I swivelled to face the desk, where my Mac was still switched on with the e-mail running from yesterday. Cathy had taken Ellie and the dog to the park. Sadie was out somewhere.

Two e-mails and five phone calls, four with messages.

Funny. It hadn't occurred to me until now, but it was weeks since I'd even thought about listening to a Beatles track, let alone played one. Not even a CD from the boxed sets I kept downstairs for everyday use. And generally it *was* every day. In fact, in the long months after Dean's accident, I would spend countless hours after dinner lying on the couch gazing at the badly artexed ceiling in my music room in Headingley, outsized earphones glued to my cranium, working my way through the singles and EPs and albums and promo and anniversary pressings in chronological order. Of course, there was nothing weird about looking for comfort in your favourite music. But for a long time – though I didn't have the heart to pick up my guitar or touch my Wurlitzer, or even hum along with the record – it seemed to me that the songs were really all that was left of Dean. I hadn't thought about it before, but I realised now that the songs were really all we'd ever had in common – all we had to explain to the world why we'd managed to be best friends for so long. So it followed that the songs *were* the memory of Dean, or at least you could say that no memory of Dean came without a soundtrack in three-part harmony.

Of course, even before Dean died, I might find myself bingeing for days and nights on one particular album, listening from new angles, coaxing out fresh nuances and incorporating them into my mental karaoke until eventually Cathy would put her foot down and threaten to leave me or at least take a rolling pin to my records when I was out at work. Under normal circumstances – until recently – I would rarely go more than two or three days without listening to something, usually just plonking a CD on in the sitting room when I was reading or drinking tea or staring across the lawn at the rusty washing machine that I had now at last managed to get out of the shed but not to the dump.

I eased the album back into its sleeve and replaced it on the shelf, shut down my computer, picked up the receiver on my red trimphone and punched in the number. It only rang three times – three times was the sign of a small dwelling with white lacy knickers draped over the radiator, I thought – before the now familiar greeting on the answering machine clicked in: *Hi, this is Ruth, I'm not here right now but if you want to leave a message, you know what to do.*

I held my breath as I waited for the beep. '*Hiiii*, it's Matt again. I'm guessing you're not back from your holiday yet. Blimey, where did you go – Australia? Anyway, if you want to, give me a call at work, or mail me! Bye.'

I closed my eyes. *Australia?* Did I really say that? Six calls, two e-mails. *You know what to do* clanged in my ears. Setting the phone on three rings was of course more likely to mean she only answered if it was someone she wanted to speak to. She could be sitting there painting her toenails. I was old enough to remember that the original USP of answerphones was that they allowed you to be in when you were out. How long did it take before everyone started using them so they could be out when they were in?

She probably *was* on holiday, though she hadn't mentioned it. The desk secretary at the *Echo* didn't actually say so, just said Ruth was off for a couple of weeks. But where *was* she, I wanted to know. Who wanted to know, the secretary wanted to know. Good question. Who was I? What was I to Ruth? What was she to me? What's it to you, I felt like saying to the secretary, but I didn't. I put the phone down before she could ask me again.

The Ruth question, I knew, could not go on. Even on the train back from Leeds, even as the goat inside me still reared half rampant in self-congratulation, my higher faculties were flying warning flags, fearful of a snowballing of what mustn't be allowed to snowball – fearful of the abrupt arrival (*blip!*) of a cheery, perhaps sexually improper e-mail from Ruth on Monday morning. I feared and feared and feared until, gradually, imperceptibly, the fear was on the other foot. Why didn't she mail? Why didn't she call? Where was she? I wanted her. I didn't. I did. I didn't. I did.

'Cheer up, Matty,' Alex had said on Thursday, slapping me between the shoulderblades as he passed.

'Fuck off, Alex,' I replied wearily, without looking up. I immediately regretted it but only because I expected Alex to come back grinning, looking for a wound to stick his finger in. But Alex just shrugged and went off with a bewildered, almost injured look, leaving me with the novelty of feeling bad about Alex's feelings for the rest of the day, which had to be a sign of how flaky things were getting.

I was standing at the kerb outside Bond Street station waiting to cross the road. There was no way I was actually going to buy a designer juicer costing God knows what from an Italian kitchenware shop near Wigmore Street, but I could easily walk to The 34 club via there and just spend a minute or two looking in the Italian kitchenware shop window at the things vain and fashionable people spent their time talking and writing about as though they were World War Three.

Then I saw Sadie. She was on the top deck of a bus waving madly at me. She laughed at the surprise on my face as I looked up and saw her. Then I remembered it was half-term and realised that she was obviously on her way home from the Saturday job that she'd extended for the holidays. A shoe department. She was miming something, interrogating me with hand signals at the window. *What are you doing? Where are you going?* I showed her the empty-handed gesture that meant 'I don't know' or 'that's life' and then waved her off, which took seconds and more seconds before the bus yielded to the slow pull of the evening traffic. I realised that my heart was pulsing. It was as though I had almost been caught by my daughter in the act of doing something irredeemably bad; as though there was nothing but luck between this occasion and one in which I might have been spotted not standing alone minding my own unblemished affairs but sauntering near King's Cross enjoying the delicious rapport of a woman young enough to be my daughter's favourite TV presenter.

When she got home she would say, 'I saw Dad in London.'

'Really – where?'

'Oxford Street.'

'What was he doing?'

'I don't know.'

And Cathy would shrug and perhaps wonder. Though I had never mentioned The 34, it was precisely the kind of place Cathy might, under normal circumstances, expect me to go occasionally and have too much to drink, as a slightly irritating but tolerable prelude to coming home and falling asleep in the chair in the middle of taking my shoes off. But now it was too late in the day for such an innocent construction of things. And now that it had become too difficult to tell her, she would doubtless, in the way of Hollywood conceits, find a book of matches with The 34 logo in my dark-grey suit jacket (while checking my pockets on the way to the dry cleaners), remember the neon 34 sign from *Cheating Hearts*, find something inconsistent in my testimony ('I thought you said you interviewed this *Lawrence* in that Elvis Presley place?') and connect it eventually with activities incompatible with my status as a happily married man with responsibilities. I didn't have the mental agility to cover the tracks that I'd made trying to cover my tracks the first time. It could happen. She did see everything. Cathy could easily have been one of those girls she knew at Oxford who hadn't stupidly got pregnant but had gone on instead to become lawyers or derivatives dealers or forensic scientists.

I didn't stay long at the club. When I arrived, Lawrence was already as out of things as I had ever seen him, though it was not yet 7.30, and was sitting in his usual spot with the girl who I recognised as the one in the red leather skirt I had seen twice before but never quite been introduced to. She was wearing the red leather skirt again.

'Matt, this is Tanya,' he said. 'Tanya, this is—'

'I *know* who he is, Lawrence,' she said, shooting him an impatient glance. She turned to me. 'I was the producer on *Cheating Hearts*? We talked on the phone?' She managed a regretful smile.

'Ah, right. Of course.' I felt awkward. All the impressions I had so far gained of *this* Tanya – red leather, the kind of dippy friend Penelope would have, someone with the kind of understanding with Lawrence that allowed her to be pissed off with him in public – collided with any polite career enquiries I might have made of the Tanya I had once spoken to on the phone – professional, impartial, sober. 'But I've seen you here before,' I said lamely.

'Oh, Tanya's never out of here,' Lawrence said, his eyes suddenly widening as if he'd seen something astonishing on a distant horizon. He grinned. Tanya said nothing, but nursed her drink, gazing idly around the club, as though Lawrence and I might have things to talk about that didn't involve her, though the situation was already too weird to fall into anything but silence.

'Look, I can't stop long,' I said. 'And you guys are obviously . . . engaged in something.'

'Hey, mate, mate, sit down, sit down.' He pulled me down and slopped wine into a glass. Tanya shook her head resignedly and stood up. She took her drink to the bar and joined a group that I now saw included Graham and Claricia.

I watched her go. 'Look, I—'

'Hey, don't worry. See her later. Me and you, Matt.' He put his arm round my shoulders and squeezed desperately. 'Did I ever tell you about my wife, Matt?'

'You did, actually. Horses, swimming pools, that kind of thing.'

Lawrence stared at his shoes for a long moment, then grinned. 'Fuck her,' he said. 'Let's have some fun.' He waved to a waitress, who arrived at the table. 'Champagne, methinks.' He turned and called to the group gathered at the bar. 'Graham! Get over here, man.' Graham came over reluctantly with Claricia in tow trailing cigarette smoke. 'Let's go dance.'

Graham pointed at his watch almost theatrically. 'But there's no DJ till ten. It'll be completely dead up there.'

'Oh for fuck's sake, man. *We'll* be there, won't we?'

Graham looked to Claricia for support but she was sitting on the back of Lawrence's couch facing the bar, exhaling smoke, waiting for someone to get in and drive. The waitress was hovering.

I rose to my feet. 'Actually, I have to be making a move.'

Lawrence leapt up. 'Matt, Matt, don't, please. You've got to stay. Come on.' He was nodding emphasis with every word. 'Please – come on, Matt. Buddy. Brother. Penelope's coming later. It'll be *cool*.' He stopped talking, staring into my face, his eyes far away in some fucked-up place, his hands awkwardly gripping my jacket sleeves.

I pulled myself away, forcing a laugh, but suddenly thinking of Sadie on the bus and of Cathy, looking up in mild surprise. *What was he doing?* 'Next time,' I was saying to Lawrence, laughing now as though things *were* fun and cool. 'We'll do it next time.'

We had to go round to Vicky's for dinner, and obviously I'd been *really* looking forward to this one, especially since Cathy managed to prise the truth from Mum about the shitbag

Richard, who it seemed had gone and shacked up with some woman half his age – well, mid-thirties anyway, which was no less amazing given Richard's lack of obvious attractions in every department with the possible exception of home brewing. So naturally, I was thinking this was bound to be a story of unavoidable late nights all alone with some fawning female minion with an unfortunate squint and negative promotion prospects, but according to Mum, the other woman in question turned out to be not some low-level minx looking for a leg-up in her job but a co-boffin on the sales side, respectably divorced with eight-year-old twins! I almost burst out laughing with disbelief when Cathy told me, which wasn't the thing to do, mainly because Cathy had become very Mother Hen lately with regard to Vicky and obviously thought I was being Mr Callous, when in fact I was being Mr Realistic. The point was, this situation had completely fucked Vicky up, because she and the shitbag Richard had been trying to have kids for years, so it was like the ultimate betrayal. No wonder I couldn't get a civil word out of her when I saw her up in Leeds, and why she was so weird.

But when Vicky opened the door my first thought was that we'd got the wrong house. 'Well?' she said. 'Are you going to stand there gawping all night or are you going to come in?' Cathy sailed in right past me and gave Vicky a big sisterly hug, leaving me to lug the travel cot in and fetch Ellie from the car (we'd had to bring Ellie because Bev had very conveniently taken Sadie for an evening of dry-ski-sloping somewhere), so by the time I got inside Cathy was stepping back and eyeing Vicky in an exaggerated up-and-down fashion and saying how *fantastic* she looked. And sure enough Vicky had shed about eight stone and was standing in front of us very neatly packed into this slinky velvet number to go with her glossy new hair (bizarrely, exactly like Cathy's) and supermodel facial administered by the best pointers and trowellers in Luton. I didn't know about fantastic, but she was certainly in good shape for a woman who was supposed to be older than me and a few short weeks previously was starting to look like Meat Loaf. God knows what she'd been doing. Not eating, I imagine. Working out, presumably, and on this evidence no one did aerobics as furiously as a woman scorned.

I hadn't actually opened my mouth yet because the last time I tried she bit my head off, but I figured it was safe to offer a small 'wow', though I refrained from following it up with an appreciative whistle. She was doing a girlish twirl to show us that she wasn't just a thin facade with all the fat stapled up at the back, and glowing with such self-belief that I was starting to think she might be just happily tranquillised, but this was before she took us through into the sitting room and introduced us to . . . Steve. Steve? Before I had the chance to think who the fuck Steve was he was leaping to his feet. He was so tall he nearly hit his head on one of the horrible executive chandeliers Vicky and Richard had all over the house. He stepped over to give me one of those crunching handshakes that are supposed to demonstrate to other men that you're not a homosexual. 'Hi,' he bellowed, which I'm afraid told me all I wanted to know about Vicky's current giddiness.

'Ouch!' I said, only half-jokingly buckling at the knees, which prompted Vicky to tell me to watch it pal, because Steve played rugby. Surely not, I said with mock shock, but Vicky was too flipped-out for irony. Yes, *rugby*, she cooed – even though Steve was getting to be an old man of thirty-two (*thirty-two!*), she added, presumably for our benefit, because as far as I know there's no upper age limit for having a size 17 shirt collar and singing in public. 'And he's a policeman,' she trilled, as a mischievous afterthought.

My God, what was happening to her?

Anyway, it turned out Vicky met her young policeman in the juice bar at the gym in the leisure centre, an encounter they now decided to recount together in fits of giggles (though, oddly, none of this story was remotely funny, and giggles are slightly unnerving coming from a beefy policeman) while the four of us were tucking into Vicky's pork chops in cider, which I seemed to remember was what she cooked for us the last time we came, though obviously I was too courteous and too busy nodding and smiling politely at Vicky'n'Steve's goofy togetherness to mention it. Cathy liked the juice-bar story because it gave her the opportunity to break the ice further by telling them how I came home recently and presented her with the impromptu gift of an Italian electric juicer that she couldn't get to work and now had to be taken back to the shop. (Yes, I know.)

The evening went quite well, though of course the more we drank, the more Steve became as openly rude about journalists generally as I was privately rude about him in particular. ('Nothing personal,' he kept saying every time he was obliged to use the 'scum' word when quoting one of his colleagues on some atrocity perpetrated on this or that innocent celebrity paedophile by rapacious tabloid reporters. Oddly, we managed not to touch on police brutality, but I did take comfort in noting that he ate like a pig and was afflicted by fast-growing chimney-sweep-brush hair, which very probably covered his whole body.)

'So, don't the police have their own gym?' I said.

'Yes,' he said, bristling in more ways than one. 'Why?'

'Oh, no reason,' I said casually, gnawing on a bone, licking my fingers. 'But . . . well, you use the gym at your local leisure centre as well, right?'

He gave a sort of twitchy shrug with the side of his head. 'When I'm off-duty,' he said, meaning, of course, when he was off trawling for emotionally unstable women. 'Why, what's the problem?' he said, his features just starting to twist into Mr Hyde's.

'Nothing,' I said, grinning and leaning towards him. 'I just wanted you to help me with my enquiries.' The four of us looked at each other for a moment. This was *such* a shite witticism that I could hardly believe I'd said it, but of course it really cracked him up. God knows why. He couldn't stop laughing and, of course, neither could Vicky, because now she thought we were all going to be friends.

There was one point for about ten seconds after Steve had gone for a slash and Vicky was getting the coffees when Cathy hissed at me across the table. 'Do you think they're . . .' She made an impatient sign that I assumed meant 'on shagging terms'.

'Of course they are – he's not the lodger, is he?' I mean you don't have to be a behavioural scientist to spot a couple on the first rung of sexual discovery, especially when you consider that, a) Steve kept sticking his nose in Vicky's ear, and b) what the fuck *else* would he be doing here, because as a dining companion he made Richard look like Oscar Wilde (whom, actually, Richard *had* come to resemble slightly in recent years, come to think of it).

Cathy gave me one of her exasperated looks. 'No, I mean do you think they're *serious*,' she said, to which the only response was cruel laughter, but I had to stifle it because he was coming back and Cathy went out to help Vicky in the kitchen, while Steve tried to explain, with the help of a dozen mint imperials, the uninteresting though happily neutral subject of how the offside rule pertained in rugby league.

And actually it was all very sweet until it started getting sour around 11.30 when Vicky started laying into the absent Richard with lurid tales of his low sperm count, which she had agreed not to tell anyone about, but fuck *that*, she said crisply. I looked at Cathy but she was nodding in a sisterly way. Steve had Vicky's hand in his big hairy mitt now, which I imagined meant he wanted her in the kitchen over one of Richard's barrels and he wanted her *now*, but Vicky was well into her stride, knocking back her goldfish-bowlful of Sainsbury's Cabernet in big rhetorical gulps, each putting the seal of disapproval on some unforgivable shortcoming of Richard's.

'And of course our sex life was practically non-existent anyway,' she blurted, squeezing two of Steve's big fingers in her own mottled fist.

'What's wrong with that?' I said, grinning, and turning to Cathy, who wasn't grinning, possibly because she wasn't drinking (she was driving us back to London), possibly because she didn't like casual references to our sex life suddenly materialising like a surprise guest on Jerry Springer.

Anyway it went on like this, with Vicky seething and claret-faced, as if the wine had *literally* gone to her head, and Steve puffing on a small cigar. By the way, Steve, who had been clean-shaven and quite sanitary-looking when we arrived, had by this stage grown a field of black stubble and kept having to mop his big sweaty face with a napkin. I had this sudden disturbing image of him naked and fully-furred, climbing on top of Vicky, and I don't know if it was because it was almost midnight now but I felt a Cinderella-like urge to make a move before things turned ugly.

Odd, but in my mind's eye I'd always seen Vicky as very together and wry and knowing. Afterwards, when I thought about her, she was always in that doorway waving us off with Steve's ape silhouette towering behind her with his head in the chandelier. It was all very bad. Cathy didn't say anything as we pulled away, not even when we got on to the motorway. Obviously I was really happy for Vicky and her new romance, but to be honest I couldn't see it lasting as long as the next afternoon, and thought at least one of us ought to be busy casting doubt on the enterprise. 'Just wait till he finds out how old she is,' I chuckled.

I could tell as soon as I'd opened my mouth that something was ticking over. 'You really are a shit sometimes,' she said eventually. This was a full minute later, and she could I suppose have been referring to anything, and I really couldn't be bothered to find out what, which was a slight bore because, of course, it then looked as though I'd accepted that she might have a point.

Ruth was at Eamonn's. Ruth. She couldn't be. Shouldn't be. But Jane was standing there at her desk taking off her coat telling me she was, so it must be true. She'd just seen her. Just now.

'Is she still there?' I had the three o'clock page deadline at the back of my mind, but the front of my mind was already busy trying to guess where Ruth-at-Eamonn's was staying tonight, and whether this was a day I would have sex with her. (You might ask what I was *thinking* of, but that would have been the answer. The rest was a blur of anticipation.)

Jane shook off the drizzle of outdoors and unloaded her lunchtime purchases on to her desk – a takeaway from Pret a Manger, bags from Boots, the Body Shop. 'I don't know,' she said. 'I saw her wandering about in reception earlier when you were out and then I saw her again ten minutes ago, through the window at Eamonn's.'

'In reception? Why is there no message? Are you sure it was her?'

'The girl you were showing round the other week, from up north? Ruth, right? Weren't you expecting her?' Jane took a plastic fork to a gluey parcel of raw fish and plugged it into her mouth for a big chew.

'Yes. Well. She said she might call in. If she was in town.' A grin sprang to my face. Jane shrugged. I pulled on my jacket. 'I suppose I'd better go and find her,' I muttered as nonchalantly as my clumping heart would allow. Isabel held me up with a proof that needed initialling. 'I've got to go out – five, maybe twenty minutes,' I said. 'Send the pages if you have to.'

Isabel opened her mouth.

'Don't worry, I'll be back.'

At the front doors Jeremy was coming back from lunch with some of the marketing people. I nodded hi and stepped to one side but Jeremy halted and turned. 'Oh Matt, I saw your young friend this morning . . .'

'Oh yes, thanks – it's OK, I'm on my way now,' I said, waving over my shoulder, hurrying on, up the street and across the road towards St John's Street. How come everybody had seen her except me? I was confused. Why hadn't she rung ahead, or left a message when she found I was out?

I reached Eamonn's, catching sight of my puffy, breathless face and damp hair in the window as I stepped inside. I stood for a moment and took in the mildly surprised expression in Ruth's eyes and then the half-comic beckoning of Alex, who was sitting at the other side of the small table they were sharing, a bottle of wine between them, empty plates, pepper, mustard pot. 'Mattie . . .' Alex was calling and gesturing with a sweep of his arm.

I went over, looking at Alex, then at Ruth.

'Hi,' said Ruth, raising her hand in a little wave. She didn't stand up.

'Get yourself a glass from the bar,' said Alex. 'We might need another bottle of this?' Alex didn't know anything, which was good, but also bad, because there was now no chance he would just fuck off and leave us to it.

'I can't stay, I er . . .' I turned to Ruth. 'Jane said you were here.'

'Yes, I saw her.'

'Don't worry, Matt,' said Alex, 'I've been taking care of my new friend from the north, haven't I, Ruth?'

I ignored him and looked at her. 'Are you staying in town?'

'I am,' she said coolly.

'With a friend or?'

'Tell you what,' she said. 'Why don't I give you a ring at some point?'

'OK,' I said, finding myself nodding. 'Super.'

At some point. We looked at each other for a long moment, me hoping for a sign, Ruth in the guise of someone I might have known slightly from a previous job and nothing more, someone who might give me the time of day but not her phone number. But was she in character? Was she playing a part too well, or not at all? It was clear that my finding her here had nothing to do with her needing to be looked for. She showed no indication of needing to be extricated from Alex's serial joshing. From my earlier giddy excitement and morbid anxiety – about being tripped up, found out, about her suddenly arriving on my doorstep, and yet needing to see her in a way I would have thought pathetic in anyone else in my position – I suddenly felt like an idiot standing there with damp hair, not being able to speak freely, or explain for Alex's benefit why I had left my desk with a deadline looming to dash up here in the rain to see an old casual acquaintance who meant nothing to me in particular and then not even stay for a drink. And, in any case, what *was* my position exactly?

Alex himself was in no hurry. He'd filed his fifteen hundred words before lunch. There was no pressing need for him to go back to the office, and therefore no pressing need to leave Eamonn's. 'Well?' he was saying, holding up the bottle.

Ruth smiled. 'Why not?'

I stayed for a moment then left, telling *her* in a disinterested way to give me a call some time. I stood across the street on the corner, watching the door. By the time I got back to the office, my section had gone.

'Where have you been?' Isabel said. 'I had to send the pages.'

'Sorry,' I said. 'I needed to do some stuff. You know.'

I looked blankly at the proofs she put in front of me and said they were fine. I spent the rest of the day watching for Alex, but he didn't come back. The next day and the one after that, I waited for a call, checked my e-mail with pathological regularity. Alex came and went with a smile on his face and said nothing about Ruth. It was Jane who told me a couple of days later that, incidentally, Ruth had apparently been in on the morning of Eamonn's because she'd had an appointment to see Jeremy. According to Jeremy's indiscreet secretary Geri, Ruth had rung on spec with a couple of ideas for features and he'd invited her into the office for a chat. I left another message on her answerphone. On Tuesday there was an e-mail at the office. Not from the *Echo*. Just a set of initials at an AOL address. I felt my skin warm and the swell of nausea from inside as I read it, not moving, my eyes taking it in and yet not taking it in. 'Matt, I think it's probably best if . . .' the message began. It finished with R. No kisses.

falling

I closed the front door quietly behind me, stepped out into the street and broke into a slow run. My first ever run. Or at least my first ever voluntary run. My first ever voluntary run not designed to get me to the bus stop before the bus pulled away, or to a train before it left or to an already breasted, broken and fluttering white ribbon tied to a distant winning post in the fathers' race (tenth out of twelve) one windy sports day at St Bede's, with Sadie (thirteen) on the sidelines squealing with embarrassment.

So. My first ever voluntary run with no clear impetus, point, or negligible chance of a silver cup. The kind of run that would draw attention to itself with its lack of experience, its uncertain attempts to determine a comfortable pace, elbow position, angle of upper body, tilt of head, all aimed not necessarily, I realised, at efficiency or ease of execution but the basic appearance of those things to regular street users who were hurrying less ostentatiously about their business, people who were (in the normal run of things) blind to practised joggers-about-town but would divert their gaze at the spectacle of a ridiculous puffing billy on the crisp horizon, in the same way that sharks can detect the false beat of a struggling fish two oceans away. I saw the movement of my electric blue and gold Adidas trainers beneath me slapping against the pavement, my lumpy knees not quite bumping into each other, and felt the effort of my lungs already wondering what the fuck was happening. I turned into the refuge of the park, a forgiving place of singular pursuits that explained to casual onlookers the mystery of someone not wearing trousers in public or carrying a baseball bat. I banished with an intake of frosty air a possibly unwarranted image of the rapacious Alex, engaged with Ruth in some indistinct carnal act, as I passed the empty skateboarders' rink.

I had no route in mind. I set off for the trees at the far side, dimly aware of lone dog-walkers, a homeless person, teenage schoolboys determinedly without coats on taking their time about taking a short cut, a fellow jogger – the only other visible – at a safe distance, passing the tennis courts and slowing for the incline back up the side of the field nearest the road. Running, I had read somewhere, raises your serotonin levels, though obviously, I thought, only if it doesn't kill you first. There was no history of fatal heart disease in my family, but it could start with me right now, pulling up suddenly, hand to my chest, losing radio contact with my legs, stumbling sidelong into the undergrowth, perhaps to be discovered by someone walking their dog, as dead bodies so often were. And then how would she feel? Indifferent, I imagined. Regretful at best. Not guilty for sure. Not her. Miss Ruth Appleton had been in the summerhouse with Alexei the groundsman when the fatal blow was struck and had enjoyed only marginal sexual dealings with the deceased, and even then only in the matter of a favour more than handsomely paid for in two equal instalments.

And Cathy, whom I could hardly bring myself to talk to ('What is *wrong* with you?'), who in the end had retreated from my impervious gloom, circling warily, attacking occasionally with sudden complaints about my spending ('And what *is* this – 34 Club £55, Chez Georges £62, cash £150 . . . Matt?'). I couldn't know what her senses told her and she couldn't confront me with what it was. She couldn't accuse. It only had the appearance of something. That was the trouble with instinct. It was just the first stage; and of course Cathy needed to get closer to the detail. I had once asked how she taught her sixth-formers English Lit. I asked out of politeness because she had once accused me of not taking an interest in what she did, as though teaching was somehow less important than covering council meetings for the *Echo*, she'd said. But then she'd looked at the ceiling for a moment before she answered me, even though she must have known what she was going to say, because once she'd said it it was obvious she'd said it before – in a classroom, I imagined, full of her adoring girls – so what was it, this gauche attempt to turn routine into spontaneity? Whatever it was, it made me warm to her need and made me feel bad for asking out of politeness and not genuine interest. 'Take what you feel, then say what you think,' she said. She drew me a diagram marked 'text' and 'first impressions' and 'analysis' and 'thesis' and arrows linking one thing to the other. 'Of course,' she says, 'you can prove whatever you want, really.' So here she was now, looking at first impressions and saying what she thought. Or some of what she thought. 'Matt, what is it – work?' she said. 'Are you unhappy? I thought you liked it here. We could go back to Yorkshire. There's no shame, you know . . .' I shook my head. 'I'm fine.' ('Is it money? Gambling? What? What?') Gambling! She didn't have any other vices to suggest. Murder, perhaps. Embezzlement. Though not the other thing.

'It's nothing,' I said, raising myself as far as politeness, with its implications of feigned interest. 'I'm fine. Just feeling a bit low.'

But my brooding sighs filled the space between us, emptying it of possibility. I couldn't do anything about it.

And then Sadie, so oddly radiant now I had stopped saying no to everything that she hardly noticed the billowing cumulonimbus above my head when she came to me with some triumphant pronouncement of forthcoming events on her young person's social calendar or to twirl in her new giraffe-skin microskirt or display her triply pierced navel ('Everybody in the school has got three, Mum. Dad doesn't mind . . .') before racing away, happy enough in her sealed world of happiness to take my unchanging countenance for approval or at least an absence of its opposite.

Running was good for your serotonin levels. Running made you slightly happier than not running. Scientists said that elation and obsession and depression all came out of the same reservoir of chemicals, which was sometimes overflowing or sometimes not full enough. Loving someone and being dumped by someone were the same thing. They called it 'over-valuing an idea'. What a brilliant thought. It was true. Once, here was a woman hot to the touch, and now she was an idea. Ruth the Idea. I accepted that. But there were some ideas you couldn't get out of your head. I stopped to take in oxygen at the tennis courts, and walked up the slope, past the little café, boarded up until the spring, past the fountain, past a woman without a dog coming the opposite way. She was in her fifties, and in her I momentarily saw myself in ten or fifteen years' time, when I would be her age, when Ellie would be Sadie's age, when Sadie would be Ruth's age, when Ruth would be my age. I caught her wary eye as she hurried by, taking in my appearance, my bare legs, my dampness. Not a pervert. Just someone who couldn't run very far. But tomorrow I'd run a bit further, then the next day further still. How many miles could it take before I was so happy that I'd be back to what used to be normal and as far from a pervert as you could be – back to loving my wife without thinking about it, happy to be moaning at having to get up at four to change Ellie's nappy, and laying down the law to my eldest daughter about tattoos? How many miles before I cared enough to even want to get back to that level of happiness?

'I was talking to Laura Farrow this morning.'

She was standing at the window with her back to me. I was sitting in an armchair, an empty coffee cup on the table beside me, my head in the *Guardian*. 'What did she say?'

I sensed Cathy turning, appraising, her head at a critical slant, turning for effect. 'That's an odd response. Why not *how is she?*'

'OK. How is she?' I didn't look up.

'She said Mike told her you were seen out in Leeds.'

'Seen by who?'

'Don't you want to know who you were seen with?'

'OK, who?' I noticed Cathy's breathing. She was controlling her breathing as she paused.

'Tony saw you. He told Mike. Tony services Mike's car. I thought you might have worked that out at least.'

I was silent for a moment. 'So? Dean used to service that car. I don't know what he's trying to prove, driving a ridiculous car like that at his age.'

'He said you were in a hotel bar with some woman.' She paused. 'Ruth, was it?'

I lowered the newspaper to my lap, the better to put the challenge in my eye and not my voice, the better to be not caught looking astonished at whatever stage illusionist's trick this was that could, without the use of mirrors, lift a name so cleanly from my own mind and transfer it to my wife's lips. 'Tony told Mike who told Laura I was with some woman called Ruth?'

'Well, were you?'

'You mean it was such a big deal that he remembered she was called Ruth and then told Mike who told Laura?'

'No. And I didn't say it was a big deal. I'm just asking.'

'What do you mean *no*?'

'I mean Laura didn't tell me she was called Ruth. I'm asking if that's who it was.'

'Fine. So if he didn't tell you, how come you've decided it *was* someone called Ruth?'

She paused again. 'Because someone called Ruth's *number* is all over our telephone bill.'

'*All* over the phone bill?'

'So I rang the number. A Leeds number. *Hi, this is Ruth . . .*' Cathy had clearly planned to go through this slowly and calmly but she had blown it with her exaggeration of Ruth's voice, the involuntary nod of her head that followed, sending the ball spinning into my court, the tremor in her voice that took her to the brink of something that suddenly *was* a big deal.

I skewed my mouth to one side. Being patient. Indulging her. Humouring her. Waiting for her. Making sure she'd finished saying her piece. Being fair about that. Because there was nothing to worry about and she was being foolish, and if there was something, well to hell with it. 'So what are you saying?' I said. 'The woman works for the *Echo*. We met for a drink. We talked about work. I gave her some names that might be useful to her.'

'In a hotel you did this. When your dad was ill. When your dad was lying in hospital.'

I rolled my eyes. I got to my feet and dropped the newspaper into the chair. 'I really don't have the energy for all this.'

'Tell me nothing happened,' she said suddenly.

I looked at her, shaking my head, my eyes incredulous and pitying. As if not believing she could ask that. As if pitying her being so unaccountably untrusting out of the blue.

'It wasn't a hotel, it was a hotel bar.'

'Tell me you were back at your mother's the same evening.'

'Nothing happened.' I looked to a corner of the ceiling where a cobweb swayed in the air, suspended in the agitated current of what was going on.

'Tell me you were back at your *mother's*.'

'Nothing *happened*.'

'Look at me!' There were tears in her eyes, and she looked at me, looked right into me.

Then I knew what she knew, and knew it didn't look good. But it wasn't photographs. It wasn't DNA. 'Oh, for Christ's sake. It's Vicky isn't it? What did she say? You know she's fucking deranged at the moment.' I waved my arm in a lame gesture of impatience. 'What did she say? Come on.'

'That was her, wasn't it? At the theatre. That was her. I'm not stupid, Matt.'

'What are you talking about?'

'I'm talking about there's no such fucking PR company as Tapir. That's what I'm talking about. There's no Tapir running corporate hospitality, and no fucking *Helen*.'

Helen?

'Look at you. You don't even remember, do you? You said her name was Helen. God, you're pathetic. I really don't know who you are any more.'

The dog ran into the room, sensing strangeness if not strangers, barking, sniffing, hunting under the table, clamping her jaws eventually in puzzled disappointment, tail hitting the chair legs. Ellie was crying upstairs. I opened my mouth to speak, but I had lost my bearings and could only stare blankly at the course of my lies suddenly dividing off and running in different directions. Cathy turned and left the room before I could decide which lie led to the higher ground of not having to deal with something.

December the first. I sat on the edge of Caroline's desk and started leafing through a magazine, not looking, just turning the pages. Caroline was on the phone. She raised her eyebrows at me in a neutral gesture that could have meant 'hang on a minute' or 'not you again'. Alex passed by, singing something, grinning. I ignored him. Caroline put the phone down and picked it up again and started dialling. 'What's he so happy about?' she said, staring past me across the office.

'Is he happy?' I said. Alex was leaning into the fashion cupboard chatting and laughing too loud. I watched. My empty stomach churned with an unwelcome thought.

Caroline waited with the phone in her hand for someone who wasn't there, then put it down with a sigh. 'What can I do you for, Matt?' she said, taking the magazine off me and putting it back on her pile of magazines.

'I was wondering about someone. Ruth Appleton. Ring a bell?' I said. 'Freelance?' I picked up a Christmas snow-scene paperweight sent by a PR and gave it a shake, putting an eye to the curve of perspex and watching the little squall of flakes swirl and settle around a thumb-sized Canary Wharf tower inside. I shook it again.

'Yes,' Caroline said without evident interest. 'Someone Jeremy knows. He sent me her CV and a couple of features she's written. Why – who is she? Why do we care?'

'Are you going to use her?' I peered into the chunky hemisphere and watched the snow teem and fall, then shook it again.

Caroline took the paperweight off me with a polite grimace and balanced it on a stack of undealt-with mail and PR handouts and press releases. 'No idea. I haven't had time to look at it yet. My guess is not. Jeremy's always sending me rubbish to look at. Makes him feel useful.'

'I heard you and he were the best of friends,' I said.

She swept her hair back behind her ears and sighed. 'Do we have any other business, Matt? I'm a bit pushed . . . season of goodwill and all that.'

I went back to my desk and signed off the pages Isabel and Isobel had piled up for me, scanning the detail cursorily, not wishing at this stage in my life to see a picture of Billy Crystal above a caption describing him as Billy Joel, which statistically could easily happen. After five minutes I snatched up the phone and called Ruth's number, hardly breathing, tapping my pencil on my mousemat. I waited for the answerphone to kick in and the now faintly mocking invitation to leave a message and that she would get back to whoever I was. I spoke quietly, aiming to set my tone at a casual, jocular pitch, or at least not one that sounded hollow, desperate, calculating, rushed, needy. 'Hello, it's Matt. Look, Ruth, I really do think you owe me a call. And, you know, obviously I don't want to get a reputation as a sex-pest or anything, but I would like a quick chat, if that's not madly out of the question. Bye.' I hadn't rung in a week. I wouldn't ring again. That was it. I didn't want her back or anything. That wasn't it. All I wanted was . . . What I wanted was closure. *Closure*. Listen to it. A word to do with therapy and psychiatrists, a word seized upon by Hollywood screenwriters and opinion-formers and sent out into the world to spread the word about itself until everyone was using it. Closure was a handshake, a funeral, a signature, an end-of-term report with marks out of a hundred, an explanation offered or expected for ungracious behaviour, your own or someone else's. It was the opposite of dangling from a tree at the end of the movie with the credits rolling and your parachute still in the branches. It was coming down to land, even with a bump. The Americans saw a gap in the market and invented a new word. Closure. Brilliant.

Alex was meandering between the desks. 'I get no kick from champagne . . .' he was singing.

'He'll get a kick from me in a minute,' Isabel muttered.

'Cheer up, Mattie, my old mucktub,' he said, sauntering over.

I swivelled my chair and rolled it against the books cabinet to avoid a fatuous slap on the back. 'Cheer up?' I said coldly. 'But then there'd be two of us going round annoying everybody.'

'Sorry, mate, can't help it.' He leaned towards me. 'A new someone special in my life.' He looked over my head as he whispered. 'Can't divulge. Not one to trumpet my sexual conquests all over the office. Not after the first date anyway.' He winked. 'Especially those involving a mutual acquaintance.'

Somehow I was on my feet. 'Why don't you just fucking grow up,' I said. I thought I'd merely said it. But it was louder than that and my finger was prodding Alex in the chest. And now I was aware of a time-lapse, a silence while the ball travels through the air in slow motion before it hits the basket in high-school movies, aware of Milo standing up with his pen in his mouth to see what was going *down*, of Jane's eyes following me, of one secretary murmuring to another, of Jeremy a mile upstream of me, a broadsheet page lowered, looking over, wondering at the raised voice, or the vacuum of quiet that followed, sucking everyone's attention behind it like the opposite of an echo.

'*Fuck* this,' I muttered, finding myself striding off towards nowhere in particular. 'Just *fuck* it,' though I could not say what in particular should be fucked. Everything perhaps. Why couldn't Alex have kept his mouth shut and let doubt prevail; let there still be a chance that he and Ruth weren't, hadn't . . .

But it was out now and you couldn't get toothpaste back into the tube. (Bad secondhand words, but this was no time to think of new ones.) Fuck him. Fuck her.

'Matt, it's Ruth.' A voice that meant business.

'Oh. Hi, I didn't . . .'

'Don't say anything, Matt. I really don't want to hear it. I'm not ringing to give you a chance to have a conversation. I'm just ringing to say I'm bloody annoyed. I'm ringing to tell you that, actually, I have absolutely *nothing* to explain. You have no rights here. You're not married to me. We had two one-night stands and by definition that's one too many. I don't *owe* you anything. OK?'

'I'm not saying that. I'm saying . . . Look, I brought you in, showed you round, introduced you to Jeremy. Didn't I give you his number?'

'Yes, and obviously I'm really grateful that you spared half an hour of your valuable time for a young nobody from nowhere. But then – hang on a minute – didn't we go out and have a nice evening? In fact, didn't we even sleep together? I'm not saying I didn't enjoy it or anything but, I mean, how many times do I have to say thank you?'

There was an embarrassed pause, her anger dissolving into the hum of silence like the fizz from an open bottle, leaving nothing to say that wouldn't sound anticlimactic or conciliatory or apologetic. I spoke first. 'I just think you might have mentioned that you'd been to the office. I mean that Jeremy had agreed to see you. That sounds quite promising by the way,' I added weakly.

'Look Matt,' she said, weary not wary now. 'I don't *want* you to take an interest. You're not my uncle – it's too late for that now. OK, yes, if you'd been around, we'd probably have gone for a drink. But you weren't. We didn't.'

'You'd already gone for one, of course.'

'There's really no need for this, Matt. You're a married man, I'm a free agent. It's not a big deal. The truth is I don't have any lasting feelings about it. It never happened, OK?'

'I'm . . . I'm not asking for anything,' I stuttered. *Married man*. That was me. 'I'm not even asking who you're sleeping with,' I said.

It was a stupid thing to say, like a last, desperate, pathetic shot from the halfway line against the run of play. I saw her standing her ground, calmly waiting for it to sail high into the crowd behind the goal.

'So, no more calls?' she said at last.

I thought of our first meeting here in this office. Me on top. Her underneath. It was amazing how half an hour of sex could change everything so quickly and irreversibly.

Cathy had had her hair cropped and dyed red. She had stopped wearing her wedding ring. Her movements and speech had become brisk and efficient. She clattered pots and pans in my presence. 'Sort out your life,' she said. 'But don't ruin Sadie's, like my father ruined mine.' She handed me a letter from the bank and a clip of bills. 'And you can sort these out too.'

I had come through that first unresolved row, and the others that followed, similar in tone, almost with an air of detachment, even sometimes puzzlement; wondering, as we sparred pointlessly, at the way proceedings seemed so uncannily to be not exclusively ours but rather to resemble the rows you saw on TV or read on a page; as though, with no experience of our own to call upon, we had reached for the staple conceits of melodrama and popular fiction. A row of marriage-breaking proportions seemed to demand its own staging and frequency and wavelength and script. But where to get all that at short notice? Cathy had not yet torn into my wardrobe with her theatrical costumier's shears – the green shirt and charcoal grey suit from Next that had been draped over a chair of a room smelling of sex at the Ivory Gardens were still intact. No one had taken a hammer to my Ringo Starr eggcup. But she *had* shouted: 'I don't know who you are any more!' Worse, she had called me a bastard and a shit – not her kind of words at all, but ones learnt elsewhere – words out on loan from a communal repository of abuse. I felt ashamed that I had driven her to use language whose power to shock lay only in its banality.

Our communications had dwindled to curt exchanges of information. Bev was in constant attendance, filling the kitchen with unspoken contempt whenever I entered. I ate at Eamonn's. I came home late and kept to my side of the barbed wire in bed or slept in my attic room, surrounded by Dean and the Beatles and the dust of my life. We kept up appearances for Sadie. 'Don't you think Mum's hair looks great, Dad?' she said, bouncing into the room and kissing my cheek before disappearing for a sleepover at Jade's, snatching a banana or a pear from the fruit bowl as she skipped by.

I saw myself in a series of vignettes: Matt at the office, maintaining a one-sided feud with Alex, who carried on as though nothing had happened; Matt betraying no sign of surprise (though I was surprised and felt an idiot for not guessing) when Jane told me, in passing, that Milo's primary function at the *Post* was to keep Jeremy supplied with recreational drugs and (less predictably) to get him VIP tickets for boxing matches, where the proximity of sweat, violence and criminal types allowed him to imagine himself at the very heart of real newspaperly endeavour; Matt seeing Caroline coming out of a restaurant in tears and crossing the road to avoid her; Matt ploughing his way through the week and his work like someone going down with an illness or recovering from an accident; Matt coming home drunk and confronting Cathy in the kitchen with the photograph of herself, pregnant, in the garden; Matt coming to regret it . . .

'Remember this?'

'*What?*' she said impatiently. 'What are you talking about now? What is there to remember?'

'See the shape?' I was about to be rambling and pathetic. I knew deep down, even as I spoke, that I was about to do a terrible thing. To my wife. To the memory of my dead friend. Something to make something happen. 'Look, that's Dean's camera. Dean had this picture in his special drawer with his Beatles stuff. Why does he keep a photograph of you pregnant in his special drawer? Why are you looking so annoyed in this photograph? Look at your face. Think back.'

'What's your point, Matt?' she said wearily.

'Had you had a . . . *row*?' I left the word hanging there like a challenge, a meaty lump of sneery sarcasm, dripping blood, to snap at if she dare.

'What do you mean?'

'You and him. Were you?'

She looked at me. 'Were we what?' Then she gave a mirthless laugh. 'Oh, *please*. I cannot believe you're stooping to this. What – Ellie was Dean's baby? No. You're insane. When did you dream this one up?'

'Why not? You slept with him before you slept with me.'

'Yes, once. A lifetime ago. I mean how *dare* you drag that up!'

'Once?'

'For God's sake, Matt, this isn't about me, it's about you. Dean wasn't in my life, he was in yours. Dean was a child. He didn't want to grow up. We never had anything to say to each other.'

'So what's this about?'

'*Nothing*. It's not about anything. It doesn't have a narrative. I can't remember. It's not important. Now just fuck off and leave me alone, Matt. You're drunk.'

I slumped in the chair, my head in my hands.

I expected Cathy to go, but she hovered nearby, and then finally spoke again. 'If you must know, he'd got some poor idiot girl pregnant.'

I looked up. 'Who? What girl?'

'Some girl he'd been going out with was having his baby and he wanted her to get rid of it. She didn't want to, and I had a go at him about it. That's it. That's all. I don't know who she was. I don't know what happened afterwards. It was only a few weeks before the accident.'

I looked at Cathy, and then at my shoes.

She inhaled deeply through her nostrils and rolled her eyes towards the ceiling. 'He was waiting for you to arrive. As usual. But he was winding me up about how pointless having children was, how they ruin your life. Look at you two, he said, having to start all over again just when Sadie's old enough to fend for herself. Of course I was bloody annoyed at him. There I was, six and a half months pregnant and he's giving me this . . . this, this *rubbish*! I didn't want to hear it. He took a photograph of me. I have no idea why – probably because I was annoyed and he wanted to annoy me more. Then he came out with it. About the girl and the baby. I didn't want to hear it. I don't know why he told me. I don't care.'

'Why didn't you tell me?'

Cathy looked suddenly defeated. 'Because you would have been mad at him for upsetting me, and I just didn't want the responsibility and the hassle of it.'

I felt tears welling up in my eyes. I looked at her.

'Oh for God's sake go to bed,' she said.

I was sitting in the almost empty downstairs bar of The 34 in yesterday's shirt. Milo was ten feet away in the corner talking on his mobile, listening and nodding, looking at the big ceiling fan turning, smoking a roll-up, every now and then scooping a handful of salted cashews from the bowl on the counter. I hadn't planned this, had no reason to be here (though I had no reason to be anywhere else), but Milo had insisted, recalling vaguely my interest in coming here weeks ago, taking vaguely into account my low spirits, dismissing vaguely my vaguely formed intention of seeing a film after work. 'Yeah, what film?' Milo had said. I sighed, shook my head. 'Come to The 34 instead. Got to see a couple of people there. Few beers. Music. Et cetera. Be great. Come on, we'll get a cab . . .'

Jackie Wilson came muted over the sound system, following Dusty, Georgie Fame, the Everlys, Traffic, the Nice. Milo was squinting impatiently at his mobile now, cigarette still drooping from his lips, prodding buttons, trying to get a function to function. He came to sit down, slid the mobile across the table with disgust and grinned. We talked about office politics, office philosophy, office economics. We talked about the logistics of

Jeremy having Caroline over the photocopier in the confined space of the archive room on the second floor.

'She was in tears last week,' I said.

'He strings her along. Married, you know. Well, separated. Two kids, twenty-four-hour nanny to pay for.'

'Who, Caroline?'

'Ha! No, Jeremy. You wouldn't guess. Did you know that the average middle-class professional man spends twice as much of his leisure time out of the home as the average woman in the same line of work? In fact did you know the average professional male spends thirty-six minutes a day in a place of refreshment?'

'I think you might have mentioned it.'

'They eat out more. Presumably with their non-middle-class secretaries. Not Jeremy I don't mean.' He waved his hand, dismissing whatever it was he did mean. 'Can't understand some people doing marriage. Kids. All that. A lot of people just aren't built for it. What do you think?'

I shook my head. Dean surfaced in my mind. Dean wasn't built for it, but what about the girl? What about the baby she was having? I drummed my fingers to 'Oh Happy Day' on the arm of the sofa, looking. 'What's Alex's story?' I said, turning. I felt my stomach tighten as I asked. 'Speaking of men and their leisure time.'

'Ah. Well, you know his wife left him. Tragic. Walked out one day after a couple of years. No explanation. Pretty hard to take, I think, him not really understanding why. Rejection, you know. And now every few months or so he falls for some poor doe-eyed student journalist or other hopeful he finds hanging out at Eamonn's.' He laughed. 'Then he walks around the office whistling tunes and singing and telling jokes. Until all of a sudden . . . *Puh*!'

'Puh?'

Milo upturned his thumb as he drained his glass. 'That's what'll happen with Amy. Give it another week. You can't tell of course. Alex is a secret depressive. That's why he seems so cheerful. Denial. Probably cries himself to sleep, is my guess, every night.'

'Amy?'

'Yeah, Amy. From fashion. Amy.'

'Alex is seeing Amy from fashion?'

'*Shagging* Amy from fashion. According to Jane. Who knows all. Beer?' He pointed at the glass in my hand.

'Oh God.' I shut my eyes, resting my fist against the bridge of my nose.

Milo punched my shoulder. 'Don't worry. He'll get over it.'

We drank. Milo regaled me with more anecdotes from his lost years on the music press in the early '70s on tour with Rod and Genesis and Queen. 'Queen were the business,' Milo told me, waving at someone passing through the bar. 'Course, that was before they became a comedy act and made a shitload of money.' He stubbed his cigarette out. I told him I thought my marriage might be collapsing. Milo nodded, gulped down another beer and wondered whether I had ever read *Diary of a Rock and Roll Star*, which he was re-reading and was a quite funny book for its time, about Mott the Hoople gigging round the States buying up cheap vintage Strats and Les Paul Juniors in pawn shops. Milo absented himself sporadically, perhaps to procure drugs for a network of media chums, and had been away for twenty minutes when Lawrence rolled in some time after nine-thirty, trailing his rambling entourage of Penelope, Graham, Claricia, and parked himself near the low-tinkling piano. I saw him beginning to scan the room but I avoided his eyes and swivelled towards the bar, my arm resting on the back of the chair. I didn't want anything more to do with Lawrence or Penelope, though if that was true what the fuck was I doing here? There were more alternatives than this to going home. And few more likely to make things worse. 'Hey, Matt.' Lawrence was motioning. I took a last glance around for Milo. 'Hey-ee,' Lawrence said. He was drunk. 'Hey-ee,' Graham repeated. I got up and went over. Penelope patted the cushion beside her. They'd come straight from a book launch in Piccadilly for one of Penelope's clients. She was wearing the black dress or a similar one, her hair up, peroxide wisps escaping from a silver grip. The conversation turned on Lawrence's favourite obsessions, sliding in a familiar pattern from gentle ribbing into something else. Penelope sat close to me, her crossed legs leaning against mine, purring, pouring drinks, topping up, going to the machine for cigarettes. 'I hear you've been spotted at the opera, Matt,' Lawrence said loudly. Penelope tugged Lawrence's ear with mock disapproval as she passed. He turned and laughed. The others laughed. I said nothing. 'Seriously, though, I have to say I do envy your happy domicile. Very nice. Cathy, young Sadie. Nice. How are things? Blissful, perfect, idyllic, restful?'

I blinked a signal of mild annoyance, then offered a thin-lipped smile. 'You guessed it.'

Penelope returned and collapsed on to the sofa beside me again, her eyes glittering with unaccountable mirth. 'What's so funny?' I said.

'Tell me I'm wrong here, Matt,' Lawrence was saying. 'Sex. Married sex. Trouble is, it gets to the point where every time you do it it reminds you of all the millions of times you don't, right? Puts you off, in a way. It's like any performance. You need to get a run together to settle in. Otherwise it's first-night nerves every time? Except you haven't got the adrenalin and excitement of a real first night. Just the dread. Isn't that right, Matt? And *that's* why.'

I smiled, as if pityingly, and shook my head, glancing at the others, but their eyes were on Lawrence.

'Point being, there's so many women and so little time,' he was saying. 'We can't help it. Darwinian impulse. Evolutionary necessity. Survival of the fittest sperm.'

Graham cackled and blew smoke at the ceiling. 'Best swimmers.'

'Don't take my word for it, ask the apes,' Lawrence said.

'We don't have to be apes,' I replied. Penelope was idly twirling my hair, ironic, teasing. I could smell her. I could be an ape. All I had to do was gibber and make a grab for it. 'We do have a choice,' I added, remembering that I had never actually, positively fancied her. I tried to remember the black hairs sticking out of her nose and the dry trail of saliva as she lay half asleep.

Lawrence rolled his eyes comically towards Penelope. 'Aha! But do we choose wisely? And if not, why not? Sociologists tell us that men are more willing to have sex with a total stranger than take one out to lunch.'

I didn't say anything but I didn't move my head away from Penelope's ironic twirlings either.

'Of course,' Lawrence went on, 'alcohol helps. Or perhaps a mild non-prescription drug. Just enough to get a chap into a state where a sexual indiscretion can seem possible and amusing.' He stared at the table, as if reflecting, then looked up brightly. 'Matt, let me get you another.'

'No, I've had enough. Got to get home . . .' But I didn't move.

'Hey. Tell you what – come and see my office. I've got to pick up a little parcel,' Lawrence was saying. 'Five minutes from here. Come on. I'll show you round.'

He told Graham and Claricia to stay on at the club while Penelope and I followed him out. The cold air hit, made me aware of a sudden flush to my face, of the unwise switch from beer to wine. We walked quickly, Lawrence ahead, with the overcompensating gait of someone under the influence, talking loudly, Penelope clicking along in stilettos, hanging giddily on to my arm, her coat wrapped tight around her body, her body leaning heavily against mine, making me stumble and her laugh. We turned off the main road and descended into a half mews, stopped at the rear entrance of an incongruous beige-brick 1960s building sandwiched between redbrick mansion blocks. Penelope and I huddled together while Lawrence fumbled for his swipe card at the metal gate, the fine drizzle animating fuzzy halos round the street lamp overhead. We negotiated the short flight of stone steps to the basement, then another key and into the warmth of a lighted corridor. A suite of basement offices surrounded a recording studio with baffled walls, speakers, panelled room-separators. It was smartly high-tech and bore the sweepings, crud and recent odours of an evening session. Screwed-up notepaper. A pot of coffee, ashtrays, beer bottles, a towel draped over a door handle. Nicotine fumes clung to the furniture. Lawrence unlocked the door to a control room with swivel chairs and a vast mixing desk with pin lights on flexible stands. A cream leather couch just behind. Beyond, through the glass, were microphone stands reaching out into the empty space and cables along the floor. Lawrence disappeared and came back with a bottle of champagne and glasses. He poured, and reached overhead to pluck a blank CD from a rack stencilled 'masters'. He slotted it in. 'See what you think of this,' he said. 'Use the cans.' He handed me a set of headphones and touched the controls on the desk, winking at Penelope and pulling her towards the door. 'We won't be long.' I opened my mouth to speak but nothing came out. Penelope turned briefly, her deliriously laughing eyes empty of inhibition, regret – anything. She blew me a kiss and closed the door to follow Lawrence. The music kicked in, pulsing suddenly, the bass registers sending a thud to the base of my spine and back up again like the strongman ringing the bell with a hammer at a fairground. It was a species of modern dance music that I was happy to know nothing about. *Booosh, baboom, baboom, baboom, babooosh, baboom*. I thought about Penelope or rather her absence and took a luxuriant gulp of champagne and poured more, sending the fizzover sloshing across the desk, stretched out my feet and rested them on the console. I sighed, closed my eyes and allowed the rhythms under my defences, the high electronic hisses and low underbeats flooding into my ears and head and body, establishing a shape, repeating on and on, before switching to a new, subtly-altered shape and repeating again. I felt the room rotating and I blinked and sat up, one eye closed now, focusing with the other on the ceiling, concentrating on tracking my eyes against the direction of the movement one way and then the other, trying to balance clockwise against anticlockwise, like a car that you had stop from rolling backwards, using the accelerator, using the clutch, using the accelerator . . . But now the music plooped to a halt, and the untreated voice of the sound engineer or the producer broke in on the tape, mid-sentence. I narrowed my eyes to slits, aware of the dim space of the studio, a drum booth just visible from where I sat, the peak of a high-hat, cymbals, mounted tom-toms. 'Not quite there,' said the voice in the headphones. 'Let's run it through again. Ready?' A pause. 'OK, one . . . two . . . three . . . four . . .' I squinted, puzzled, my mind struggling with the queasy movement and the voice. The guitar and vocal came together. No intro. Straight in. I knew what it was almost before it had started. '*Yes*-terday . . .'

I blinked to clear my muddied head, alert to the song, which was already retrieving from my mind the echoing place where I had first heard this version, lying in the bath, the sound bouncing off the goldfish tiles. Hearing it so clearly now, through these deep, expensive monitors, crisp, loud, every breath audible, I knew it could not be – and therefore was not, and never had been – Bob Dylan. The idea was laughable. The guitar was hopelessly wrong – more wrong here than it had been through the ear-trumpet of my post-Ivory Gardens hangover – and the vocal . . . a near impersonation, but betrayed at this proximity as just that. That nasal whine, those line endings crudely flattened Dylan-style, McCartney's escalating melody cropped and detuned in a parody of that mumbled Dylan talk-sing. It went on to the end, my flustered senses taking in what it meant, but looking for a reason for it to be something else. Was I wrong? The engineer cut in at last, a rude tinny interruption at sharp variance with the tinkered mellow timbre of the song, like a metal grill opening and the sound of Lawrence shouting into a cell. Because Lawrence it was. 'Excellent, mate, that was great, terrific . . .'

The recording stopped with a reverberating clunk and as it did, and as I clumsily pulled off the headphones and readjusted my senses, I became aware of a rattle of percussion and, surmounting that, a counter-rhythm – *uht-uht-uuuuh* – the pant-and-moan overdub of a sexual act, not recorded but live. Out there. I suddenly realised and saw half in my mind's eye, half in the studio dimness, a faintly quivering high-hat, a busy arse or knee playing urgently against the splayed chrome tripod of its stand. Lawrence had left the mikes live. I could hear the pair of them now, full on, fully coupled. *Uht-uht-uuuuh* . . . A little echoing reverb on everything. Their little joke. Laughing as he enjoyed it, the joke, the sex.

I felt sick. I lurched to my feet, out, down the corridor, up the stone steps, out into the cold, a race against nausea. A woman in leather trousers waiting on the other footpath eyed me curiously for a moment as I hurried swaying up the mews in the cold, sleety drizzle. I was away, quickstepping through the late, cruising traffic, took a right at the next corner and a left and another left. Then I saw George Street and staggered down it, half realising that I had come a meandering circle, wondering for a moment why I knew it. George Street . . . Drunk with everything (drunk on the revelation that Alex and Ruth weren't an item even of the temporary kind, but drunk also with shame that it meant something to me when I knew the rule was that it should have meant nothing, and drunk with self-pity that, having let myself and others down, I too was let down and made a fool of), I found another street name I recognised and beyond that, another, yes. The club was back down that way and so this way should be . . . I stood on the corner just staring, rocking slightly, until my vision and the words on the sign locked together. City of Westminster. Montagu Square. Yes. I lurched forwards a few steps, fixing my eye on the numbers. Then I stopped. Number 34. The real 34. I bent forward to retrieve my wits and my breath, belched and went up the steps. No heritage plaque announcing the site of legendary happenings or marathon drugs binges. Just graffiti, pathetic in biro, on the paintwork. *Hendrix was here*. Well, yes, but McCartney. Lennon. Yoko too. The original cast. But wasn't it the basement? I stepped back down to the pavement, then opened the black iron gate, half falling, grabbing the rail as I went down. The blinds were down, grimy-looking. I tried to peer through. It was quiet. But there was a light in there or a reflection. I imagined them all back then, long-haired and successful, cross-legged on the floor swathed in the velvet and denim of the age, listening to demo tapes and nodding in silence as one or the other held forth on Agent Orange, capitalism, avant-garde literature. Perhaps Paulie would let them hear his embryonic 'Eleanor Rigby'. No strings attached. Just him on the guitar, the chords still new in his head, words yet to be hammered into shape. What joy in that. New song. *See what you think* . . . And, later, what excellent bollocks they must have talked with their dope and their joss-sticks burning and their LSD trips. What acts of cultural subversion planned here in the name of peace, love and enlightenment.

Above, the sound of a car braking, footsteps urgent on the path. 'Hey, what the *fuck* you doing down there?'

I looked up affably. A group of three, four men, standing at the gate silhouetted against the light, one already vaulting down the steps. I didn't get a chance to speak, just took a blow to my stomach that took the wind out of me. I doubled up, gagged, heard others arrive, jabbering in something foreign, Arabic, Turkish. They had hold of me, pulling me up the steps.

But then a girl's voice. 'Matt, Matt – what are you up to? Come on, we'll be late!' I looked up and saw nothing, but the grip on me relaxed.

'He's with you?'

'Sorry – he's a bit drunk.'

There was a white Merc with its engine running at the kerb with the radio or stereo going and something Middle Eastern keening sharply out of it and people on the pavement – a girl with her back to me who I didn't know arguing with three men in eastern clothes. I thought I saw Milo sauntering into view, but my stomach reacted first and I felt the tang of bile in my throat and I turned instinctively, leaning over, bent against the railings, heaving and retching uncontrollably.

'Fucking *hell*, man!' someone barked disgustedly.

Milo's voice came to me now. 'Tarik! Berhan! *Matt?* You guys know each other?'

'He's with you?' someone said.

I stared blankly into the mess of vomit steaming in the frost, a lariat of snot hanging from my nose. Someone offered me a tissue. I took the tissue and wiped my nose, my sleeve, the toe of my boot. I turned to find Tanya holding my arm. 'You okay?' she said.

'No,' I said, blinking at her. 'What are you doing here?' Milo came into view. 'Fuck.' I shook my head. 'Where did you spring from?'

Milo waved a hand casually, in the direction of back there, towards the brow of the mews I had started out from before arriving here drunkenly, circuitously. 'Had to run a small errand,' Milo was saying. 'I thought it was you. Don't worry about these chaps. Very nervous with strangers.' He sniffed. 'You can't be too careful round here.' The Arabs or Turks stood watching, dark, mustachioed, wearing chunky jewellery and lumberjack shirts, trainers, incongruous Ali Baba trousers. One of them spat on the ground and they all got back in the car.

'Let me get you back to the club,' Tanya said.

'No. No club,' I said.

'Coffee then.'

And then everything got worse.

The deal was that I would pay all the food bills (rent was right out of the question, no matter how much I protested) and occasionally pick up ready-to-eats from the M&S food hall or the Italian deli on my way back from the office. ('Here's the list – and make sure you get the pancetta, not the prosciutto.') I wasn't expected to cook, just to consume and to share my convalescent musings and to stack the dishwasher afterwards, all of which was no great hardship under my new regime of lunching in the canteen, drinking only moderately and leaving most of my earnings sitting in the bank for Cathy to squander as she saw fit in the absence of any formal financial arrangement, which she had yet to inaugurate via her legal appointees whose communication I awaited daily at the office with a leaden heart. A van arrived on Saturday during *Football Focus* with an experimental Internet order of organic vegetables, fruit for the bowl, lamb for the freezer. Otherwise the thing was to shop locally. ('That's the advantage of living in a village – all these brilliant little specialist bakeries and everything else right on your doorstep.') I twisted my mouth slightly, playing the doubter, a bulwark against enthusiasm, a monkish presence in this temple of light, not only because it suited my current mood of reflection and self-abnegation, but because someone had to do it. 'And Stoke Newington is a village in what sense, exactly?' I said.

'Stoke Newington? Hey, *Mattie* – Greater Islington, if you don't mind.'

I couldn't quite work out how someone as irritating as Alex could live in such a brilliant, spacious flat, with no clutter, or dog hairs, or smudges of make-up on the mirror, or stray nappies on the landing, or the latest flamenco-heeled orthopaedic boots from Miss Selfridge clogging up the doorway. Just seamless chrome living, with matching white sofas, cube storage, gadgets, beech floors, a staircase that bent upwards through the kitchen ceiling and a bathroom with the plumbing hidden away behind Moroccan tiles. And although the place was so fucking spotless and I felt like the slobby Walter Matthau half of *The Odd Couple* merely by taking up *space* here, Alex never once turned into Jack Lemmon – not when I replaced his Chemical Brothers CD (half of the first track played) in the rack under 'S'; not when I sent a small nut of butter looping into his four-slot Dualit toaster during a forceful gesture at breakfast concerning the respective merits of *Godfather*s *I* and *II*; not even when I dashed out to work leaving the shower running all day.

Milo was wrong about Alex. Not wrong about Amy from the fashion desk, whose ardour faded, as predicted, in reverse proportion to Alex's much-broadcast infatuation. But Alex was far from miserable ('Plenty more Amys in the sea, eh Matts?'), and seemed to get genuine pleasure out of trying to pull me from the mire of my own sorrows – me, who he had found trailing to a B&B in King's Cross with my guitar and a rucksack full of ironing. Jane, whom I had told, had immediately spilled all to Alex, against my unequivocal wishes. Alex, amazingly, had come after me, coat billowing in the wind, taken me back to his place, bathed my wounds, anointed my feet with oils, given me a beer and a fold-down designer bed in the spare room. I felt like weeping. In fact I did, more than once, though not with him around.

'What you need is another woman. You'd be amazed what a new sex life can do for your self-esteem. What about that girl Ruth from up north? Nice body. Quite bright. I would.' He gestured with a sweep of his arm. 'You're better off out of it, mate. Look at this. Peace and quiet, space to think, widescreen TV.'

'I'm not looking for another woman. I want my marriage back.'

'Well, how did you lose it?'

'How did you lose yours?'

Alex answered without a pause, cheerfully. 'Loved her too much. Too possessive. I think I've got the hang of it now.'

I shook my head. I shook my head a lot at that time. There was self-pity and there was self-loathing and there was the realisation that the very best I could hope for began with the terrible pins and needles of emotional recovery and a marriage that at best would only ever walk again with the aid of a stick. But it was the home-alone quiet of it here too. It was only when Alex was absent, the flat empty of his confident wittering, that I realised with horror that the price to be paid for all this bachelor loveliness – which I myself had pre-emptively forfeited by very astutely getting married and having children before I had the chance to contemplate material luxury – was the deathly stillness of solitude. There was no noise until you made some. Nothing moved unless you moved it. A teacup left on the stair would still be there fourteen years later if you, personally, didn't carry it into the kitchen. It was a numbing thought. What was it like for Alex suddenly to have someone around helping to fill the air with sighs and the occasional cough? Did Alex talk so much at the office by way of compensating for the lack of air currents at home?

'Come on, what happened, Matso?'

I shook my head. You could be touched by someone's kindness, I realised, and still be right to think it would be mad to tell them anything. So I didn't. Whatever there was to tell was too tainted with my own stupidity to bear the scrutiny even of those disposed to be sympathetic. Sex *was* like a terrible drug. It was something you believed in for as long as it was making thrilling promises, no matter how wild and unlikely. It made you do stupid things.

There was a story I'd read on the wires (there was always

one like this) – some halfwit picked up by the police for standing in a woman's garden in the middle of the night. It turns out she knows him, he's crazy about her, though not quite crazed. He's not really doing anything, just looking up at her bedroom window like some idiot dog pining at the graveside of its dead master. Naturally she doesn't want him there. Who is this guy? What is he up to? When did he stop being someone who just fancied the woman and start being some kind of hopeless stalker? Or worse: when does he stop being some kind of hopeless stalker and start being some sort of hopeless complete lunatic who might strangle her on the way home from her hen night? We don't get it. By definition, an overvalued idea is one nobody else will buy. But, in a parallel world, perhaps that could have been me standing there, outside Ruth's house, aching (there was no other word) with jealousy, looking for silhouettes at the window, perhaps urinating with devotional significance into her flowerbeds? I couldn't rule it out, though obviously I would draw the line at strangling. And then there was Penelope. Had I sought her out? No. Had I been truly in the market to shag other women? No. Had I always been the kind of man who looked at women in the street and wondered what they looked like naked? No. Admittedly, I was not entirely blameless in finding myself in the wrong bed at the wrong time and with the wrong kind of stimulants in my blood on that one particular unlucky night, suddenly free of scruple, suddenly willing to have sex with a stranger and even then only to keep up appearances in the pure guiltless light of anything goes. But how did I get from that to how it made me feel to have Penelope fucking Lawrence practically in front of me across a darkened studio? What was she to me? Had the market conditions changed so much? Had the seeds of letting Cathy down and making a twat of myself as a person formerly known as having principles been sown entirely by chance on that unending evening? Could I not have just walked away from that one-off experience and gone back to my old non-transgressing life? Or were there other forces at play? Ones that made it happen in the first place.

'You have to remember the manoeuvres Lawrence was making,' Tanya had said, when we were drinking coffee in a kebab house on Edgware Road in the aftermath of the Arab–Turk fiasco. 'Lawrence hates losing. He doesn't care how he wins, and he doesn't stop until he has. He sucked you in. I'm really sorry you got involved.'

'And how did *you* get involved?' I'd asked, holding my aching ribs.

She sipped her coffee and answered a different question. 'He made that Dylan recording in about half an hour with a musician friend, Luke, who hangs out at the studio. I was there. It seemed harmless enough. But he found a way into you through that. He had to have you.'

'Why?'

'Because of what you said you were. You stood for the opposite of what he is. It was like a challenge. You can't both be right, so he had to turn you into him. It's like alcoholics, or other kinds of addicts. They don't want to be judged. If everybody else is as bad as you, then nobody's bad, right?' She shrugged. 'That's what I think.'

That's what Tanya had said. I sat in the house when Alex was out Christmas shopping and listened to myself breathe. I didn't care about Christmas itself. I hadn't asked Alex about his plans, because it would seem that I was angling to figure in them in some way, which I wasn't. And I had none myself, though there was the question of telling Mum what had happened, adding to her burden of disappointments, adding to my burden of being disappointing. I would say it was my fault. She would guess why. And at Christmas too! she would say, if she said anything at all. And what about Sadie? I wished I knew. Though perhaps it was better I didn't. How many ways could you go wrong?

Tanya had gone on to sketch out the mechanics of my

duping, the anatomy of my folly: look at this; this is what happened at this point; these were the lies. It was almost amusing. Setting out to corrupt a person seemed otherworldly and anachronistic. Faustian. That was it. (Year One English Foundation Course, Oxford Poly.) You know you want it – that was the hook. It's what they did to Michelle Pfeiffer in *Dangerous Liaisons*, presumably because back then social death was brutal and permanent and therefore enormous fun for everybody else. But here it was – intrigue! – popping up in the digital age: no Dylan tape, no tragically dead keyboard-playing brother to match my own long-lost confrère. Of *course* – hadn't Lawrence had the Beatles conversation with Cathy? How could she not have mentioned Dean? (I thought of Dean now. That pregnant girl. His baby.)

'But in a way,' I said, 'Lawrence was already like me – I mean he'd already bought into marriage and the hearth and home and swimming pool. He said he loved all that too.'

'I'll tell you something. Off the record. Seriously.'

She waited for me to concur. I nodded, though I was hardly likely to advertise my own gullibility to the world for the sake of a story in the *Sunday Post*.

'Lawrence split from his wife and kids two years ago.'

'What? But on your programme . . .'

'I know. Let me tell you. Briefly. I knew Penelope at university. We shared halls in the first year. And when we started working in London, I'd bump into her occasionally. She was in PR, me in television. So when we were researching *Cheating Hearts* and I was casting around for possible subjects, she came up with Lawrence. He seemed plausible, convincing. He had a philosophy to share. He was confident. Articulate. Carried no guilt. He was perfect.' Tanya shrugged. 'But. Here's what I didn't know. Penelope was phenomenally badly into coke, and Lawrence was her Prince Charlie. So obviously she'd do practically anything for him, right? I got the feeling they'd had a relationship, but by the time I came along it was just drugs. Anyway, she introduced me to him socially, I got romantically involved, which I know was a mad thing to do – not least because of the wife and kids. But I liked him, and even when we had to go to The 34 and put up with that fool Graham and numerous other stiffs he got associated with, it was fun. Lawrence was fun. It was fun right up until the morning I got called in by the head of programming and told that they had evidence that the whole Lawrence story was a hoax. I couldn't believe it. And they could tell I knew nothing about it. So even then I could probably have saved my skin if . . .'

'If?'

'If they hadn't also found out that I was sleeping with him. So they fired me with a decent pay-off, tied to confidentiality.'

'So why did you carry on seeing him?'

'Well, he apologised, of course. Needless to say, I was incandescent. But he said it was just a kind of joke that had got out of hand. Then he helped me get a contract through someone at the BBC. Smoothed things over. And remember, we were pretty close by then. But, after that, once he'd won me over, he started getting cooler with me. We've been a bit semi-detached. I knew something was going on with you, and eventually Penelope told me what he was up to. She seemed to think it was hilarious. But things were getting sticky for him. His wife wasn't letting him see the kids. She was asking for more money. There were a lot of legal headaches. So he's doing more coke too. The two of them screwing tonight in his studio doesn't mean anything. It's the drugs. And the game they're playing . . . pathetic really. I probably won't see him again.'

'Probably?'

She shrugged.

The odd thing was, though, Tanya told me, that Lawrence had genuinely liked me. Probably still did. We had stuff in common. We were on a wavelength. 'He often talked about you as though you were best mates,' she said. 'When he wasn't slagging you off.' That was a surprise. The blood brother who couldn't quite commit. Couldn't quite make the cut.

I got the feeling that Tanya would have stayed in the kebab house all night, though in the end she got a cab back to the club.

And when I had finally arrived home there was a note from Cathy to say that she and Sadie and Ellie were at Bev's and wouldn't be back until I had packed my bags and gone. 'Listen to your messages,' the note said. I went to the phone. Not Ruth, of course, as Cathy thought. Just Penelope inviting me to come back and have some fun, Lawrence cackling, the fake 'Yesterday' playing in the background. Game over. Tilt.

I was in my own kitchen, cigarette smoke drifting provocatively across the ceiling, Bev's dog wandering from room to room, wagging its tail as though there was something to be happy about, Kite excitedly circuiting my legs under the table, nuzzling, panting, licking my outstretched hand, delirious at this unexpected show of warmth, this unwonted affection, this sudden windfall of sentiment. 'Hello girl, have you missed me? Have you? Have you?' I held her head in my hands and pressed my cheek against her neck, smoothed and patted her sleek coat, pushed and pummelled her with the determined playfulness of someone who knew how to do it but didn't do it too often. Kite, whose duo of loving mistresses had been cruelly snatched away by forces unknown, joyfully reunited with the master of the house! Ellie, on the sofa asleep with her bottle in the next room, purring softly, exhausted following a grumpy round of the park with her estranged father of two weeks, little pellets of snow swept by the wind along the path in front as I pushed the buggy. I wished Ellie had the dog's capacity for enthusiasm. But it was a homecoming of sorts.

'I wanted to talk to you,' Cathy's mother was saying. She had the habit of lighting a cigarette and then leaving it smouldering in the ashtray to get up everybody else's nose, and there it was, not even in an ashtray but in one of our blue saucers from Habitat. Under normal circumstances, I would have made pointed observations about the growing incidence of respiratory problems in pre-school children. But this was different. She wasn't here as Cathy's annoying mother. She was here to look after Ellie and the dogs while Cathy and Bev took Sadie off for a pre-Christmas skiing trip to Romania. She was the lady of the house, and therefore authorised to smoke up every room in the house if she wanted. I only had visiting rights.

She poured the tea and pushed a plate of assorted biscuits my way. 'Now, I don't know what happened . . .' she said.

'*Nothing* happened.'

'Matt, please.' She looked impatient. 'I don't know what *happened*,' she repeated, 'but obviously *something* did, otherwise I wouldn't be here, and you'd be with your family where you belong, and not sharing some squalid bedsit with a person you hardly know.'

'I wouldn't be skiing, that's for sure,' I said.

'And neither would they! Don't you think poor Sadie deserves some small consideration for all you've put her through? Are you happy with the kind of daughter who goes out stealing from shops? To my mind, we were lucky she didn't go off the rails again. Can't you see that Sadie is going through an extremely sensitive period of her life, and that this is precisely the kind of traumatic event that could send her over the edge? And we all know what that means. Drinking, drugs, pregnancy – is that what you want?'

'Well, I was hoping she'd get through her GCSEs first.'

'Look, if you're going to be flippant . . .'

I sighed. 'Look, did you want to talk about something in particular? I have a squalid bedsit to get back to.' I gazed pointedly at her cigarette in the saucer. The ash was an inch long.

'You really don't see it, do you? This same thing happened to Catherine in her teens, when *her* father abandoned us both for another . . . another life. He too thought the grass was greener on the other side.'

'Hang on, I'm not the one who left. That is, I didn't want to leave. Anyway, Cathy turned out OK, didn't she? She has all her own teeth. She doesn't drink gin before six. She doesn't live in a cardboard box.'

'We expected better things of her.'

'Oh. Thanks very much.'

She was silent for a moment. 'It was a way of getting back at her father.'

'What was?'

She lit another cigarette from the first one and looked out of the window at the snow blowing around.

'What – you're suggesting she got pregnant on purpose? You're mad.'

I wafted the smoke away from my face. She didn't say anything. As though it had alrcady been said.

fixing

I did try talking to Dean again.

OK, let's get this over with, I said. And nothing but the truth. New Year resolution, clean slate, I said. Admittedly, in the interests of self-preservation, some of the business brought forward from the last century had had to be written off against gross moral turpitude and given a new identity under a one-off special plea-bargaining arrangement I'd made with myself, but to be honest (because that was the general idea) at the moment I was too busy being deliriously happy to be back on the domestic treadmill to feel bad about the details. But, I explained, we should do this anyway, not only because Dean was one of the few people who would listen without interrupting, but also because he was not entirely out of the blame zone himself. After all, who was it that got me into this?

So. A false start, yes, but a new beginning. You hear the gun, you rush forward, the crowd groans, you get another chance. So it was probably best not to make too much out of it. I didn't have to learn to walk again, just go back a few squares. As I said, this was not the stuff of high drama. For every marriage that crashes to earth, another hundred pull out of the dive and says, fuck, how close was that?

And Cathy? Well, better a lie that she could bear than a truth that she couldn't. And if that sounds like a clean slate apart from the shite on it, look at it this way: you might tell all, but how much could you actually explain? You might establish the who, the what and the when of chopping down her cherry tree, but where's the why? And if it ever grows back, she's thinking, what's to stop you chopping it down again? You can say sorry, and you can say it'll be different next time because next time you'll have the memory of how bad it was this time. And of course you can tell her you love her. Because, of course – lest we forget – I did love her, even more now that she had agreed to have me back subject to a new contract with draconian new clauses governing my social life and sexual ambitions. Plus, I had always *told* her I loved her too. I was never the cold, unfeeling husband. I'd always told her. *I love, I love you, I do, I do, I do*. And in a way that was part of the trouble. The more you used it as an everyday greeting, the less infinite the variety of its possible meanings. You drain it down to the shallows over the years, then wonder why there's nothing left for emergencies. So confession – I mean to Cathy – was out of the question. Why? OK, yes I would have lost the burden of not being able to stand in the same room as her without breaking into a sweat but then *she* would take on the burden of not being able to trust me any more. The pain doesn't go away. It just moves in with her. That's why sometimes the right thing to do is the wrong thing to do. That's why it's not just about cowardice. It's about the other person too. Though, obviously, cowardice might come into it.

I wish to Christ she'd lied to me.

*

I would have liked to have asked Dean about the girl and the baby (where are they, Dean? Why didn't you tell me about it?), but of course he didn't do the answering thing, so we had to talk about me. We didn't get very far.

The point was, if I had told Cathy everything, she would have expected me to say it didn't mean anything. But it had to mean something. I don't mean Ruth – that was just temporary insanity brought on by the sudden proximity of available sex with a live woman. She meant nothing, really. Well, eventually she meant nothing. But going off and actually deciding to do it meant something, just as going off and deciding to walk across the Gobi desert would mean something. We spend our lives not walking across the Gobi desert, so, clearly, I could have said no, but on this occasion, when everything else was saying yes, I suddenly felt like giving it the benefit of the doubt. It was like a sudden realisation. It was somewhere I'd never been, and if I didn't go now, I wouldn't have another chance. It was like suddenly seeing myself out of context – not as Matthew Anthony Lewis and all the births, marriages, deaths and driving licence application forms that stick to you through life and make you a model citizen and perfect husband, but more like, I don't know, something more basic, more primeval, a body, a blob, a kind of visceral . . . I don't know what. Anyway, when it came to it, when I was finally granted five minutes to explain myself, I couldn't bring myself to acquaint Cathy with that kind of unfocused picture.

'Get on with it, Matt,' she said, sitting there, unsmiling for effect. She looked fantastic of course, in the way that women do five minutes after they split from their man, as if somehow it's living too long with the wrong person that's been keeping their beauty repressed and unwanted. But now suddenly she was blossoming – snow-tanned, fit, spanking new short hair modelled on I'm not sure who, though I should have if I knew anything about TV. I was half-expecting her to have started smoking, like Vicky did, but she probably spent the first two days back home peeling her mother's nicotine off the walls and didn't get past the coughing stage.

I hadn't been re-admitted to the house at this point (we were sitting in a quiet pub in Crouch End, Monday evening, about seven) and there was no way I was going to get back in the house that night. She was impatient, edgy, angry. Angry that it had come to this, in the absence of being able to be angry about something more specific, because, after all, she had no specific proof yet that I had done anything specifically heinous. And even if I convinced her tonight that nothing heinous had happened (and I knew I could only do that by giving up something slightly less heinous, so she could still be right and I could still be wrong, and rightly so), I could see straight away we weren't looking at an unconditional discharge and immediate release from custody. On the other hand, she was meant to love me, right? You couldn't just kick the habit of fourteen years on the strength of a few unsubstantiated tarty phone calls.

Don't get me wrong. I'm not trying to wriggle out of anything or plead mitigating circumstances. Not in my heart anyway. I knew what I'd done. I'd spent endless days and nights over Christmas and New Year with nothing left to think about but what I'd done, nothing to do but beat myself with the big stick of what I had done, wishing like a child that what I had done could be magically undone, buckling under the weight of it, and the even more unbearable weight of not knowing whether Cathy would ever have me back, knowing I should be at home with her and the kids, knowing that it was my fault that the four of us would not be together at Christmas in this year to end all years. When Ellie grows up and asks what we were doing when the new millennium dawned I don't know what I'm going to tell her. All I knew was that, without Cathy, whatever I did I was going to do alone.

Alex went off to his parents for Christmas and then afterwards to stay with old chums from university who he said had this huge castle up in Cumbria and were having an equally huge party. He practically begged me to go with him. 'It'll be heaving with women,' he said, slightly missing the point. I think he was worried he might come back to find me in his bath with my arteries slashed. But I was touched by his concern. St Alex of Assisi. If there was anything to be salvaged from all this it was to discover that goodness and insensitivity are not mutually hostile states of being. But it had to be solitary for me. Bread, water, hard labour. I deserved that at least. I unplugged the TV, drank no alcohol, ate no turkey, listened to no speeches, witnessed no celebrations. I spoke to no one except to call Mum and Dad on Christmas Day, which I kept defensively brief. I did read a book (I was magnetically drawn in WH Smith to *Disgrace* by J. M. Coetzee, the tale of an unrepentant sinner, as it turned out), and I struck out every day on long walks across London, lost in the sales crowds, alone in the park and on the riverside. I shed six pounds in weight, which in my new ascetic cast of mind I saw as a physical badge of the transformation going on inside. Self-abasement, restraint, purification. I wanted to be stripped down.

On Christmas Eve I wandered up and down Crouch End's main drag with presents for Sadie and Ellie in two carriers, not daring to knock on my own door, fearful of making things worse, fearful of triggering rejection before I had the chance to have my application considered, fearful of looking as though I expected to just buy my way back in. I waited, hoping to catch sight of her mother in the street, or even Bev, buying last-minute tinsel or candles or Yuletide treats for the dog.

I wanted to take the punishment but I wanted it to end too.

Eventually, five days into the year, I rang and Cathy answered. 'I have to see you,' I said and, before she could put the phone down, added, 'I love you.' So when at last there was just an ordinary pub table between us it seemed like a miracle. I just wanted to reach out, touch her arm, but even that seemed fraught with jeopardy. Instead I just looked at her, not sure where to start. In the absence of questions, what were the correct answers?

'I haven't got all night,' she said, meaning presumably that in the hiatus between kicking me out and going skiing, she had erected a whole new life-schedule that threw up a plethora of pressing engagements. New boyfriend? Karate class? Tarot reading? It did make me wonder, of course, for a fleeting moment.

'Bev's sitting for me,' she added, still possibly reading my mind out of custom rather than consideration, but the minute she said it I could tell she was biting her tongue, wishing she'd kept me guessing.

So I told her about the Lawrence saga. I tried to tell her without too much sordid adornment. Doleful, penitent, eventually blinking back tears that I brought along for the occasion but didn't really need to use. I told her how, through a complete freak accident of trying to follow up a legitimate story, I got as far as definitely not having sex with Penelope in Lawrence's flat or anything approaching it. I told her about the drugs, which I could see disappointed her even more than what followed, which – the way I told it – sounded like high jinks of the schoolboy kind. But I did get serious. I said how I'd felt professionally tarnished by events and emotionally confused and that I couldn't tell her because too much else seemed to be going on, and how I got drawn in, and how things escalated, by which time it would have looked as if I had something terrible to hide.

None of this was a black and foul lie.

And I tried not to change the subject. I didn't bring up the absurd stuff her mother was hinting at regarding her deliberately getting pregnant by the first idiot she met at college, not just because this was supposed to be her day in court, so to speak, but it would have been slightly pushing my luck pathetically asking for reassurance that she loved me for my personal qualities back then, at a moment when those same personal qualities were being called to account right now over a red spritzer (hers) and a corrective Diet Coke (mine). Still, for all that she was supposed to be in a fantastic hurry to get back to Bev, we were there until about ten, and at one point we were sharing a bag of crisps, which I think was quite symbolic.

Which just left the question of the full identity and role in the proceedings of the mysterious Ruth, whom I had reduced in Cathy's mind to the thing that always looks bad on top of everything else but has an innocent explanation all along; Ruth as the wrong turning taken as a result of Cathy reading the map upside-down; Ruth as the dark cellar with a bad smell that turns out to be nothing but a dead chicken. It was just circumstantial. Let's not go there at all. She was an ex-colleague who happened to answer the phone at the *Echo* when I rang from my mum's; someone who had harangued me for the names of people who might help her, careerwise. Yes, it was a dubious idea to go out on the booze when Dad was ill but, hey, wasn't Vicky driving me nuts? Wasn't I entitled to cope with the imminent death of a parent in my own way?

'I do love you,' I said.

'I know,' she said, looking at the floor.

I was out with Caroline for a quick half of Guinness during happy hour at Eamonn's, which of course was the height of irony since the poor woman was misery incarnate, with Alice Cooper eyes from being in tears all afternoon and half-pissed after a lunchtime session with Jeremy, who by all accounts took her out to L'Usine, so you'd think she'd show a bit of gratitude. 'What a *bastard*,' she was saying, gulping some horrific giant cocktail down. I was looking at my watch the whole time because Cathy was at home rustling up something hot and Moroccan out of Nigel Slater for dinner, as part of our twelve-step marriage rehab programme. I'd like to report that sex – as well as dining together – was part of the treatment, but it wasn't. Our counsellor . . . did I not mention Teri? Ah. Our counsellor, Teri, was one of the conditions of our *entente cordiale.* Teri couldn't overemphasise what a serious mistake it would be to rush things. Teri said marriages that had become weak and moribund (her favourite description) needed plenty of nourishment, warmth, shelter, encouragement, repose, patience, imagination, stamina . . . I can't be fagged to list it all. When did the sex start, I wanted to know? In fact, when did Cathy and I get to sleep in the same room? When did I get a chance to see the new Cathy naked? Teri was someone Bev knew, and had, I guessed, been heavily leaned on to keep me out of the marital bed for the statutory hundred hours' community service. So here I was, scrubbing the years of graffiti off our life together, happy to be on the straight and narrow, determined not to reoffend.

'*Jeremy's* a bastard?' I said.

The reason I'd asked Caroline for this quick meeting was to discuss the possibility of moving my feature-writing career onwards and preferably upwards, following the slight misunderstanding about the piece I'd done on cheating husbands, because it had all gone a bit quiet for me in that neck of the office. But now she was busy collaring the barman and sending him for another large one, only this time in green, with a slice of orange, no straws and no swizzle stick. 'I mean, shouldn't I have control over my own section?' she demanded. 'Is that so *fucking* unreasonable?' She actually said 'fucking' under her breath, but in a spitty way, and two people gassing at the next table gave us the odd telltale alarmed glance.

'Of course,' I said, soothingly. 'That is, of course it's not unreasonable.'

'Shouldn't I?' she said, catching me for a moment half thinking she hadn't heard me and half that she might be thinking I was on *his* side. 'Why not, for God's sake? I mean, can you imagine him interfering with Sport or Business, laying down the law on what stories they can and can't run? What does he know about it?'

I sat back and gave her my sympathetic grimace. I was trying to be a calming influence and the best way to do it, I figured, was to act as though there was no fire. 'Features are like football,' I said. 'Everybody thinks they can put their oar in.' I admit this did sound quite lame as well as metaphorically mixed, but she just looked at me impatiently and lit a cigarette really quickly, as if her heart was about to instantly stop if she didn't get one in her mouth *right now*.

'I know what this is about,' she said, puffing smoke all over the place. (I think I may have been getting a thing about smokers.) 'He's such a lying toad.'

But now there was a space in her thought processes and I took my chance. 'I was wondering,' I said. 'I think I need to raise my profile a bit on the paper, perhaps a few interviews or profiles. Maybe another big feature.' I waited for her to respond but she was clammed up now and staring at a wall mounted with hockey sticks (or hurley sticks, I suppose), so I found myself going on and on about how much more I felt I could contribute creatively and how my talent was being a bit under-exploited, especially as being TV Editor wasn't exactly what I imagined it would be. I had not mentioned my bid, currently still pending, for the big prize of the 'Weekender' and 'Watch It' columns because that would have meant saying the 'Jeremy' word, which would set her off again, and I figured that as long as she was staring at the hurley sticks – and therefore at least theoretically giving the impression of someone who might just conceivably still be listening to me, albeit in a distracted way – there was a chance she wouldn't turn me down flat and tell me I'd be better off looking for something else, perhaps in waste disposal, or compiling crosswords. But then when I'd finished my spiel, she pointed at my drink. 'Same again?'

I couldn't of course. I had to get home. 'Tell you what,' I said, 'maybe you could just have a think about it. Maybe have a coffee tomorrow . . .' I got up and she followed, both of us pulling our coats on. But then she really started. 'He's seeing someone. I know he is,' she was saying. 'That's what's at the bottom of all this shit.' She was snuffling now, and kind of falling towards me, and I felt obliged to kind of put my arm round her in a non-threatening, brotherly way, as we were heading out into the cold. Which was a mistake, because before I knew it she'd got her head kind of tucked in under my chin and shoulder and was hugging me. I mean we were just standing outside like this on the pavement at seven-thirty in the evening, and I can tell you she was *quite* drunk. And, of course, I did have this prior engagement. Then she lifted her face and started searching my eyes in that meaningful way when you know what's going to happen next, though of course it didn't happen because I managed to extricate myself and started madly flagging for a cab. 'I think you ought to get home,' I was saying. She was holding my hand and I had to practically shake her off. 'See you tomorrow,' I said. 'Don't worry, everything will be fine . . .'

I was fleeing the scene. Cathy would have been proud of me. Or she would if I'd chosen to tell her. Which would have been unwise under the circumstances. Trouble was, I was starving hungry from sheer exhilaration and panic now, so I stopped off at a Greek shop and bought three samosas to stuff down my face on the Tube, before arriving home to an aromatic candlelit couscous with tender lamb and apricots with Cathy.

'You smell of garlic,' Cathy said when I greeted her in my new enthusiastic way and pecked her on the cheek.

'Do I?'

I was sorry for Caroline. I knew what Jeremy was up to too, because it took someone like me to know someone like him. What he was doing was distancing himself professionally so he could dump her personally.

In the kitchen afterwards, while I was helpfully stacking the dishwasher and putting the slops in Kite's bowl, Cathy gave me a long kiss, and I really thought the moment had come when I got to put my erection to some intimate use with the new woman of my dreams. Luckily, Ellie woke up for her hourly bucket of milk, which meant I had to go scampering off and be the perfect father. Teri had thought of everything.

Vicky rang with the news about Dad. And now, next morning, she was downstairs with Cathy while I stuffed some things in a bag so she could drive us both up to Leeds. As I mentioned, I was hardly playing any Beatles music now. For some reason it didn't seem vital any more. But I did put on *Revolver* while I packed, just to hear 'For No One', the track Dennis Brain didn't play on. On the phone, Vicky was telling me what she thought had been at the root of Dad's problem. It started years ago, back in the 1980s when he'd parted unamicably from his brass band – that was the moment he'd parped his last note on the French horn. The band was supposed to have saved his life, she said. The band had given him a reason to wake up in the morning after he'd retired. Given this, it wasn't surprising that Dad was fiercely ambitious for the brass band. He nagged his fellow trumpet-heads into trying out more classical pieces, to go upmarket a bit, to team up with the local choral society, to make a recording, to enter competitions. But this was a modest band from a little mining community. They just wanted to wear clogs and do local galas and play snooker in the social club in the evenings. Dad never really fitted in. He was the outsider, trying to muscle in with his fancy ways, making them listen to Dennis Brain, getting them to play in time, disturbing the social balance by pronouncing all his words properly. I don't know if they fired him. He wouldn't have said. But there were irreconcilable differences.

The point was: it wasn't his bad health that stopped him playing. On that following Sunday, when he should have been donning the flat cap and heading off in his old Morris Traveller to Pontefract like someone out of Wallace and

Gromit, he was sitting in the garden staring at the lupins. A week, two weeks, three weeks later, he had taken up a similar, more or less permanent, position in the front room. The cough came with the armchair. And once the cough had established itself as a companion more faithful than his grudging, stubborn bandmates, it gave him the reason to do nothing.

OK, I admit this seems fanciful. I mean he'd always had a bit of a smoker's cough in the mornings, so it didn't just come from nowhere. But the doctors found nothing physically wrong with him when he went complaining to them about chest pains or wheeziness. He was fine. Well, until he had the stroke.

'How come you know all this?' I said to Vicky.

'Everyone knows,' she said.

We talked a little bit about Richard, who had come scurrying back to Vicky now, presumably having found out about the laughing policeman in his bed. I was wrong about the policeman. In the end, it was Vicky who'd packed him in, presumably on the grounds of his not quite having evolved enough. Richard had taken up swimming, she said. Saturday mornings. She couldn't quite work out why. I said it was probably just some kind of unconscious desire to show that he was a changed man by doing something that he wasn't doing before (something wholesome, I was thinking, which would by definition exclude shagging other women). There was a silence at the other end of the phone. 'You could be a psychiatrist when you grow up,' she said.

Richard was supposed to be driving up with us, but as luck would have it he'd gone down with a touch of flu. I don't know what happened to his genteel divorcée. Maybe the reality of children was too much of a shock for him so late in life. I could understand that. I'd been talking to Sadie, trying to explain things without actually telling her anything, which was quite tricky. She came clomping up to my den with a CD for me that she'd very thoughtfully found in some cut-price emporium of the senses in Muswell Hill. A '60s compilation –

Kinks, Marmalade, Small Faces, Wayne Fontana, Dave Dee Dozy, Gene Pitney, Vince *Hill* for God's sake, Cat Stevens. A kind of belated peace offering I think. She put it on, then talked all the way through it.

'Hey, that's a Boyzone song!' she said.

'How can Tom Jones be so old when he's still around?' she said.

'Were Freddie and the Dreamers cool?' she said.

'Paul's dad likes the Rolling Stones. You don't, do you Dad?' she said.

'Who's Paul?'

She was on the top step, holding on to the door frame and swinging in and out of the room. 'Oh, just a friend. He's invited me to Denmark for Easter. I mean with his family. Can I go? It wouldn't cost anything.'

'He's Danish?'

She looked at me as though I was an idiot. 'No. His dad's a lawyer.'

I wasn't crazy about the idea of Sadie on holiday with her boyfriend, especially in Denmark, which is after all famous for letting consenting children have sex together, so naturally I was playing for time here. I didn't want to go all the way back to my old Edwardian-father persona, who would rather shoot his offspring than see them taking drugs and having anal sex, but on the other hand, I needed to distance myself from my more recent laissez-faire parenting announcements, try to avoid the kind of expedient, rash half-promises that might get me into trouble with Cathy and therefore defer the resumption of full diplomatic relations.

'What does Mum say?' I said.

'She said to ask you.'

'Mmm. Is this the Paul who comes round here to smoke pot?'

She flicked her hair out of her eyes defensively. 'I'd have my own room and everything.'

'Well, why would you think that I'd think you wouldn't?'

She ejected the '60s CD, put *Revolver* on, and sat on my desk. She took the little rubber ball out of my mouse and rolled it between her finger and thumb. She ejected *Revolver* halfway through 'Taxman'. 'Dad, what did you and Mum row about?' she said, not putting either CD back in its case. 'Why did you have to move out?'

'Oh, I think Mum just needed some personal space,' I said. 'Have you asked her about it?'

'She said *you* needed some personal space.'

'Well, that's it. Maybe we both did.'

'So what now?'

I made a point of putting the CDs away. 'Now we live happily ever after.'

'Really?'

'I think so.'

'So can I go to Denmark?'

'Tell you what. I'm not saying no. But I'm not saying yes. OK?'

'Brilliant! Thanks Dad.' She kissed me and rushed off punching the air – *yessss!*

I was quite looking forward to the trip up north with Vicky, even though as a point of principle she had to drive faster than everybody else. I didn't know how much Cathy had told her about us. Nothing, I hoped. I had been incommunicado on the subject with my extended family. I thought it would be nice to see Mum, who was still in shock after the most recent business with Dad. As she told it, she woke up to a racket going on downstairs, leapt out of bed and dashed down to find Dad standing in the living room at the back in his dressing-gown and pyjamas, just looking out into the garden, and, yes . . . *playing his French horn.*

That was the news.

I saw Ruth. I saw Ruth and I had a rush of feelings, mostly

bad ones, feelings that put me in a low mood for the rest of the afternoon. She saw me but didn't come over to speak to me. I don't want to overstate it, but it's like thinking you've recovered from some tropical disease, but then you get out of your sickbed and can't get to the bathroom without falling over. I know it sounds crummy, but when I got home I just had to get close to Cathy, physically. I was like Scott of the Antarctic or someone and she was like the roaring log fire that you can't get too close to. I was following her all over the house. She just couldn't shake me off. She probably wondered what the fuck was wrong with me, but she didn't say anything. I suppose she thought I was just being reassuring in my cloying way, as I had been recently, because of everything. I had a terrible night's sleep. But then in the morning, when she'd gone to mother-and-baby group with Ellie, and the house was quiet, it came to me. I went up to my attic and took Dean's signed Lennon tea towel off the wall.

I knew that this was all very melodramatic, and that one day I might regret it (the day I come to my senses and flog everything at Sotheby's), but it seemed the only way to take a step forward. It was freezing out in the garden, and I suppose I could have done it inside, but an elemental ritual deserved a natural setting, I thought. Plus I wasn't sure about the fumes (that's a clue). There. I burnt it. I took it out of the frame, found a bottle of white spirit in the shed, soaked it and threw a match on (just to prove that none of this was premeditated, I had to borrow the matches from Jonathan next door). Up it went – *puwh!* – like the little popping sound of the gas lighting on the hob. Lennon in that cap with his leering laugh. Terrible inky drawing. The great man's autograph in felt tip. I didn't even inspect it closely and think – wow – Lennon really touched this. But then Dean touched it too. I didn't think anything. *Puwh!* History ablaze. Lennon's, Dean's, in that order. The flames quite took me by surprise.

I'd wanted some kind of crucible to burn it in, but all I

could find was a watering can, which was plastic and I didn't want to take the risk of it melting. I didn't want Cathy to know. So I just burnt it there on the patch Cathy had turned over for organic vegetables, and afterwards I dug the ashes into the soil as best I could, which was practically impossible because the ground was like concrete and the tea towel didn't really turn to ashes, just burnt material. Then I realised I was still holding the authentication certificate that came with it, so I burnt that too. I didn't want to tell Cathy. It wouldn't work if I told her. I decided it was a bit like being an anonymous donor. I wanted to keep it pure and instinctive and religious. I didn't know if it would work, but you had to have faith in something.

forever

Dad's opening words were always 'How's work?', as though 'work' were notoriously provisional, susceptible to being pulled from under your feet, as it had been for him. But it was great to hear him say them again. Work was brilliant, I said, patting him on the hand. Mum came in, followed by Vicky with the tea tray. 'He's going to put an ad in the *Echo*,' she said. 'Has he told you? Tuition, all levels. The consultant says he should keep active. Problem is keeping him still at the moment, isn't it, love?'

She chuckled delightedly, an old husband restored, just like Vicky – and like Cathy too, though of course Mum didn't know about what had happened between me and Cathy. She poured the tea. Dad rolled his eyes theatrically for me, man to man against the ambient fussings of wives and daughters. 'Listen to this,' he said, animated now, wanting to show off his new lease of life. He had a CD player now and a small collection of CDs, and busied himself selecting one from the rack. 'Listen to the sound. It's digital – the clarity's marvellous. Listen to this passage.' He stood by the window and pointed the remote control carefully, his lips tightening in anticipation, eyes focused brightly on the cornices as the music came trumpeting in.

'Don't you find that you lose some of the resonances from the original recordings?' I said, asking a question from the goldrush days of CD.

'You lose the crackling, I know that much,' Dad replied, his right hand falling and rising in time as he waltzed comically back to the sofa. Was it a miracle? Who could guess that he'd hardly stirred out of his armchair in God knows how long. He was only sixty-eight! Young enough still to do something. Younger, certainly, than he had been the last time I saw him, eating yoghurt in the hospital. The stroke had left him with some stiffness in his left leg, but everything else seemed to have been improved by it.

'The stroke reminded him of death,' Vicky had said in the car. 'He's decided he doesn't want to die after all. You know what it is, don't you?'

I was dozing. 'Mmm . . .'

'It's like a second midlife crisis for him. The first was losing his job. The second was this stroke. And in both cases . . .' She pulled on to the sliproad, foot down, indicator, '. . . it's been a question of pick up thy horn and walk. He got a second chance. It's been good for him.' She shifted the plush, fat, silver Audi into the outside lane and held it at a stately eighty-five, squinting at the upcoming road, barking out opinions as though she belonged to them and not the other way round. She had changed, I thought. Something had reminded her of death too, to be talking like this, her scientist's certainties evaporated overnight to be replaced with the what-nows? and how-much-time-have-I-gots? of growing older and less attractive. Losing Richard had been the big fright for her. Misfortunes mushroomed into disasters when life was running out, even though everybody knew life was always running out for everybody. Hadn't life been running out for Dean ten years ago, five years ago, two years ago? If he'd known, he might have gone to university or taken up water-skiing or walked across the Gobi desert. Made another few marks before it was all over. I Was Here.

Vicky lapsed into silence, inviting a contribution from me, her eyes flicking to the mirror, grim-lipped, measured in her movements, signal, manoeuvre. But I didn't want to join in with this. There was no point. You could never see death until it was almost upon you. You couldn't know twenty years ago what you know now. Youth was like this huge, sleek, noiseless car we were in, moving relentlessly on, bend after bend, forward into who cares where, sheltering its passengers from brute nature, allowing no real appreciation of how fast the ground was moving. But then – before you knew it – suddenly you found yourself bumping along in an '85 Ford Fiesta with nothing left on the clock. Suddenly, you saw and heard everything for the first time, loud and close up and frightening.

Watford. Peterborough. Milton Keynes. And then Vicky had grimaced, as though she'd just remembered something, and switched on the radio, but it was only music. The metaphor was upside-down, of course, because it was eighteen-year-olds who drove '85 Fiestas, while here *we* were, a pair of over-forties, eating up 200 miles of motorway in under three hours. But it still held true.

'Listen to this,' Dad said. We listened. Through the double-glazed patio windows I could see Dad's French horn lying on a chair, and a music stand with a score open and flapping in the breeze of the fan heater.

Mum made more tea.

'So, how's work?' she said.

'Great,' I said, though it wasn't great. It hadn't been great for a while. And it hadn't been made any greater by my impulse decision on Wednesday morning to present myself at Jeremy's office door urgently seeking an audience, asking if he was busy, asking could he spare a minute.

'A minute? Sure, sure, come in, sit down.' Jeremy had looked at his watch and clicked a smile on and off. 'Five minutes? I've just got one or two things looming.'

'Sure, sure, fine. I was just wondering if you'd had a chance to look at my ideas for columns. Whether you'd come to a decision.'

Jeremy narrowed his eyes. 'This is for . . .'

'For the TV pages? I left you some samples?'

'Ah, right. Yes. You did. And they were very good.' He was frowning now, clasping his hands together on the desk, shaping his thoughts into a refusal designed not to hurt too much. 'But. Two things. Well, three things. First. We're not sure you've really put your stamp on the listings yet – I mean really made them as sharp and bold and inviting as they might be. And there are still a few silly mistakes creeping in. People notice. Looks bad. I don't know how happy you are with your current team there, but I do feel you're going to have your work cut out, especially with changes in the pipeline. We still think that's your best area of opportunity, to be honest.'

'What kind of changes?'

'Hang on. Second thing. I wasn't going to bring this up, but I was slightly disappointed by the way you came in and *entirely* re-nosed the New Cads spread that Caroline and I spent so much effort putting together. I mean, we don't edit copy for the sheer fun of it. We had a problem with the tone, we changed it. That's how it works. You must know that.'

'Ah, yes, I can explain that—'

'Hang on. OK, I know Caroline has already spoken to you on the subject, and I was more than happy to leave it at that. Except . . . well, now it seems that you knew this chap socially. Which is slightly tricky – in terms of ethics and so on?'

I opened my mouth to speak, but Jeremy put his hand up to stop me.

'Don't worry,' he said. 'I'm not going to ask for details or even ask if it's true. I'm the last person to give lectures on who you should mix with or sleep with. I really don't care. But conflicts of interest are – you know – bad for the paper? Point being, this is probably a time to keep your head down for a while. If you get my slant.'

'But who's been saying that I've—'

'Doesn't matter. You get all kinds of nods and winks in this game. Some fully attributable, some anon. E-mail and suchlike – the new way of dishing dirt. Normally, I wouldn't dignify it with a response. Perhaps the chap himself took exception. I couldn't say.'

Which meant what? Lawrence?

'Third thing,' Jeremy was saying. 'I'm thinking of turning the current column space to new media, get a younger person in who's quite switched on with these things. Someone who can give us the definitive round-up of current thinking in screen-based media – which is, after all, practically everything now. I think we need someone who's already got a handle on the whole e-commerce thing, online movies, MP3 technology, the dot-com um . . . merry-go-round. I mean, could you offer that kind of coverage? In all honesty? You've got to be absorbed in it to an extent, or at least be familiar with the implications. I'm no expert myself obviously, but if we get a new, young face up there . . .'

My heart sank. 'But what about our "Watch It" slots? Surely we'll still need TV recommendations?'

'Oh, for sure. But we can just have a star system – you know, four stars for unmissable, one for crock of shit and so on. I mean who really needs more than that now? Especially when the TV audience is so fragmented and the best output gets trailed on the features pages anyway. Though we might make a few tweaks there too. Get a bit more *Zeitgeist*-led, a bit less PR puffery.'

'So, you've got someone in mind for the new column?' I was desperate for him to say no. Just that word. No, no, no . . .

'Obviously I can't really say at the moment. But we do need to strengthen the squad.' He paused. 'I'm thinking maybe a woman. Youngish.'

Christ. Something told me then. Even if I hadn't seen Ruth appear like a mirage that same afternoon to send me home to Cathy in a sick panic; even if I hadn't watched her walk the length of the editorial floor in that chalk-blue business suit, and watched the heads turn as Jeremy ushered her into his office and asked the secretary for coffee just before the door closed, and watched Caroline at her desk, watching with a glacial expression; even if Ruth hadn't so pointedly averted her gaze when she saw me. I knew.

'Listen to this one,' Dad was saying, slipping another CD from the rack.

'I've got something for you, Dad,' I said. I unzipped my bag and pulled out the rolled-up score of 'For No One'. 'Here.'

He opened it out, turned the pages, humming the melody under his breath.

'You probably don't know this,' I said, 'but the Beatles wanted Dennis Brain to play this on one of their albums. But he got killed in a car crash before he could do it. He could have been a star.'

Dad looked up, coughed and then laughed. 'What? He was already a star. Best horn player in the world. Britten wrote for him, Malcolm Arnold. But the Beatles couldn't have helped,' he said.

'Why not?'

'Why not? Well, because Dennis Brain died in 1957. First of September. It was our fourth wedding anniversary. I was sitting right there with your mother drinking sherry when it came on the radio, late bulletin. It was terrible. Long, long before the Beatles were thought of, mind. Someone's got their sums wrong.'

'But it was in McCartney's book . . .'

'Ha! They might have wanted him, but they couldn't have had him. He was a lovely, lovely horn player. Thirty-six years old. Had his whole life in front of him.'

She wasn't difficult to find. She was right there in the phone book, and I rang the number before I had a chance to change my mind. When she answered, she was polite, then bewildered, then angry. She could do without this, I could tell. She didn't want to talk. 'Look, I know how you must feel,' I said gently, 'but all I'm asking for is just a few minutes of your time – no strings. We stop when you want to stop. *Please.*' She sighed. I suggested her house. 'No,' she said. 'Somewhere else.'

I arranged to meet her at the lake in Roundhay Park. The small lake. A bright, cold January afternoon. The ducks were out, and paddled alongside me as I walked, quacking hopefully. It was that kind of day. I wished I'd brought a bag of breadcrumbs. It would have made things less awkward, maybe. I sat on a bench. Then I saw her coming, pushing a buggy, slowing up as she noticed me. Nice-looking, early thirties, wrapped in a cream duffel coat. Wearing a fleecy hat and gloves. I stood up. I was suddenly really nervous.

'Mandy?'

She forced a smile. 'This is Annette. Sorry she's asleep.'

'Annette. That's nice.' I looked at the child. For some reason I'd been expecting a boy. I had the sudden idea of one day presenting him with Dean's old Rickenbacker. *This used to be your dad's* . . . I tried to see some resemblance in the little pudgy cheeks and reddish curls but couldn't.

'People say she's got my looks,' Mandy said.

'I have two girls – Ellie's about eighteen months,' I said.

The ducks were out of the water now and coming across the path. 'I meant to bring some bread.'

'Don't worry, we thought of that.'

We strolled around the lake in the cold breeze, and further, to the big lake, throwing bread on the windblown ripples. Annette didn't wake up.

Mandy told me she worked three days a week as a legal secretary in town. She earned good money. Her parents helped with the baby. They were happy enough. She was financially sound. She had no regrets. She had a boyfriend called Danny who she'd been going out with for four months. She and Annette lived in a decent two-bedroom Victorian terrace house two streets from where she was born and grew up.

'When I found that Dean didn't want me to have the baby – that he wanted me to have an abortion – I couldn't have anything to do with him,' she said. 'We'd only been seeing each other a short while. I agreed to meet him a couple of times. He said that obviously he'd support me financially, but I didn't want that either. It didn't seem right. I knew I could manage. I was thirty years old. I had money in the bank. I just wanted a baby. And then, out of the blue . . . there was his name and face in the paper.'

'That must have been hard for you.'

'It was a shock. But in the end, I realised nothing had really changed.' We walked to a kiosk and bought cups of tea. 'How did you find me?' she asked.

'You were at the funeral. You signed the book. It was the only name I didn't know, though when I saw it I vaguely recognised it. He would have mentioned you. I only found out about the baby recently. I mean I didn't know whether you would have . . . gone ahead with it.'

'I just went to the service,' she said. 'I didn't know anyone. I felt weird about the whole thing. I remember your reading at the funeral. Your wife was pregnant. He told me about you, you know. He said you were mad about the Beatles.'

'He said *I* was?' I smiled. 'The reason I wanted to find you and talk to you. I've been to see Dean's mother. Obviously she doesn't know about the baby. I mean it would be upsetting to start with. But Dean was an only child. And I think . . .'

'I can't,' she said, looking away. 'I'm sorry, I can't. It's too late.'

'Couldn't you at least think about it? Think about Annette. I mean this is her grandmother.'

'Do you think I haven't thought about it?' she said with a pained expression. 'Sorry,' she said, closing her eyes. 'It's not your fault. It's just that me and Danny. We're quite serious. We might get married. He knows about what happened to Dean, but . . .'

'So what's the problem?'

'I don't know. It just complicates everything.'

'In what way?'

She didn't answer.

'Look, have you got a photo of him?' I said.

'Danny?'

'Dean. For Annette. Let me send you a picture. And take my number.' I dug in my wallet and scribbled on the back of a card. 'Tell me you'll think about it. Ring me.'

We walked to the gates in silence. She seemed reticent now, embarrassed, I think, at being unfairly tracked down, unfairly confronted with unpaid dues, unfairly found wanting in remorse and generosity of spirit. But I couldn't be sorry about that. I wanted to do something right. I looked at her standing in the cold, a picture of not knowing what to do for the best. And Annette there, fast asleep with Dean's signature right through her. The remains of his day. His flesh and blood. His memorabilia. His living proof.

Peace and love. You can't beat it really. From up here, it all seems pretty clear, even in the Saturday post-matinee darkness, lights as far as your senses can take you, the concrete walkway below with its tourists, homeless people, queues for the wheel, South Bank promenaders in winter coats pointing up at the glass pods, and then the little fuming boats stretching down the black Thames, the black, broad bend of water intervalled by illuminated bridges and edged by toytown parliaments and greenlit glassy buildings. The London Eye, it's called, because up here you can see everything. Sadie, body-pierced and confident, hanging on my arm, indicating, enthusing, wishing for binoculars. Cathy, no head for heights, down there somewhere in the theatre bar, happy to wait for us to come back to earth, sipping her latte, reading the programme notes, re-absorbing the performances, remembering production details, mentally sifting, comparing this *Othello* with past ones, better or worse, richer in this, poorer in that. And to the north, Ellie asleep by now, knowing nothing but familiarity and its opposite, Bev in the kitchen, reading Annie Proulx. Look at it. Family ties, love, friendship and the great in-between of pub regulars, shoppers, fellow Crouch Enders, ticket collectors, newspaper sellers, co-commuters, people in passing, people whose only personal details are the ones they stand up in; then the Lawrences, Penelopes, Tanyas, Grahams, people who have great foreground but no hinterland, people who might fuck you up on a temporary basis but can't really betray you to death, because you never know them well enough for it to matter that much to your life as a whole; then the Ruths, the confusing ones who can change their appearance to attract mates, discourage predators, survive extremes of climate. All out there. The big picture. Life slowed right down from that rush towards death as only revealed to the no-longer young.

'Dad, look at St Paul's . . .'

We look at St Paul's, and then the other way, up-river, searching out landmarks, settling for an impression of things, the satisfying sprawl of it.

The big picture doesn't have Dean in it. There's no point

looking. You might find something similar but it can never be the same thing. Whatever me and Dean were was the result of years of customising and tuning. You couldn't get the parts now. There wasn't time to put the work in. The expertise was lost. Forget it. It's gone. I know now that this is the moving on bit. Having sex with other women wasn't moving on; that was just trying to have some of my past again differently. And now what all the horoscopes are saying is Don't Hang On To The Dead (Dean, Yellow Submarine alarm clocks, etc.) and Don't Let Go Of The Living (Cathy, Sadie, Ellie, the dog, etc.). Forget what absence makes and what familiarity breeds. Look forward to a glorious new year, the horoscopes are saying. Reap major benefits in the weeks ahead! The truth is, you can choose novelty without abandoning tradition entirely. Look out there. Wasn't this whole city my crack at the French horn, my conversational French, my Gobi desert? Wasn't that the idea?

Sadie is pulling at my arm in her jokey aggressive way. Pulling at my arm like this had become her preferred way of saying something. Intimacy posing as aggression. It kept us in touch. It brought us together without the need to hold discussions about whether we liked each other at the moment. 'Look, Dad, it's Mum – wave!'

I look down into the crowd and follow Sadie's cheerleading enthusiasm, waving energetically, arms above my head. Cathy is squinting up, one of many, but of course not like the others. She isn't waving back, just smiling in a general way that you might when you're watching strangers enjoying themselves in public. But the wheel is turning now, taking us down, turning slowly. Turning so slowly that it's impossible to say whether it is moving at all.

SLAB RAT

Ted Heller

Zachery Arien Post is a fraud. A lazy but ambitious magazine editor who toils in one of New York's skyscrapers, or 'slabs', Zachary is struggling to work his way up the masthead of *It*, the shallow, glossy magazine at which he's an associate editor. But his ascent has stalled: he can't seem to get promoted. So when determined new boy Mark Larkin begins to get himself noticed and promoted, Zachary realises that something must be done. Mark must be destroyed . . .

'Heller's satire on American magazine journalism is written to the same high standard as his father's first novel, *Catch-22* . . . this is the funniest and sharpest novel about journalism since Jay McInerney's *Bright Lights, Big City*'
Daily Telegraph

'A biting, hilarious satire in the footsteps of Bret Easton Ellis, Jay McInerney and Tom Wolfe'
Big Issue

'[A] wonderfully smart, funny and juicily cynical dissection of mad American office life'
Heat

'Black comedy of a very high order . . . terrific'
Daily Mail

Abacus
0 349 11375 0

WHATEVER LOVE MEANS

David Baddiel

'Touching and strange and funny'
Sam Mendes, director of *American Beauty*

Like most people, Vic Mullan can remember where he was and what he was doing on the day of Princess Diana's death. Yes, he can remember it particularly well: he was at home, beginning an affair with Emma, Joe's wife.

The opening sections of David Baddiel's second novel chart the history of an intense and passionately sexual liaison set against the background of the most hysterical time in recent memory. But as the months wear on, and life and love return to normal, so things become more complex between Vic and Emma. And then, tragedy – a real, local, small-scale tragedy, as opposed to a national, iconic, mythological one – intervenes.

'A complicated, compelling look at connections between sex and death, loyalty and love, this is an impressive and intelligent book from a novelist who deserves to be taken seriously'
Dominic Bradbury, *The Times*

'Compelling, inventive and, best of all, there's not a cheap gag in sight. Funny man, serious talent'
Mariella Frostrup, *Mail on Sunday*

'Insightful, funny, profound, funny, moving – and did I mention funny?'
Jonathan Ross, *Guardian*

Abacus
0 349 11392 0